TOUCH
THE
LION'S
PAW

By the Same Author

Angels in the Snow

The Kites of War

For Infamous Conduct

The Red House

The Yermakov Transfer

TOUCH
THE
LION'S
PAW

DEREK LAMBERT

NEW YORK
SATURDAY REVIEW PRESS
E. P. DUTTON & CO., INC.

LIBRARY OF CONGRESS CATALOGING IN PUBLICATION DATA

Lambert, Derek, 1929–
 Touch the lion's paw.

 I. Title.
PZ4.L2218To3   [PR6062.A47]   823'.9'14   75-12504

Published simultaneously in Canada by Clarke, Irwin &
Company Limited, Toronto and Vancouver
ISBN: 0-8415-0391-5

To Joan, Ray, and Debbie

Acknowledgment

I read many books during my research for this novel. I am particularly indebted to Eric Bruton for his exhaustive and fascinating work *Diamonds* published by N.A.G. Press Ltd., London. If there are any mistakes they are mine, not his.

Part 1
CASTING

Chapter 1

The legend hanging in the booking hall of the airport said Welcome to Antwerp, the World Diamond Center. The man in the camel-hair coat acknowledged the greeting with a slight inclination of his head, because it was here that he intended to make preparations for the biggest diamond robbery in the history of crime.

The date was Wednesday, December 19, 1973, his first day out of retirement, and already he was instinctively planning: counting the number of footsteps from the customs barrier to exit doors; assessing his fellow passengers as they left the British Island Airways Herald from London, identifying those carrying diamonds.

If you were in the diamond business—mining, buying, selling, cutting, or stealing—you could always tell. Most of them carried the stones in the inside pockets of their jackets, which were distinctively misshapen. Their overcoats flapped open, and their hands repeatedly returned to those inside pockets.

The more dashing, a minority in the trade, carried

their stones elsewhere. Johnny Rhodes noticed the polished white knuckles of an elegant, grey-haired man in a velvet-collared coat holding an airline bag stamped In Safe Hands with Sabena. He wondered what sort of fortune the bag contained. Fifty thousand pounds worth of uncut gem stones, perhaps, on their way from Hatton Garden, in London, to a favorite craftsman on Antwerp's Pelikaanstraat; from there to the showcases of Cartier's, Garrard's, or Tiffany's, transformed from undistinguished crystal into chiselled fragments of rainbows. Rhodes' pulse quickened; diamond fever had returned. He walked to the exchange counter, eighteen steps from customs, and changed fifty pounds in notes—never traveler's checks, which could be traced—into Belgian francs.

A plump, middle-aged woman counted out the notes with a cashier's distaste of other people's money. She always assessed customers by their waiting hands: Rhodes' hands were strong and lightly furred, with long fingers and clean nails. She approved and said, "Your first visit to Belgium?"

Rhodes nodded and smiled. This smile and the long, powerful fingers were two of his greatest professional assets.

"English?" The woman shifted her gaze from hands to face; she still approved, and, for a moment, her expression was flirtatious and her face young.

"No, American."

"Ah, then you must visit Rubens' house."

Rhodes grinned at the assumption that an American must be on the culture circuit. "I'll certainly do that," he said.

"And the diamond showrooms on Hoveniersstraat."

"I certainly wouldn't miss those," he said truthfully.

She watched him sadly as he strode purposefully to the glass doors. Twenty years ago, even ten. . . . The next customer had broken nails and fingers stained

4

with tobacco tar; she didn't bother to look at his face.

Outside, Rhodes calculated the distance to the road. About two hundred yards. He waited while the other passengers climbed into taxis; he liked to get the feel of every possible key point before a heist; the little airport at Deurne, a branch line on the world's jet network, was the number one key point.

Five minutes later he made his way across the parking lot to the bus stop. The man with the Sabena bag was waiting there; he had calculated, Rhodes assumed, that it is easier to hijack a cab than a bus. The last time Rhodes had been in New York, a dealer carrying a bag of diamonds along Forty-seventh Street had been attacked. But the bag had been chained to the dealer's wrist, and the thieves had cut off his arm. Rhodes and the man in the velvet-collared coat eyed each other warily.

It was a grey and white morning: a few flakes of snow peeling from the sky; gulls floating in from the North Sea; smudges of frost on the rooftops. With its cold colors it was the correct sort of day to plan a diamond robbery.

Eight minutes passed before a number 16 single-decker bus arrived. Rhodes; the man with the Sabena bag; an engineer in blue denims; a boy with a runny nose; and a girl of about twenty with loose, careless hair paid the driver and took their seats. It was cold in the bus, and Rhodes' feet felt as though they were weighted with ice.

The bus jolted along a wide street flanked with squat, flat-roofed apartments sprouting with TV aerials. Rhodes took out a street map issued by the Belgian Tourist Board in London and marked the route with a ball-point pen, using a code to indicate traffic lights, open spaces, building sites, awkward intersections, and vantage points for a sniper.

The traffic thickened, the buildings became smaller and older and more cramped as they approached the heart of Flemish history and prosperity. Rhodes felt happier than at any time since his last job eight years ago. It had been stupid to retire at thirty-two, but then it had seemed the only sensible course of action. Like boxers, thieves should know when to quit, especially when they are champions. They said boxers never came back; but the difference between a fighter and a thief is that the fighter's wits are blurred by his profession, whereas a thief's are sharpened. Retirement had dulled Johnny Rhodes' senses, and if he hadn't decided to make a comeback, he would have died of an atrophied brain.

Suddenly, Rhodes realized the bus had passed two blocks and he hadn't noticed anything. With his ballpoint pen he recorded the position of a yellow-caped policeman on duty.

The man with the Sabena bag got off at Pelikaanstraat, which separates diamond territory from the railway. Rhodes stayed on the bus while it passed the museum hulk of Central Station and got off at Franklin Roosevelt Plaats, the last stop. With hesitant flakes of snow settling on his shoulders, he walked back to Pelikaanstraat along cobbled streets lined with patisseries, kosher food shops, and bars with girls smiling from the window. Much of this city, the world's third largest port, was ancient and much was clinically new; the two had married well. He emerged opposite the Century Hotel on De Keyserlei, the short, broad street of hotels and restaurants protruding onto the sidewalk like ships' cabins. In these "cabins," diamond-rich women, shipping-rich women, oil-and-chemical-rich women, sat in their furs sipping coffee or chocolate and eating cakes before going to the sauna baths to shed calories.

Rhodes noticed that like so many facets of the diamond business, Pelikaanstraat is shabby—like the brokers and merchants in their nondescript suits; like the cutting and polishing workshops in dingy attics;

like Hatton Garden; like uncut gem diamonds, which look like grubby bottle-glass. The industry seems to be apologizing for its wealth, donning a grubby disguise before handing over its end-products, which will sparkle from crowns and coronets; wink from cool fingers; hang warm and heart-shaped on noble bosoms.

Pelikaanstraat overlooks the railway and the cavernous seventy-year-old Central Station and has absorbed their gloom. Its fortunes are hidden behind insignificant façades, the occasional shop window of jewelry standing out like a whore in a laundromat. The pedestrians, many of the Orthodox Jews with beards and black hats, have a preoccupied air about them—which is hardly surprising when, on a street corner, they may just have concluded a fifty-thousand-pound deal.

Amid all this ordinariness the Diamond Club at number 62 has the air of a distinguished guest—a justified distinction, the glacial block being one of the biggest sorting houses of diamonds in the world. Johnny Rhodes paused on the opposite side of the road and scrutinized the building.

He didn't linger long; the diamond barons are proud of their discreet security, and the Belgian police claim they can seal off the area within a minute. Already he had probably been observed on closed circuit television.

He dodged through the traffic (not a Rolls or a Cadillac to be seen), and entered the portals of the Diamond Club. A uniformed guard with a pistol at his hip stopped him. "Can I help you, sir?" No hesitancy with language; Americans and English are as easy to spot to the trained eye as policemen at a gangster's funeral.

"I have an appointment with Mr. Benjamin Volkov at noon."

"If you would care to wait a minute, sir."

The guard conferred with two men at the reception

desk, one of whom picked up a telephone. Two minutes later Volkov's secretary—a stout woman with a healthy face and pale, stiffly lacquered hair—crossed the foyer at a brisk waddle. "Delighted to meet you, Mr. Rhodes. Please come with me."

One minute later Rhodes was in Volkov's sparsely furnished office on the fifth floor of the block overlooking Central Station. God, he thought, couldn't these people make any concession to their wealth? A Gobelin tapestry, a Sevres nymph, a Pirelli calendar? Volkov's grey carpet was wearing thin, and his filing cabinet looked as if it had been hit by a truck; yet on the window sill stood a hunk of crystal, patently quartz. From the wall a picture of King Baudouin and his queen surveyed the scene gloomily.

Volkov stood up and stretched out his hand. "Hello, Johnny, marvelous to see you after all these years." His eyes belied his pleasure.

"Hi, Benny, nice to see you, too. How's business?"

"Making a living," Volkov said. "Take a seat. A drink? Scotch, gin, anything you like." He was forty-six, short but broad-shouldered with features that were somehow both glossy and lined; his voice was surprisingly high-pitched.

Rhodes asked for a gin and tonic; its blue tinge reminded him of a blue-white Jager stone. It had the airs of a diamond, too: cold, sharp, and aloof.

Volkov opened a cupboard and poured the gin and tonic and a Stella Artois beer for himself. He had to summon his secretary to fetch ice.

Rhodes said, "Why don't you spread yourself a bit, Benny? You've got the money."

Volkov stared unhappily at King Baudouin as if they shared a secret. "It hasn't been a good year, Johnny. . . ."

"Like hell it hasn't," Rhodes interrupted. "The value of a good-sized, well-cut gem diamond has rocketed in the past twelve months." He sipped his drink, savoring its clean taste. "In fact it's been a very good year for compressed carbon, Benny. Why so tough for you?"

Volkov averted his gaze from the King and stared out the window. Sparks from an electric train spluttered thickly; snowflakes paused outside the glass before falling into the wind tunnel of the street. Despite the heating, you could feel the cold outside.

Volkov said, "This and that, you know. The fuel crisis, the dollar, the Mideast War."

"You stashed away enough to invest it and survive a couple of nuclear wars," Rhodes replied.

Volkov held up his hand. "Please, Johnny." He checked the intercom in case it was live, then lit a cigarette, which he held between thumb and forefinger as if it were on a pin.

Rhodes said, "Don't worry. I'm not here to make trouble." His voice was kinder; he had forgotten about Benjamin Volkov.

Once Volkov had been the young wolf that his name implied. He was a Ukranian Jew, and when the Germans poured into Russia in 1940, he was captured. He worked as a double agent, flitting between Nazi storm troopers and the Red Army with figures of troop deployments. But, in the end, Benjamin Volkov knew that either side would kill him, not because he was a traitor or a double agent but because he was a Jew. Volkov the wolf became Volkov the fox. When the Russians halted the Germans on the outskirts of Moscow and counterattacked, Volkov stole a dead German soldier's papers and uniform and retreated with Hitler's frozen army in the footsteps of Napoleon.

When he reached Berlin he planned to disappear among the tooth stumps of buildings and give himself up to the British or Americans. But his Jewishness was discovered, and he was handed over to the Gestapo for some sport before the final German defeat. They pulled out his fingernails, squeezed his testicles with nutcrackers, and passed electric shocks through him. They were using him for target practice with Mauser pistols when a Russian $92\frac{1}{2}$-pound Katyusha rocket hit the school they were hiding in. All the Gestapo were crushed by a girder, but Volkov escaped with one German bullet in his thigh.

Volkov the fox surfaced eleven months later in Vienna with a limp and sharp instincts for survival. He was trafficking in black market cigarettes, scotch, and penicillin when Belgian and Dutch diamond experts arrived searching for loot stolen by the Nazis from Antwerp and Amsterdam. The thieves had left behind meticulous records of the distribution of the diamonds, and one of the caches was in Vienna. The antennae in Volkov's survival kit twitched; here was the chance of a future. The diamonds had been moved to a secret hide-out in Vienna just before Germany capitulated, and Volkov offered his knowledge of the city's underworld to the retrieving party, most of whom were Jews. Within a week he found the diamonds in a white medicine chest in the X-ray department of a hospital on the banks of the Danube.

Volkov was allowed to handle the cut diamonds—one thousand carats of them—and was hooked. With a loupe borrowed from one of the Dutch dealers he gazed into flawless crystalline depths; he held the stones to the sunlight—thereby displaying his ignorance—and was dazzled by the fires; he examined their facets—fifty-eight to each stone—and marveled at their luster.

Love and lust stirred; he was like a young man aroused by the first breeze of spring. But Volkov knew that this was no spring-time affair that would be exhausted by the heat of summer. This was for ever. Perhaps his ancestors had cut and polished diamonds in central Europe before moving to the Ukraine in one of the continent's endless population shifts.

In their gratitude, the diamond experts offered Volkov a job in Amsterdam. Three days before he was due to leave he learned that all his family in the Ukraine had been killed by the Russians.

He was nineteen when he reached Amsterdam. By the age of twenty-seven he was one of the most renowned craftsmen in the Dutch capital, working for a small company called Van der Werffs, which specialized in cleaving stones for timorous manufacturers. It was the smallness of the company's capital, a touch of arrogance, and one glass of Bols gin too many that brought about Volkov's downfall.

One hot August day in 1954, Van der Werffs was asked to cleave a sixty-carat gem diamond from Oranjemund. They gave it to Volkov and told him the company's future depended on him. Like Joseph Asscher, who had cleaved the giant Cullinan in Amsterdam at the beginning of the century, Volkov took several weeks to examine the diamond. The weather grew hotter, and he sweated in his workshop, which faced north for the light. The scar in his thigh throbbed; there was an empty ache in his damaged thigh; and he took to drinking lemon gin, redcurrant gin, straight gin.

Halfway through September he decided to cleave. He marked the stone with India ink; cemented it into the end of an eight-inch stick; and, with a sharp diamond mounted on another stick, rubbed a nick, or a kerf, on its surface. Then he fixed the stick holding the big diamond into a tapered hole on his workbench and picked up knife blade and rod. Sweat poured down his face; his hands shook.

"Are you sure you're all right?" Van der Werff senior asked him.

"Never felt better," Volkov replied, wishing he could have one more nip of Bols.

"There's no hurry. . . ."

"No time like the present," Volkov said.

"Are you sure the grain is right? Our livelihood, *your* livelihood, depends on that chunk of carbon."

"Sure I'm sure. Now, stand back, please. Here goes."

One swift, deft tap, and the diamond, together with Volkov's livelihood, shattered into fragments.

Volkov acted the mouse. He fled to London and got a job sorting diamonds in Hatton Garden. It was nearby in Henneky's wine lodge in Holborn that Johnny Rhodes found him and persuaded him to cooperate in a diamond robbery that netted him £200,000—enough to set up his own business in Antwerp, the center of the world's diamond industry.

The last person Volkov the squirrel, hoarding his riches, ever wanted to see again was his benefactor, Johnny Rhodes. Now here he was, six days before Christmas, sitting on the other side of the desk, talking about "money stashed away." Volkov shivered.

Volkov said, "How about some lunch?"

Rhodes held out his empty glass. "What about another aperitif first?"

Volkov filled the glass, frowning. "Just what can I do for you, Johnny, after all these years?"

"I'd just like you to show me around the building."

"You're not. . . ."

"No," Rhodes said, "I'm not."

"Then I don't see. . . ."

Rhodes picked up the ten-power loupe on Volkov's desk and gazed into his gin and tonic. A few flaws—bubbles and feathers. "You don't have to see, Benny. There's nothing to see"—because, he thought, the plan is flawless.

Volkov's secretary knocked on the door and entered without being asked. Rhodes knew the sort: the meddling power behind the throne. Had she been listening? He doubted it; diamond people were so proud of the trust and honesty in their midst that it was their weakness.

Volkov snapped, "What is it?" His voice rose an octave.

His secretary said, "It's Paul Verhardt with the tickets for the Christmas lottery."

"Buy fifty." Volkov waved a hand dismissing her. The power behind the throne looked aggrieved.

Rhodes said, "So times are hard, huh, Benny? Funny, they told me you had a summer place at Ostend, a house at Ghent, and a castle in Spain."

Volkov gestured with his hands, which were very expressive and which he used a lot. "Like I said, there are many factors. Now the Russians are moving into the business. They're going to occupy a new building around the corner."

Rhodes finished his drink. "Nothing to worry about there, Benny. They won't flood the market. You know, they want to stabilize the price as much as anyone else."

Volkov made a gesture with one hand as if he were throwing a handful of sand, a Russian gesture. "You can never tell with those bastards. I should know." He stood up. "Some lunch?"

"Sure," Rhodes said. "Why not?"

They walked along the silver-and-white corridor on the fourth floor and entered the elevator. It took forty seconds to reach the ground floor, a fact Rhodes recorded mentally just in case.

Volkov hesitated in the foyer. "You want the full tour?"

Rhodes nodded. "The treatment."

More lines seemed to have appeared on Volkov's glossy face. "Just as you like. But first something to eat." His stomach made a noise like escaping bathwater.

He signed Rhodes into the Bourse, the diamond stock exchange of which there are four in Antwerp, and they went into the restaurant. Volkov chose an empty table in a quiet corner. After a waiter had taken their order he leaned across the table. "Why, Johnny?" he asked.

Rhodes gripped his wrist. "You've got nothing to worry about, Benny, I promise you." He remembered Volkov's nightmares when he awoke screaming, believing he had been castrated. "I promise you," he repeated.

Volkov relaxed a little. "But you said you'd quit forever."

"Who says I haven't?"

"Then what do you want to see around this place?"

"Believe it or not," Rhodes said, "I'm writing a book about investment and I need to know about diamonds."

"How to steal them?"

Rhodes took a letter from his jacket pocket. "Here, read this." It was a letter from a London publisher confirming a commission to write a book; it had cost Rhodes, an old friend of the publisher, a lunch at Rules.

"Is this on the up-and-up, Johnny?"

"On the up-and-up."

The waiter brought them two Stella Artois, followed by steaks, French fries, and green salad. As he ate, Rhodes watched with fascination the scene in the Bourse on the other side of the plate glass windows. Some two hundred dealers and brokers sat opposite each other at long tables placed at right angles to the long windows, facing north away from the sun. They looked as if they were playing chess; but the pieces were gem diamonds, and they were examining them for the four Cs—cut, color, clarity, and carat—and bargaining with each other.

In between each couple, glittering on white paper, lay the merchandise. Beside the gems lay the folded sheets of paper in which they had been carried, sometimes lined with pale blue for brilliant-cut stones and black for rose-cuts.

Rhodes concentrated on two men: an Orthodox Jew with luxuriant black curls, gentle features, and a black hat, and a little man with a walnut face and a small hat perched on his head like a vaudeville comedian. The bargaining was animated. Then they suddenly both relaxed and slumped back in their seats.

Rhodes pointed at them and said, "Looks like they made a deal. What happens now?"

Volkov looked up from his steak; his war-time ordeals had taught him always to be hungry. "They've agreed verbally for payment to be made on a certain day. Now they'll seal the goods and take them to the Bourse office, where they'll be weighed and put into another sealed envelope with the weight and date written on the outside."

"Supposing someone has second thoughts?"

"Any disagreement goes before the Board of Arbitrators. If you don't accept their decision, you're disbarred."

"Hard people, you diamond merchants."

"As hard as diamonds. But there is a right of appeal." He looked at Rhodes almost shyly. "How are things with you, Johnny?"

"Fine," Rhodes told him. "Just fine. I retired after our last . . . experience. I deal in antiques, but I have a lot of time to travel, play golf, go skin diving. You know, the whole bag."

"Doesn't sound like you, Johnny. Don't you get bored?"

"No," Rhodes lied.

Volkov looked around surreptitiously before asking, "Don't you ever miss the old game? You know, the scheming, the excitement?"

"There's not too much excitement in a penitentiary."

"But you never got caught. You were the king."

"And I abdicated. I always said when I'd made enough I'd get out and live the sweet life. Life is very sweet now, Benny, as sweet as honey. I don't want it to go sour."

Rhodes heard again the wail of a siren in New York; saw the light flashing on a police car; felt the polished hardness of brilliant, baguette and emerald-cut diamonds in his pocket; saw the hijacked police car waiting on the corner of Lexington and Thirty-fourth; jumped from the speeding getaway car and scrambled into it. The stolen getaway car, driven by a Hollywood stunt man, careened down Thirty-fourth toward the East River; Rhodes and an accomplice, followed by two other police cars, took up the chase. The getaway car made a sharp right, and Rhodes flung the police car round the corner so that it slid around, blocking the pursuing police. The stunt man, followed by Rhodes and his accomplice, ran for it. Six hours later they met the stunt man in Brooklyn and paid him ten thousand dollars.

Rhodes felt a pulse beating in his temple. He thought, I could use the police-car angle again.

Volkov said, "I've lost you, Johnny."

"Sorry, Benny, meeting you takes me back."

"You didn't look as if you were minding it."

"Does anyone mind looking back into their childhood?" Rhodes dipped his spoon into the lemon sherbet.

"I do," Volkov said.

Rhodes apologized; he had forgotten again.

After coffee Volkov took Rhodes through the Bourse, pausing at the bulletin board where the names of members disbarred for bankruptcy and other offenses were displayed on green slips of paper. The names were also displayed in the other ten bourses of the world: two in London and New York; one each in South Africa, Amsterdam, Tel Aviv, Milan, Vienna, and Paris.

"You see, we have our own laws, our own punishments," Volkov said in his squeaky voice.

16

"A secret society?"

"An exclusive society."

They took the elevator to the first floor and visited the Diamond Club's committee room, with a picture of Kimberley's Big Hole on the wall, and Room 1411, the Diamond Office.

Rhodes concealed his interest. "So this is where the diamonds are delivered from London?"

"No, next door."

Volkov took him into a bleak room furnished with a long table and a dozen wooden chairs. On one end of the table stood the thick white candle stained red with sealing wax.

Volkov said, "That's what they use to seal the envelopes containing diamonds."

Rhodes glanced at the locks on the doors. They looked rather flimsy. He said, "So this is where it all happens?"

"Every consignment is delivered here and checked."

"That's a hell of a lot of carats in one room."

"The biggest consignment in the world."

"And they arrive ten times a year from London?"

Volkov looked at him suspiciously. "How did you know that?"

Rhodes shrugged. "I may have been out of the business a long time, but I've got a good memory." He removed a globule of red wax from the candle. "And after this they're distributed to the various buyers?"

"Of course."

Rhodes forced a yawn. It was as he had thought: the diamonds would have to be lifted before they reached this room, while they were still in one container.

In the foyer, watched by the armed guard and plain-clothesmen, Rhodes shook Volkov's hand warmly. "You've been a great help, Benny. I'll be over again soon."

"You meant what you said, Johnny?" Volkov's hands fluttered nervously.

"I meant it, Benny. I'm respectable these days."

Volkov looked doubtful.

Rhodes took Volkov by the arm and led him into the street. "There is just one thing," he said as they stood together, isolated in the preoccupied crowds hurrying through the gathering dusk. He paused because he didn't want to say it; but it was a precaution that had to be taken, one of many hundreds that would have to be taken. "Don't get me wrong, Benny. I'm not threatening you or anything. But don't ever mention my old career, will you? You know, you're set up now, and I wouldn't want anyone to know about you."

For a moment the fangs of Volkov the wolf showed. "Don't say things like that to me, Johnny. Have I ever let you down?" Snow settled on his thinning hair. "I don't know what you're up to, but I want no part of it. You reappear from the past and start threatening me after all these years. Just who the hell do you think you are, Johnny Rhodes?"

Rhodes was sad that it had been necessary to warn Volkov. "Don't worry," he said softly. "It merely occurred to me that, seeing me like this, a lot of memories might start overflowing. Maybe you wouldn't see any harm in telling a few buddies that the guy writing this book was once a diamond thief."

"I won't tell anyone," Volkov said stiffly.

Rhodes smiled. "I know you won't. So long, Benny."

"Good-bye, Johnny."

Rhodes turned and strode off, leaving Volkov standing outside the Diamond Club with pedestrians pushing past him. He looked very vulnerable, Rhodes thought.

First Rhodes stopped at an antique dealer—the ostensible reason for his visit to Antwerp. Then he walked rapidly down De Keyserlei, crossing the broad

Frankrij Lei into Leysstraat and Meir. To the left lay Rubens' house; but although he liked to collect pictures and antiques, Rhodes was in no mood for culture. Whenever he was excited he liked to walk, his sensibilities sharpened so that everything around him seemed more vivid.

The snow was still uncertain, the streets streaming with light. He turned into a maze of side streets, fancying he could smell a breeze from the Schelde River, and stopped for a beer in a warm bar where men were playing dice on green baize tables.

His mood was familiar, surfacing from the past like an old man's memories of youth, closer than the immediate past. He drank two glasses of draught beer, watching the tumbling dice. Then he headed back toward Pelikaanstraat. When he got there he was slightly out of breath.

He hailed a cab to catch the 8:35 flight back to London. He was more relaxed now, gazing at the shop windows decorated for Christmas. It would take a year, he decided. He hoped Santa Claus would be generous in December 1974.

Chapter 2

Several factors had combined to entice Johnny Rhodes out of retirement before he decided to make the trip to Antwerp. The first occurred eleven days before Christmas. With Marie, the French-Canadian girl he loved and planned to marry some day, he was heading for the Strand to pick up a taxi after eating in an Italian restaurant near Covent Garden. It was 10:35 P.M. They were tired after a day in the West End, shopping and observing the way Londoners were re-acting to their gravest crisis since 1939. Gas, coal, and electricity were in jeopardy; the floating pound was sinking; shares were falling, and a three-day work week was imminent. All day Oxford Street, Regent Street, and Piccadilly had been solid with traffic; the shops were crammed, and the pubs were foaming with booze. It was, Rhodes thought, as if Neville Chamberlain had just stepped off his plane to announce, "Peace in our time."

Now most of the traffic had departed, and lines were forming outside the few gas stations still open. The air was sharp, the stars hard and cold. Marie was clinging to his arm, complaining about her sore feet, when they heard two shots and an alarm bell. Rhodes sprinted to the corner of a narrow street. He could just make out the figures of two men loading bags into the back of a car waiting at the curb. A Fiat 124 Sport, he noted; it was the sort of car he would have used—neat and nippy.

Marie joined him at the corner but he pushed her back. "Get out of the way for God's sake."

Did an ex-thief try and stop colleagues still active in the profession? It was only much later that he realized he had gone after them because they were using guns, something he'd never done.

The driver was revving up the car and the two men were shouting at each other when one of them noticed Rhodes. The pistol gleamed in the moonlight as the man raised it and took aim. Rhodes heard Marie shout, "Johnny . . . the gun. . . ."

He hit the ground as the bullet tore into the wall, the impact as loud as the shot. The bullet hummed around and smashed the windscreen of a parked Jaguar into a sheet of white frost. Rhodes knew the alarm bell was doing its job by unnerving them, but there was still time for another shot. He rolled to one side into the gutter. The second bullet chipped the pavement and he felt a splinter of stone sting his hand. He flung himself behind the Jaguar as the pistol swivelled around.

He heard the voice of a third man. "Leave them. For Christ's sake leave them." Rhodes stared along the street, and for the first time noticed a black shape, like a sack of coal, lying on the pavement beyond the gunmen. Another shape on the road was unmistakeable: it was a policeman's helmet.

Johnny Rhodes snarled. In the pocket of his overcoat he felt a hard, round shape: the last purchase of the day, a heavy glass paperweight.

The sack of coal was trying to crawl along the pavement toward the thieves. Only one of them was left outside the car. He threw the last bag into the back seat before turning and aiming the pistol at the black shape moving toward him. His features were blurred, as if covered with a stocking.

From the car a man shouted, "Get in for Christ's sake and let's move. We don't want a dead pig on our hands."

Rhodes sensed the man's finger tightening on the trigger. He threw the paperweight as he had once pitched a baseball. The gunman's head jerked as the paperweight hit him on the back of the neck. He dropped the pistol. The man in the back seat dragged him into the car as his body sagged. The car took off with his legs sticking out of the half-closed door, bounced off a parked Mini and accelerated down the street.

There were figures running in front of the Fiat, but they scattered as it drove at them taking the corner with a squeal of tires. More bells, whistles, sirens, shouts, a blue light flashing. A familiar combination for Rhodes.

He ran to the wounded policeman. He was a young man, and his face looked very white in the starlight; there was a pool of blood on the pavement. "You shouldn't have tried to stop them," the policeman said. "Not when they had guns."

"You did," Rhodes said. He unbuttoned the thick blue overcoat and tunic. Blood was seeping from a shoulder wound, but the policeman would be all right. Rhodes took off his coat to cushion his head and dabbed the bleeding wound with a silk handkerchief.

By now there was a crowd, and policemen were pushing their way through. Then an ambulance arrived, its siren braying like a donkey.

Rhodes stood up and put his arm around Marie. Above the window of the shop he noticed the words *Diamond Merchants*. He said to one of the policemen, "There's a gun down there. You'd better stop anyone handling it in case of any prints."

Thoughtfully, Rhodes picked up the paperweight and wiped it clean of his own prints.

All next day he was restless. The job had been so amateurish, so brutal, so unambitious. About ten thousand pounds worth of poor-quality stones, none of them weighing as much as a carat. Was there no refinement left in crime? And what was he, Johnny Rhodes—who had lifted more than £1 million worth of diamonds from New York, London, Paris, Rome, Berlin, Madrid—doing *helping* the police?

Angrily he picked up one of the newspapers lying on the sofa of his Park Lane apartment. There was a column and a half about the robbery and the part he had played in it:

> American antique dealer John Rhodes, 40, who came to England to escape the violence on New York streets, last night encountered violence on London streets—and saved a policeman's life.
>
> Police Constable Terence Dowling, 23, was lying on the pavement near Covent Garden, felled by a gangster's bullet, when Rhodes and his fiancée, former air-

line stewardess Marie Tellier, 29, rounded the corner.

One of the gang, who had broken into a diamond merchant's store and stolen gems valued at £10,000, was aiming a Smith & Wesson at the wounded constable.

Rhodes, a one-time baseball player, snatched a heavy glass paperweight from his coat pocket and "pitched" it at the gunman, hitting him on the head.

The gang escaped in a stolen Fiat 124 Sport, which was later found abandoned in Cornwall Road, near Waterloo Station.

P. C. Dowling's condition was described early today as "satisfactory." A man is at the Bow Street police station helping detectives with their enquiries.

After the shooting, Rhodes, a handsome 6-footer [Rhodes' anger dissipated a little], said: "Once a pitcher always a pitcher."

Rhodes stopped reading as Marie came in with coffee and biscuits. "Well," she said, "how's our handsome six-foot hero this morning?"

"Lousy," Rhodes said.

"The police said they'd be around at eleven."

"Then hide the silver," Rhodes said.

"You saved one of their lives last night."

"A human error."

Marie, dressed in green slacks and sweater, sat opposite him and regarded him critically. She was a small girl, stewardess-size, with greenish eyes, a pale complexion, small, firm breasts; she cooked well, dressed well, made love with abandon, was inclined to be possessive. She sulked occasionally, laughed a lot, got drunk quickly. She had told Rhodes that if he didn't marry her by the end of 1974, she would leave him. The quality that Rhodes admired most was her loyalty.

"Not exactly handsome," she said after a while. "Too crumpled."

"Crumpled?"

"A lived-in face."

"Beat up, you mean."

"I was being kind." She spoke with a slight Quebec twang.

"An interesting face?"

"To me anyway."

"A pistol whipping at the age of nineteen didn't help."

"Stop talking tough," she said. "That's all behind you now."

Rhodes didn't reply. At least, he thought, I had a touch of class. No back-street jewelers; no alarm bells unless you purposely synchronized the break-in with the time they tested it and no one took any notice; no guns; no murder raps. Shoot a policeman and you were on the run for the rest of your life. The crudest job he had ever been involved in was a smash-and-grab; but that was in the early days, and at least they had been sophisticated enough to pay a glazier to install ordinary instead of bullet-proof glass in the window.

He stood up and walked to the window overlooking Hyde Park. Beneath him cars and taxis cut up the red buses on the straight run from Hyde Corner to Marble Arch; beyond, the wealthy were walking their dogs in the park, while solitary men, who looked as if they had nowhere to walk, watched them. Lonely places, parks, especially near Christmas.

Rhodes loved London. In particular he loved Park Lane, where the old diamond magnates had lived. Alfred Beit, the shy millionaire with his Gothic bungalow at number 26; J. B. Robinson, the tight-fisted businessman who had entertained Clara Butt and Melba at Dudley House; Barney Barnato, the extrovert cockney from Whitechapel who built a five-story mansion with two billiard rooms and a school-room before jumping to his death off the deck of the S.S. *Scot* three weeks before his forty-fifth birthday.

Robinson apart, they had all died young, those self-made moguls of Kimberley mines, in the last throes of diamond fever; even Cecil Rhodes, pursued by the inexorable Princess Catherine Radziwill and taxing his weak heart against medical advice. Johnny Rhodes would have liked to have lived in those rumbustious days in the last century, when the profits from swindles, legal and otherwise, dwarfed anything he had ever attempted. But at least his parents hadn't called him Cecil.

Marie joined him at the window. "What are you thinking about, Johnny?" Her voice was worried.

"Nothing. Just looking at London. According to today's Pravda, it's probably paralyzed. They'll never learn, will they, about Britain? If the British ran out of gas, they'd adapt their cars to draught bitter."

"That's not what you were thinking."

"So you can hear me thinking?"

"Most of the time. Sometimes you leave me, and I let you go away for awhile because I know you're breaking a safe or hijacking a bullion van." She slipped her arm into his. "But that's all in the past, isn't it, Johnny."

"I guess so."

"Only guess?"

"Know so."

She smiled uncertainly. "Anyway it would be crazy, wouldn't it, to go back to that life when everything's so good for us. You don't have to steal diamonds any more, you can buy them." She held up her hand with the engagement ring he had given her glittering on her wedding finger.

Sensing that the conversation was turning toward marriage, Rhodes examined the stones in the ring appreciatively; about fifty thousand dollars worth, taken ten years ago from a jeweler's on Fifth Avenue without their permission. No sense in telling her; she was happy with that ring.

The bell on the wall buzzed. Rhodes crossed the room and spoke into the grille. "Who is it?"

The voice from the front doorsteps told him it was Detective Chief Inspector Willis.

"Okay," Rhodes said, pushing the release button for the door, "come along up." He turned to Marie. "That does it, me asking the cops up for drinks. What shall we give them, arsenic?"

Willis was a surprise for anyone who visualized all Scotland Yard detectives with pipes, bowlers, and umbrellas. The lapels of his grey suit were broad; the trousers slightly flared; the knot of his silk tie fat and loosely knotted. His hair was greying, worn long around the ears.

"A drink, Officer?"

"Thanks. Scotch please, ice and not too much water."

Willis settled himself into an easy chair, assessing the room with professional speed. Wealth, judging by the address. Good taste in the lime-green drapes and carpet, the old Mott and Company piano; the sideboard from a design by Thomas Hope and George Smith; the silver inkstand by Rundell; the Waterford whisky glass that Rhodes handed him. During his career investigating crime, much of it in Mayfair, Henry Willis had acquired a taste for fine antiques. He too would have liked to have been born in the previous century; one of the Bow Street Runners, perhaps, who made a point of retaining their share of any loot they recovered.

And his hosts? Willis' eyes flickered over Rhodes, who was pouring a fresh orange juice for the girl. He looked very relaxed in a fawn cashmere sweater and chamois leather slacks. A little too relaxed for a man being interviewed by the police after dodging two bullets by a hair's breadth? Willis was accustomed to such exaggerated casualness when it was a thin skin over wariness, guilt. Shit, thought Willis, I must cure myself of the suspicions of a lifetime; with retirement twelve months away, I must learn to live with people without assessing their form. This man saved a copper's life. And in any case, Willis liked Rhodes' looks: the strong face creased in the right places with humor and decision. A professional. But a professional what? Willis sighed.

He sipped the Chivas Regal appreciatively and said, "I see you appreciate the good things of life, Mr. Rhodes." When Rhodes made an inconsequential reply, Willis turned his attention to the girl. An airline stewardess they had said. Again he admired Rhodes' taste. There was Gallic femininity there, a hint of passion behind the chic exterior. She also had a nice bottom, and Willis liked bottoms. He imagined her in uniform; he also liked girls in uniform, which was why he had married a policewoman.

As Marie sat down on the sofa beside Rhodes, Willis said, "I've come, Mr. Rhodes, to express the gratitude of the police for what you did last night." He swallowed a mouthful of whisky. "You were very brave."

Rhodes shrugged, nonplussed. "I learned how to pitch a baseball as a kid."

"But the batsmen—is that what they call them?—weren't holding Smith & Wessons." He paused. "There were some prints on the gun, by the way. Thanks for pointing it out to the officer. Very professional. . . ."

"Common sense," Rhodes said.

"I see you also got the number of the car, not that you were the only one. And you were able to give an estimate of the gunman's build and weight. You should have been a policeman, Mr. Rhodes." Willis laughed and stared at his empty glass. Rhodes refilled it.

"We've got one of them," Willis went on. "The driver. A second-rate thief called Lou Chambers with form as long as his arm."

"Form, Inspector?"

"Previous convictions," Willis explained, his instincts telling him that Rhodes knew perfectly well what *form* meant. "With a record like that he'll be put away for ten years—unless he grasses. It's my guess he'll grass. I'm afraid we shall have to ask for your cooperation in the future, Mr. Rhodes. You'll have to give evidence at the lower court and the Bailey. The price of bravery, I'm afraid."

Rhodes said he understood.

Marie said, "You don't look like a policeman, Mr. Willis."

Willis grinned. "That's my strength." He hoped she wouldn't say anything about it being wonderful that they didn't carry guns. She didn't.

Willis went on, "The Commissioner of Police, among other people, will be getting in touch with you, Mr. Rhodes. It's a pity there aren't more people around like you." He spoke with sincerity. "Although we don't expect the public to intervene when guns are being used."

"Guns are pretty commonplace on New York's West Side, where I was brought up."

"I suppose so." Willis held up his glass, watching the winter sunlight splinter into rainbows; the ring on Marie's finger winked back. "You were born in a tough neighborhood?"

Rhodes nodded. "The kids played marbles with bullets and the babies were suckled on Old Grandad."

"I didn't mean to be offensive. You know, it's just that you seem more at home in Park Lane than Skid Row."

Rhodes said, "You can drag yourself out of it, you know, Mr. Willis. A guy called Barney Barnato was born in your East End. He was a Jew; his real name was Barnett Isaacs, and he grew up brawling with the Irish. He left the Jewish Free School at thirteen and made a living selling used theater tickets. Then he went on the stage with his brother Harry. Harry was a juggler playing it for laughs, and Barnett was his stooge. But the audience wanted more of Barney, and when it was time for the curtain calls they yelled, "Barney, too." The brothers liked the sound of that, and they called themselves the Barnato Brothers."

Willis looked puzzled.

"Barney Barnato went to the diamond mines of Kimberley, Mr. Willis, and became a millionaire. He lived in Park Lane, too. You see, we slum kids can make it." Rhodes didn't bother to tell Willis about his own struggle through night school; the fight to get the chewing gum out of his accent; the opposition from his parents, who expected their kids to bring in cash as soon as they left school, if not before. Now the old man had a place in Florida.

Willis nodded at Marie's ring. "Are you interested in diamonds, Mr. Rhodes?"

Rhodes shook his head. "Not particularly. They're a good investment, I guess."

Marie waggled her finger. "Johnny's investing in a wife."

"Congratulations," Willis said, standing up.

"You must come to the reception," Marie said.

Sensing domestic tensions, Willis pointed at a couple of Manton pistols on the wall. "You really know your antiques, Mr. Rhodes."

"They're my living."

Willis stuck out a hand, and an inch of cuff clipped with gold links shot out. "Good-bye, Mr. Rhodes. Once again, the thanks of every copper in Britain for what you did. It's good to know that the police still have some friends."

It was at that moment, Rhodes decided later, that the seed of the idea began to germinate. Subconsciously, the alibi had registered: the policeman's friend. Who would ever suspect a businessman who has risked his neck to save a policeman's life of organizing a diamond heist?

Willis picked up his sheepskin coat, smiled at them

both, and let himself out of the apartment. Waiting for the elevator, he thought about the report from the finger-print people. Out of curiosity he had given them the paperweight as well as the gun. Oddly, it was clean.

Rhodes' restlessness increased after Willis' visit. He took a hot shower, and, with water streaming over his body, took stock of himself in the long wall mirror. His waistline was thickening, and there was a suspicion of a paunch; his muscles felt flabby, there was a sheen of good living on his features.

Vigorously he toweled himself, but the self-reproach remained. He put on a blue bathrobe and examined his face more closely in the mirror. You poor, jaded bastard, he thought. So this is what retirement does to you. They wrote books about organizing your leisure after you quit your job, about enjoying the fruits of a lifetime of hard work; but they didn't cater to men who quit in their thirties, who didn't want to take up gardening or sailing or chess or stamp collecting full time.

He shaved with an electric razor and patted his cheeks with after-shave, wasting time, not wanting any harrowing conversation with Marie. He sat on a bath stool and began to file his nails; even the bathroom—with its pink tiles, gold faucets, and boudoir perfumes—seemed effete.

And as for antiques. . . . For the first time, Rhodes admitted to himself that his business was nothing more than a lucrative hobby, his substitute for bridge or growing orchids. But it was a hobby that involved more cheating and double-dealing than any clean, carefully planned diamond robbery. So what did a man, bored with retirement at forty, do? Return part-time to his old profession?

Rhodes wished he could discuss the problem with Marie, but these days discussion with Marie always had a nuptial ring to it. Retirement with children would be different, she would point out; not to mention grandchildren on your knee at seventy. It wasn't that Rhodes didn't want to marry her; with her he shared most things, and that was what mattered. But not a family just yet; there was something he had to do, something he had to prove, before that.

Marie battered on the door. "Have you drowned?"

"No," he shouted back, "I'm practicing with my snorkel."

"Lunch is ready."

"Maybe I'll catch a fish."

"We've already got fish," she said, "and it's cooked."

He combed his hair and went into the kitchen where lunch was laid. Lemon sole, green peas, tossed salad, a bottle of Reisling, and Marie in a butcher's apron with her hair disarrayed.

After lunch he picked up the papers again. One carried a report that a private detective thought he had seen Ronald Biggs, one of the Great Train Robbers, in Cape Town. The story repeated the details of the robbery. Between 3:10 and 3:45 A.M. on August 8, 1963, a post office mail van was ambushed at Mentmore, near Cheddington, Buckinghamshire, and 120 mail bags containing £2,595,998 stolen. Only £343,448 was recovered.

It was called the crime of the century. Personally, Rhodes thought it had been a mess. The hideout had been left cluttered with evidence, fingerprints all over the place; and, consequently, most of the thieves were now serving prison sentences. The crime of the century, in Rhodes' book, was the one in which no one got caught. Admittedly, the train robbery was ambitious and well planned, but it was short on detail, short on precautions, those essential ingredients that greedy, overanxious crooks overlook. And an innocent man got hurt. What was missing these days, Rhodes decided, was finesse.

Nor was the train robbery the biggest heist ever pulled, as many people thought. On June 7, 1945, U.S. Army personnel, working with Germans, lifted 728 gold bars worth £3,518,334, part of the Reichbank's reserves, from a mountainside near Einsiedel in Bavaria; and, for spending money, six sacks of bank notes worth $404,840 from a garden in Oberaer. And then there was the $13,193,000 "missed" from the Morgan Trust on Wall Street on October 23, 1969.

Rhodes knew his crimes like other men know racing forms. From the bookcase he selected a volume of statistics; it fell open at jewel robberies. On November 13, 1969, in Freetown, Sierra Leone, a gang stole diamonds valued at £1,500,000. And on New Year's Eve, 1971, at the Hotel Pierre on New York's Fifth Avenue, property worth $5 million was stolen, most of it thought to have been jewels. Rhodes' mouth watered.

No, the train robbery certainly wasn't the crime of the century. Maybe that was yet to come. Maybe. . . . Sitting among his antiques, Johnny Rhodes began to daydream. When he glanced at his watch it was 3:00 P.M., and he had less than an hour in which to drive to Guildford for a business appointment.

He took his blue E-type V-12 from the parking lot under Hyde Park and drove down Park Lane, turning into Knightsbridge and down Brompton Road, thinking that the two-seater, with its long, inquisitive bonnet, was too flashy for a man in retirement, too thirsty for a fuel crisis.

At Wimbledon he got clear of the heavy traffic but kept the speed at fifty miles an hour to preserve gas. The day was beginning to fade, with a mauve haze on the skyline and a few pink clouds without any warmth in them.

He made Guildford with five minutes to spare and went into the Angel Hotel, where he ordered tea and toast in the old-fashioned lounge beside a blazing fire. At 4.00 P.M. the retired Army colonel who would give every reason for wanting to sell a Sheraton table, except the true one—he needed the money—joined him.

Rhodes poured him a cup of tea.

Col. Francis Bland sipped his tea, holding the cup with his little finger crooked. His hands were covered with large freckles, and his eyes were vague.

It took them half an hour to agree on a price, £250 less than Bland had asked. Rhodes was ready to go, but Bland was looking forlornly at the empty tea pot.

Rhodes felt his loneliness and ordered a fresh pot.

"You're very hospitable," Bland murmured. "I enjoy my tea. You know, it breaks up the afternoon." He took a silver flask engraved with a regimental crest from his pocket. "Like a nip?"

"No thanks, Colonel. Not in tea. That's sacrilege, isn't it?"

Bland put the flask away without opening it. "Nothing's sacred any more. Strikes, slowdowns, work-to-rule, the government held to ransom by the Arabs."

"The country's going to the dogs," Rhodes said.

"No need to be sarcastic," said Bland, hearing bugles sound the charge. "Your country's not much better off. At least we can walk our streets at night without fear of being attacked and robbed."

"Want to bet?" Rhodes picked up Bland's evening paper carrying a short account of the diamond robbery and immediately wished he hadn't.

Bland glanced at the story, realization slowly dawning in his mind, which might once have been as sharp as a parade ground command. "You?"

Rhodes glanced at his watch; time to go. "Me, Colonel. But that's not why I pointed it out."

Bland looked as if he might spring to attention. "I'm proud to have met you, sir." He took a crumpled cigarette from a leather case and lit it with shaking hands.

"Nice to have met you, Colonel. Glad we could do business." Rhodes was now feeling sorry he had clipped £250 off Bland's price, even though he was still paying him £100 over the odds.

Bland then surprised Rhodes by saying, "A paltry little robbery, eh? They steal a measly £10,000 and then make an absolute mess of it. Damn it, not even criminals seem to have any class these days."

Perhaps Bland had once absconded with the mess funds. "It wasn't very ambitious," Rhodes agreed cautiously.

"Don't do their homework, that's why. I could have told them where to steal an absolute fortune in diamonds, an absolute bloody fortune." Bland sipped his tea. "They're too greedy, that's their trouble. Like everyone today. I remember. . . ."

Rhodes cut him short. "I agree with you, Colonel. If you're going to rob a bank, make it the Bank of England." He warmed his hands in front of the fire and asked casually, "What's all this about a fortune in diamonds?"

"Eh? Oh, nothing. Just something a fellow in the city was telling me. Hatton Garden, actually. His name is George Williamson, an old friend. We were at school together. He's done rather well for himself."

"And he's got a fortune in diamonds tucked away?"

Bland looked vacant. "Don't know about a fortune, old man."

"But you said. . . ."

"Ah." Bland drained the last of his tea, the leaves forming a blot on the inside of the cup. "No, I meant he told me where there's a fortune in diamonds available."

"Which a thief who uses his brains could steal?" Rhodes yawned. "I believe that's what you implied. But not the sort of petty criminals you get these days, eh, Colonel?"

"Exactly," Bland replied. "You've got my point, old

man." He leaned forward confidentially. "According to this friend of mine, consignments of diamonds are sent from London to Antwerp ten times a year. And do you know how much they send in one year?"

Rhodes said he didn't.

"About £130 million worth. Just think of that. That's an average of £13 million a consignment. Perhaps £15 million some days. Think of that, old man."

Rhodes was.

Driving back, Rhodes felt an urgent desire to put his foot down. But there was no point in breaking the law. Rhodes had known many crooks nailed because of some driving fault: out-of-date license, no insurance, a knocked-out rear light. A car could be a criminal's great ally or his greatest enemy; Rhodes thought it was as senseless to leave your prints on a safe as it was to drive carelessly.

The needle of the speedometer flickered to fifty-five. Rhodes eased his foot off the pedal. Two miles further on, two lights that had been keeping steadily behind him grew larger, flooding the rearview mirror with light, and two motorcycle cops roared past.

When he reached Fulham he stopped at a Bohemian pub where the world's problems were settled twice a day and Laurie Lee could sometimes be found playing the flute. He ordered a large Cutty Sark, because neither the darker whiskies nor the small British measures appealed to him. He sipped it slowly, oblivious to the polemics around him.

Fifteen million pounds—something like $40 million —worth of diamonds in one consignment. Adrenalin flowed, dormant instincts surfaced. He finished his drink and walked down the Fulham Road. As always, at times like this he walked quickly, head bowed, hands thrust deep into his overcoat pockets. Fifteen million pounds: if you could pull it off, all other robberies were peanuts.

By the time he had returned to the E-type, Johnny Rhodes had decided to emerge from retirement. To pull the crime of the century, the biggest heist the world has ever known; to assure himself, anonymously, of a place in the *Guinness Book of World Records*.

Chapter 3

It was Christmas Day, and in the pink-tiled bathroom Johnny Rhodes was easing his body out of retirement. First a jog around Hyde Park, where, every morning, an exclusive society of men of all ages in moth-eaten sweat shirts and running shorts loped along the paths with misery written on their faces. This was followed by twenty push-ups and thirty sit-ups, because he was taking it easily to start with, and a workout on a rowing machine. He had cut down on his drinking, on French fries, and on bread.

Marie regarded the whole performance with suspicion. Her French background demanded good food, plenty of it, washed down with wine, and frugality was an insult to her cooking. Today she had determined to make up some of the calories Rhodes had shed. Norfolk turkey, bread sauce, homemade stuffing, hunks of sausage meat, roast potatoes, green peas, cranberry sauce, followed by Christmas pudding soaked with brandy sauce, mince pies, and Irish coffee.

The smell of cooking opened a cavern in Rhodes' stomach when he came out of the bathroom, in his bathrobe, panting slightly.

"You'll kill me with all that food," he said.

"You're killing yourself," she replied, leaving the

lunch to cook by itself and pouring herself a glass of dry vermouth. "Dieting at your age."

"Forty isn't so old."

"It isn't so young either. And in any case, who wants a heap of bones for a lover? I'll cut myself on your ribs."

"It's not my ribs you have to bother about," he said, pouring himself a glass of white wine.

"Don't be vulgar. Not at Christmas." She tinkled the ice in her vermouth. "Anyway, who says that won't get smaller without its calories? I bet none of these dieticians say anything about that."

"They all say dieting makes you more virile." He patted her bottom. "So watch out."

She sat down and crossed her legs. Great legs, Rhodes thought, as she smoothed the pink suede skirt across her thighs; a beautiful body, in fact. "Hey," he said, "how about a walk? There's a pub open on the other side of the park."

"A sugar-free soda?" She gazed at him steadily. "What's all this about, Johnny? You had a run this morning and came in looking as if you'd been lying in a field of wet grass all morning. Now you want a walk. It's just as if you're training for something."

"Sure I'm training. You know, to keep you happy."

"It all seemed to start after that robbery."

"A coincidence." He finished his wine. "How about that walk?"

"It's a terrible day."

Rhodes glanced out of the window. Mist threatened to thicken into drizzle and a pewter sky. "I need to work up an appetite to tackle that meal of yours."

"On one condition."

"Yeah?"

"That you take your present with you."

"Okay. Anyway I think it's a great present," he lied. She had bought him a man's handbag from Aspreys, small, made of soft brown leather with a loop you slipped around your wrist. Rhodes thought he needed a poodle to go with it.

He had bought her a diamond necklace from Cartier's. What else?

There were children playing in the park with new black-and-white footballs while the fathers watched, wearing bright ties and woolly scarves they would hide after a week. Rhodes tried to carry his bag as if it were a transistor radio, thinking he would kill the first joker who wolf-whistled. Marie was silent and he knew that she was thinking about Christmas with children.

Rhodes let his thoughts return to the subject that now occupied them most of the time.

First of all he had made sure that Colonel Bland's facts were right. And he had to do this without arousing suspicion.

Rhodes went to his gallery just off New Bond Street and checked his customers. His man was number forty-two on the list, a diamond merchant named Ronald Massingham, with offices in Hatton Garden, who was a fanatical collector of silver candelabra. Either his storehouse was an inferno of candlelight or he was Liberace's London agent. Rhodes called at his apartment in Albermarle Street; bribed him with two Queen Anne silver candlesticks at a giveaway price; and sought information about the book he planned to write about investment in an inflationary age.

Were diamonds a good investment? Like most people in the diamond business, Massingham, a plump, loquacious man with polished cheeks, had been asked the question many times before; he recited the answer with importance.

Certainly they were a good investment if you knew what to buy; the diamonds had to have size and quality, anything from one to three carats of at least

VVS quality, river if possible. But, said Massingham, warming to his subject, you shouldn't buy them too big; an investment was only sensible if you could realize it, and it wasn't always easy to get rid of a stone larger than three carats. Personally he thought the 69.42 carat diamond bought by Cartier's and sold to Richard Burton for Elizabeth Taylor for $1,200,000 was too big.

Massingham lit some candles, and the antiques in the elegant sitting room no longer seemed like exhibits. He offered Rhodes a Turkish cigarette, which Rhodes declined. He poured some claret, which they drank sitting opposite each other in front of an Adam fireplace. The smoke from a small coal fire, the Turkish cigarette, and the candles fused into an acrid perfume.

The point about diamonds, Massingham went on, sipping his claret, was that unlike gold, which had always been associated with paper currencies, the value of diamonds was stabilized. The virtual monopoly in uncut stones prevented prices from being manipulated, and, at the very least, they appreciated at the same rate as the cost of living. "If one particular diamond bought a house at Wentworth twenty-five years ago, the same diamond would still buy the same house today," Massingham explained. "And a really top-rate stone might well overtake the rise in the cost of living."

Rhodes, who knew all this, looked intensely interested.

Furthermore, Massingham continued, diamonds were an infallible currency in themselves. They had an intrinsic value that paper money could never possess, and they could always be exchanged for cash. Slip a two-carat brilliant-cut diamond into your pocket at Heathrow, disembark at Orly, and within a couple of days, you could realize it for francs without any unpleasantness from the Treasury.

Rhodes observed the furtive beam on Massingham's face and recorded it. Here was a man who could be bent as easily as a paper clip, and one day he might need him. For another pair of candlesticks, Massingham would steal the English Electric formula for synthetic diamonds.

"What about diamond jewelry?" Rhodes asked. "Is that a good investment?"

Massingham looked sly. "Are you sure you only want all this for a book?"

Rhodes grinned conspiratorially. "I might have a few side bets."

Massingham puffed at his cigarette, slotted into an amber holder. "Well, you can't really lose as long as you take professional advice. The situation's much the same as it is with uncut stones. Provided the diamonds are well cut and set, the piece of jewelry will cerainly keep up with inflation, unlike other goodies, such as stocks and shares."

Gently, Rhodes steered Massingham toward the distribution of uncut gem stones.

"All done in London," Massingham told him. "They hold what they call 'sights,' and two hundred dealers and cutters are summoned and handed envelopes with their allocations of stones. The sales are negotiated through brokers, who pick up a fee of 1 percent. The dealers don't have much of a say in what they get, mind you, but it's all pretty fair. God knows what would happen to the industry if the supply of rough diamonds was a competitive business."

"Perhaps they'd get cheaper," Rhodes suggested.

Massingham gave a patronizing smile; he'd heard that one before. "There's only a limited supply of gem stones and already the big ones are getting scarce. It's better for everyone, including the consumer, if they're controlled. You know, if they weren't, prices would jump around like a yo-yo. It was your namesake, dear old Cecil, who first realized that supply had to be measured against demand. Then, after a series of slumps, Sir Ernest Oppenheimer, the boss of De Beers, formed the Diamond Producers' Association, which enabled all the world's diamond producers to control diamond supplies and ride the depressions that seemed to occur every eight years or so. In any case," Massingham asked, "who would want diamonds if they were cheap?"

No one, Rhodes thought. Not even a fence. He said, "So there aren't many risks in the diamond trade."

"I wouldn't say that, old boy." In the firelight Massingham's cheeks were the color of the claret. "Supposing the Russians decided to flood the market and bring South Africa to her knees? Ever since a woman found a diamond pipe called Dawn in Siberia in 1953, they've been digging them up by the bucket-ful. No one knows how many, but in 1970 it's been calculated that they marketed 2.7 million carats of gem diamonds, .9 million of near gems, and 8.4 million of industrials."

"But they wouldn't want to kill the golden goose, would they?"

"Probably not," Massingham agreed. "But you never know with the Russians. Then, of course, there are dangers in cutting or cleaving, and there's always a gamble if you buy a coated stone. You may have a flawless gem on your hands or you may have something the color of chocolate. And you don't know until you've polished two windows opposite each other and looked through."

"How does the price of a cut diamond compare with a rough?" Rhodes asked.

"Depends on the stone." Massingham began to show off with abandon. "First of all the size. Then the shape: stones, cleavages, macles, flats. Then the color: fine white, river, silver cape, light yellow. Then the flaws: flawless; VVS; SI; first piqué, which means flaws just visible to the naked eye; and so on, down to heavy spotted. And, of course, you've got to take into consideration the types of flaws: a bubble, an inclusion, a feather, a crack, a butterfly, a fezel. Those are the internal blemishes," Massingham explained. "Then there are the external ones: chips, cavities, polishing lines, scratches. . . ."

"I thought you couldn't damage diamonds," Rhodes interrupted.

Massingham came out with the old cliché, as Rhodes knew he would. "Diamond cuts diamond. Some dealers carry more than one diamond around in their envelopes and they get scratched. Many people don't know that you can burn diamonds."

Rhodes looked astonished.

"Diamonds are an unstable form of carbon, and they will burn or oxidize in heat. Bring them up to anything between 700 and 900 centigrade and they convert into carbon monoxide. After all," Massingham said, pointing at the fire, "coal is a form of carbon, and that seems to be burning all right."

Rhodes nodded as though realization were dawning.

"Then, of course, you've got to take into consideration the cut. It's got to be well proportioned. Sometimes diamonds are cut to gain weight or make them look bigger; sometimes they're downright badly cut, with an overangled pavilion or a misplaced facet. And sometimes a bad cut is hidden by the mounting— although most people in the diamond business are pretty honest," Massingham added.

"Except when they're taking stones abroad to avoid treasury regulations," Rhodes said, grinning.

Massingham smiled uneasily and told Rhodes about old-fashioned cuts. "A rose-cut, for instance. Can't get rid of them for love nor money. So, if you've got any family heirlooms in the attic, you'd better get them out and have a good look."

"But, as a general rule, you must be able to assess a rough gem diamond against a cut stone."

Massingham frowned; he didn't like general rules. "When a stone is cut, it loses at least half its weight, probably more. It's impossible to say really, but despite the loss, a cut diamond should be worth at least twice the value of the stone it's made from."

Rhodes was silent. If he got away with rough gem stones worth £15 million then, theoretically, they might be worth £30 million when cut. The chippings and cuttings shed when the rough diamonds were cut would also have their value. But this was all academic; he would get one price from crooked dealers in New York and Tel Aviv, and that would be 40 percent of the market value of the rough stones. Nevertheless, when the robbery was reported, he would like to see the value of the stones recorded when they were cut; Johnny Rhodes liked his statistics to be accurate.

He asked, "How much would a two-carat polished diamond of top quality be worth?"

Massingham shrugged.

"As a general rule then."

"There aren't any general rules with diamonds. Two thousand five hundred pounds perhaps. But don't expect immediately to sell a diamond for the price you paid. Don't forget that the dealer you bought it from has had to add on, say, 25 percent to cover wages, overheads, etc., and still make a small profit. And in this country, the bloody government deducts tax before the retailer can even sell, so he's got to add that on as well. So, once you've bought your polished diamond, you've got to wait some time before trying to sell it again."

Rhodes refused another glass of claret. "It's fascinating. We must have a few more talks before I even start thinking about this book."

"Anytime," Massingham said, "if you can help me with my candelabra."

"But tell me one thing," Rhodes said. "What about synthetic diamonds? What would happen to the value of diamonds if the market were flooded with synthetics?"

"Synthetics as opposed to simulants?"

"There's a difference?"

"Most certainly. A simulant is a substance like strontium titanate or yttrium aluminum garnet—known as "yag" in the trade—which is made to look like a diamond. Paste, or lead glass, is the best known. In the days of Gun Cotton, Blackshirt, and Bulldog Drummond, paste was always being substituted for the duchess' diamonds. Elizabeth Taylor's duplicate is made of yag, one of the best simulants, but the weight is all wrong, and the refractive index is less than that of a true diamond. The trouble with strontium titanate—also known as Fabulite and Starilian—is that it's too bloody marvelous to be true, with a fantastic dispersion. It's also too soft and doesn't wear as well as a diamond."

Massingham slotted another Turkish cigarette into the holder. "Anyway," he went on, "that's your simulant, a stone manufactured to look like a diamond. A synthetic is a stone manufactured to actually take the place of a diamond, using the same processes as nature."

"And are they any good?"

"Damn good," Massingham said.

"Then why won't they affect the market?"

"For several reasons. First of all they're more expensive than the real thing. Secondly, people always want the genuine article. You know, who wants to eat synthetic steak, even if it tastes as good as a genuine fillet? Thirdly, as far as we can make out, it will always be possible to detect a man-made diamond in a gem laboratory."

"Your trade doesn't lack confidence," Rhodes said. "I'll give you that."

"At least it has fewer fakes than yours," Massingham said.

Rhodes grinned. "You're probably right. But anytime you want a couple of synthetic Queen Anne candlesticks. . . ."

"Like diamond buyers, I prefer the genuine article."

"And where's the best place to buy genuine diamonds?" Rhodes asked, steering Massingham in the right direction. "Amsterdam, I suppose."

"Good God, no, you're a bit out of date there," Massingham said happily. "Antwerp's the center of the world's diamond industry; has been for years. I think they're a little more publicity conscious in Amsterdam."

"And how do the rough stones get to Antwerp? Through London?"

"Correct. Antwerp has the biggest consignment of any diamond center."

"I suppose each shipment must be worth hundreds of thousands of pounds," Rhodes said.

"Hundreds of thousands?" Massingham chuckled. "Millions more like. In fact, each consignment must be worth anything between £13 and £15 million. They're flown out ten times a year by executive jet from Heathrow or Gatwick."

They were silent for a few moments, listening to the flames flapping among the coal. Then, after asking Massingham not to say too much about the book in case someone else realized its potential, Rhodes left him sitting in the smoke, surrounded by his candlesticks.

The pub was packed with customers: husky young men with their pints; pretty girls sipping Campari sodas; and foreigners from the outposts of Lancaster Gate, Queensway, and Paddington. Rhodes elbowed his way to the bar and bought a Ricard for Marie and a glass of Spanish white wine for himself.

They retreated into the middle of the crowd, standing pressed together. He touched her cheek and she

45

smiled at him. In one corner a trio of young men was singing "The First No-oil."

Rhodes slipped his arm around Marie's waist while his thoughts went their own way once more.

The ideal crime is carried out by one man because every accomplice is a prospective weakness. But one man can't organize a robbery on the scale envisaged by Rhodes.

The search for partners was the toughest part of his field work. It took him to New York, Florida, Marseilles, and Spain.

To start with he went to the British Museum, the London Library, and various cuttings agencies and studied reports of ambitious and successful robberies in the past five years. None of them had the finesse he sought.

After ten days intensive research, he decided that present-day crime—unless it was organized by the Mafia, and he wanted none of that—was a hit-and-miss business. The real artists had operated during the fifties and early sixties and had, like himself, gone into retirement. No doubt, Rhodes reasoned, they were as bored with their leisure as he was, like company directors prematurely retired.

It was then he decided that instead of accomplices on a payroll he would seek partners, although he would retain overall command. Each partner would have to recruit his own staff, who would be paid off as soon as they had completed their tasks. But only the partners would have access to the master plan.

In the rear office of his showroom, Rhodes started a file on the robbery, to be known as "Operation Solitaire," using a code based on terms used in the antique trade. There was no point in researching the robberies of the fifties and sixties, because he was only interested in cracksmen who had pulled perfect crimes; if they were perfect, the thieves hadn't been caught and there was no record of them. Instead, Rhodes consulted his own memory and came up with three names.

First, there was Pierre Tallon from Marseilles, who had organized some of the great wine frauds of Bordeaux by arranging for rough plonk to be bottled and labeled with the names of some of the more celebrated houses. He had made a fortune and had loaned his expertise to the Italians when they perpetrated a similar fraud fermenting the waste from banana boats and selling it as red wine.

Tallon was a man of diverse talents, all of them crooked, and he didn't specialize, like so many criminals who eventually get caught because they leave a trademark. But his first love was diamonds. He had carried out successful jewel robberies in Cannes and Nice; and it was said he had been consulted by the Organisation de l'Armée Secrète, better known as the OAS, before they raided the Banque d'Algérie in Oran on March 23, 1962, and escaped with 23,500,000 francs.

Rhodes met him in the Langham Hotel in Johannesburg in 1960. Rhodes had discovered that alluvial diamonds—stolen from the Bushimaie and Katsha rivers in the Congo and smuggled across the Congo River to Brazzaville—were finding an outlet in South Africa. If you lifted stolen property, there couldn't be much of an outcry. So with information supplied by a spy in the Société Minière in Leopoldville, Rhodes flew to Johannesburg. Tallon's information came from a contact in Brazzaville, and the two men arrived in Johannesburg on the same day. They had a drink together in the men-only bar, drawn together instinctively as men of the same profession often are. The next day they met again in a poor white area on the route from Jan Smuts airport into town, where the outlet was said to be situated. They acknowledged that their meetings had to be more than coincidence, cooperated on the heist, and escaped with £150,000 worth of diamonds.

The second name was Moses Ferguson, a black American who served his apprenticeship in the numbers racket in Harlem. But like Tallon, Ferguson was an individualist, and the feuding within the black Mafia didn't appeal to him particularly since it involved the risk of a clutch of machine-gun bullets in your back. So Ferguson graduated to Lexington Avenue, where he got a job as a porter in an apartment building with a green marble vestibule and elevators that smelled of expensive perfume. There he studied the habits of the rich, liked what he saw, and decided to help himself to some of their wealth. He formed an alliance with four black porters in other buildings, and each compiled a dossier on the habits and security precautions of their three richest tenants. Then, over a period of twelve months, each robbed the other's territory. Thus, when the police interrogated Ferguson about the jewel theft in his building, he was clean.

But how could a black porter explain sudden riches? Moses Ferguson had seen too many operators busted after throwing hundred-dollar bills around like confetti. They had won the money at the races, they said, and the bulls fell around the interrogation room. So Ferguson took elocution lessons and moved to Europe, operating from London, Paris, and Amsterdam, where affluent blacks are not unusual. He stayed at the Savoy, the St. George, and the Krasnapolsky; scrupulously paid his bills after robbing guests; dressed immaculately; and tried, unsuccessfully, to join White's Club, in London.

He had an athlete's body, toughened during adolescence in Harlem, and carried out some spectacular cat burglaries. As a cover he opened an import-export business, which is comparable in the underworld to a whore calling herself a model or a con man a company director.

In a quiet way Moses Ferguson, whose grandfather had been a Baptist preacher, was also a schizophrenic.

Every Sunday he went to church and explained to God that he only robbed the disgustingly rich. To pay the poor? At that time Ferguson paid only himself. But one day, he promised, he would help the church.

When that day came and he had made his fortune, Ferguson returned to America, attributing his affluence to his export-import business. He bought a handsome white-framed house on Long Island and an apartment in Manhattan. But he couldn't resist pulling one last heist at the Algonquin, on West Forty-fourth Street, because it had class—as did the jewelry he had seen nestling between the extravagant bosoms of an Italian film actress, a guest at the hotel.

He chose an evening when the Blue Bar and the lobby were full of U.N. officials dining at the hotel, and from an outside phone booth, telephoned a warning that a bomb was due to explode in ten minutes. While the hotel was being evacuated, he helped himself to a master key, let himself into the actress' room, and lifted the jewelry. Then looking like a diplomat from Dar-es-Salaam—to everyone except Johnny Rhodes—he mingled with the departing crowd. Rhodes remembered seeing the same elegant black man at Luxembourg Airport waiting for a Luxair flight to Paris after a jewel robbery at Echternach, on the German frontier, when attention had been distracted by the annual firework display on July 20. Rhodes had been after the jewels himself. Nevertheless, he had admired the thief's style, and now he watched curiously as Moses—tall and impressive in a pearl-gray suit, blue shirt, and black silk tie—strode across the hotel lobby with impressive nonchalance, in view of the bomb threat, and reappeared four minutes later, walking slightly quicker. Outside the Algonquin he climbed into a chauffeur-driven Lincoln Executive. The Lincoln took off down Forty-fourth, and, followed by Rhodes in a cab, turned into the Avenue of the Americas. On Forty-seventh, the center of New York's diamond industry, the Lincoln stopped, its engine still throbbing. Moses dived into a doorway and reappeared a couple of minutes later. Rhodes' car tailed him to an apartment block in Tudor City, near the elegant United Nations Headquarters. Rhodes dismissed the cab, waited half an hour, and then went into the foyer of the building occupied by a janitor and a uniformed guard with his hand on his gun. For twenty-five dollars each they parted with the name of the elegant black man: Moses Ferguson.

My, my, Johnny Rhodes thought as he walked along Forty-second past the Daily News Building, a black Raffles.

The third name was Nigel Lawson. Lawson had been an accomplished diamond smuggler, operating from South West Africa, the Belgian Congo, Ghana, Liberia, and the Ivory Coast. When he returned to Britain, Lawson, ex-Guards and Old Etonian, moved to Dulwich Village and organized two robberies in Hatton Garden involving half a million pounds worth of diamonds. With the proceeds of the two robberies and the smuggling, Lawson withdrew into apparent retirement.

Rhodes had no difficulty in choosing two partners from the three names. During his preliminary inquiries he discovered that Lawson was now on the side of the law, acting as an adviser to the international diamond security bureau with its headquarters in Hatton Garden.

After Christmas lunch, which seemed to weigh him down to his chair, Rhodes fell asleep in front of the television. He awoke at six and made lazy love to Marie on the deep-pile carpet. They watched the "Morecambe and Wise Show," played a game of Scrabble, which Rhodes lost, and went to bed at 11:00 P.M.

Boxing Day was much the same, except that the

food was cold and Rhodes succeeded in losing his handbag in the men's room at the Inn on the Park.

On December 30 he flew to Marseilles.

Chapter 4

The girl with the Caribbean tan stood on the end of the diving board as if she were posing for photographers. Hand on hip, long blonde hair pushed off her forehead by a pair of sun glasses, she gazed across the orange groves to the Mediterranean.

The swarthy man with the cap of tough black hair shot with needles of grey looked at her with minimal interest. There had been many such girls posing beside the blue-tiled pool at Denia, on Spain's Costa Blanca, and it seemed to him they were always in uniform: goggles on the forehead, postage-stamp bikini, sheen of Ambre Solaire, pastel-colored shoes that clattered on the marble walk. Even their bodies were uniform: sharp hips, flat belly, plump breasts like fruit on their lean frames.

They all ate yogurt, drank lemon juice by day and Campari soda by night; they all read fashion magazines and the latest novels snatched from airport bookstands; they all tanned themselves with the care of a Cordon Bleu chef grilling a Dover sole; they all walked with arrogant grace, bra-less breasts bobbing; they all made a performance of lighting and smoking cigarettes; they all claimed to have met Brigitte Bardot and Princess Grace; they were all on the pill; they all made love expertly, a few with passion.

This one, a girl called Elke, from Stockholm, made love as if she had learned the art in a sex manual.

Pierre Tallon had taught her to skip the first six chapters. At the moment he was contemplating driving her to Alicante and putting her on the first plane to any city of her choosing.

Tallon was at last admitting to himself that he was bored with it all. He had retired too young.

He lit a Gaulloise, stretched and went to the open-air bar to pour himself a Pernod. His body was deep brown, his chest thick with hair curled like watch-springs and sheathed with muscle that was in danger of subsiding into fat. In another five years, if he didn't take care, he would be like a weight lifter who has turned to blubber.

He shivered. A sunny day in January on the Costa Blanca might seem warm to a Scandinavian but not to a retired gangster from Marseilles. He put on a beach robe and wandered around the pool assessing the luxuries that crime had bought him.

The house was built on a hump of land covered with wild rosemary, gorse, and herbs, in between the sea and a mountain called the Montgo. It consisted of five bedrooms, each with its own bath; a patio around a lemon tree; a marble-floored lounge with a vast open grate, in which he burned the gnarled trunks of vines; a luxury kitchen; and two terraces; one for breakfast, catching the sunlight when it first filtered across the peak of the mountain, and one for dinner when the moon threw avenues of light across the sea. Its white walls and arches were covered with purple bourgainvillia, orange bignonia, and passion flowers planted by his Spanish staff. On the old vine terraces outside, he had personally planted orange, lemon, and grapefruit, and they had all died. In the flower beds beside the pool, he had planted roses and hibiscus, and they had all gone the way of the citrus trees. The British, Germans, and Dutch who lived in the colonies at the foot of the mountain had told him that jaster daisies were easy to grow; you planted them in builders' rubble and up they shot. He planted them in rich loam bought from a nursery, and within a fortnight they had passed on. It was like an omen to Tallon. He had wooed the countryside and it had rejected him, as though he had blood on his hands. Which, he thought, I have.

He left the girl by the pool and toured the house, flip-flops slapping the marble floors. The big round bed was still unmade, and the girl's clothes were scattered over the floor, her cosmetics spread across the dressing table. The more cool and self-possessed a girl, the dirtier her habits away from public view. Gazing at the bed, Tallon recalled the Scandinavian's predecessors; saw them with hair tumbled on the pillows, thighs spread in welcome, adept at every variation of sex, moaning in orgasm, sometimes shouting so loudly that he had to put his hands across their mouths in case they disturbed the Spanish cook and her husband.

But despite the imported girls, despite the visits from friendly neighbors, the house remained cool and impersonal; full of echoes, the bookshelves undisturbed, two bedrooms untouched, the goddamned flowers dead in their beds. The house needed a few scrawls of a child's crayon on a wall, the click of knitting needles, laughter imprisoned in the rafters.

Tallon peered into the bathroom; the girl had left a line of scum half way up the bath. He dropped the butt of the Gaulloise into the lavatory and flushed it away. Somehow the leisure he had promised himself in his short, violent working life hadn't worked out. He loved Denia, with its French-style main street and boulevard cafés under the plane trees, its whitewashed alleys, its square occupied by doves and old men in berets. To him, the sound of the fishing boats chugging out to sea at 3:30 A.M., the smell of oranges, and the almond blossoms in spring always gave him pleasure. And yet he wasn't happy. A defect in his own personality maybe. Once a bandit always a bandit.

Tallon returned to the lounge. Outside he heard the clatter of shoes on marble. Elke came into the lounge pouting, invisible cameras still trained on her. "Why did you leave me alone like that?" she asked.

"It's cold out there."

"It's cold in here, too."

Tallon said, "If you don't like it, clear out."

She shrugged. "Just as you please. Call a taxi and I'll be ready in half an hour."

Tallon undid his robe. There was a scar on his belly, the legacy of a gun battle in Lyons.

"Oh no," the girl said. "If you want me to go, I go, but no more of that."

Tallon stretched out one hand and pulled her toward him by the bottom half of her bikini. "Oh yes," he said.

She went for him with her long, dark-red fingernails, and he slapped her across the face. "Oh yes," he said.

He tore the bikini off, laid her on the round bed, and took his last payment. She snarled, cried, and yelled but when it was over asked, "Do I have to go?"

Tallon nodded. "I'll drive you to the airport."

He put her on the evening British Airways flight from Alicante to London and drove back to Denia in his Jensen Interceptor along the twisting coast road, skirting the flesh-pots of Benidorm before turning into the orange groves that hide Denia and its castle from the main flow of traffic. It had been raining, and he could smell the oranges hanging in heavy clusters from the trees; many growers were turning to other crops because it hardly paid them to pick the oranges. This saddened Tallon, who thought he must have come from peasant stock that had gotten polluted by gangsters. Still, if they wanted to get rid of the trees, he could offer his services; all he had to do was touch them and it was good-bye oranges.

He drove around the square, where, during fiestas, cannonades of fireworks dispatched the indignant doves to the roof tops, past the white-helmeted policeman on point duty, down the main street with its small bars, where brandy still cost only a few pesetas, toward the harbor. It was almost dusk, Tallon's favorite time of day, when, in Paris or Marseilles, you set out to meet your girl and have an anise on the way, smelling black tobacco smoke and women's perfume. Here you smelled octopus cooking in olive oil, almond blossoms, and the sea. Denia came to life in the evening; just before the awakening, it was a soft and gentle place. Tallon glided slowly along, glancing at the girls with their long slithery hair; the stray, servile dogs; the old ladies in black with autumn-leaf faces; the cinema, where Tallon indulged his taste for western and horror movies.

Like many successful crooks, Tallon was sentimental. Most of them idolized their mothers, but, since Tallon's had been a Marseilles whore jailed for knifing her pimp, mother love presented difficulties. So he was sentimental about Denia and antagonistic toward anyone who criticized it.

He turned left at the end of the main street and passed the fish market and the harbor, its water milky and phosphorescent in the fading sunlight. He parked the Interceptor and drank a Ricard in the Blackstone Bar of the Jamaica Inn, an old pub, where the flames from a log fire threw points of light on the antiques. It was homey, unlike his villa, and he spent a lot of time there. Next he called at the Galeon, a smart bar overlooking rows of jostling yachts, where he drank more Ricard and chatted with the Cornish owner. Then he drove back to the desolate grandeur of his home—and found Johnny Rhodes sitting beside the fire.

"You!" Tallon's hand darted inside his jacket. Five years ago he would have brought out an automatic; today he produced a gold cigarette case.

Rhodes nodded. "Yes, me."

"How the hell did you get in?"

"Broke in, of course," Rhodes said. "Is there any other way?"

"But the burglar alarms. . . ."

"Pretty amateurish, aren't they."

"And the staff. . . ." Tallon remembered it was their night off. *Merde,* he thought, I'm really out of touch. "What do you want?" he asked, adding, "And how the hell did you find me?"

"The second question first," Rhodes told him. "After we've had a drink. You do have something to drink here? You haven't become a teetotaler or anything?"

"We can have a drink before you go. What do you want?"

"Scotch," Rhodes said.

"I've only got Dyk. You know, Spanish whisky. Nothing wrong with it, though, and it's less than half the price."

Rhodes raised his eyebrows. "You short these days?"

"I just like Spanish whisky," Tallon said.

"Quite the *aficionado.*"

Tallon shrugged. "I like Spain. Anything wrong with that?"

"Not a damn thing. But you weren't always the one for the simple life, not back in Johannesburg anyway."

"You can't go on living like that," Tallon said. He spoke fluent English with a slight Marseilles accent. "Who wants to live out of a suitcase for the rest of their life?"

He poured Rhodes a whisky and a Pernod for himself and added ice. Then he lit the fire and they were silent for a moment, watching the flames lick the newspaper before igniting the wood. "Well," Tallon said after a while, "what about answering that question?"

"I went to Marseilles. It wasn't difficult. You know, a few of your old haunts, a few bars like Le Paradou on the Rue de la Tour."

Nostalgia overcame Tallon. Smoky bars; black-stockinged hostesses; the sprawling docks; boat trips to the Chateau d'If; a stroll down the Rue de la Prison to La Maison Diamante, with its stonework shaped like diamonds; the lights of the old port pulled out across the water. . . .

Tallon said, "I used to own a bar in Marseilles until twenty or so customers were gunned down and the police closed it down."

"Nice place, Marseilles," Rhodes said.

"They do things in style," Tallon said.

"I asked after you at the Prefecture and the Palais de Justice."

"Don't even joke about things like that," Tallon said.

"Anyway, a guy living on Avenue Foch finally told me where to find you."

Tallon sat down, clinking the ice in his drink, sniffing the woodsmoke. "So that's *how* you found me. Now, why? You must have wanted me pretty badly."

"A job," Rhodes said.

"Forget it," Tallon said.

"Wait till you hear about it."

"I said forget it. I'm in retirement, you know, and men can have heart attacks suddenly starting work again."

"They can have heart attacks sitting around and getting fat and trying to fix the garden."

"You mean the orange trees?"

Rhodes nodded. "You haven't got green fingers, Pierre."

"You can't be good at everything," Tallon said, gazing at the firelight through his cloudy drink.

"What are you good at these days, Pierre? Apart from that." Rhodes nodded toward the open bedroom door where the bottom half of a pink bikini lay on the floor.

"I'm good at doing nothing. You know, I'm an expert, and I apply all my energies to it."

"You're putting on weight," Rhodes said.

"Snap," Tallon said. He paused. "Anyway, what is this job?"

"It doesn't matter if you're not interested."

"I'd still like to know. After all, you did break into my house and you are sitting here drinking my whisky. I could call the Guardia and have you put inside for illegal entry."

"And I could put them in touch with the Marseilles police," Rhodes said, handing Tallon his empty glass.

"So what is this job?"

"Diamonds," Rhodes said briefly.

"You still can't keep away from the ice, eh, Johnny? After all the cash you made I should have thought you'd have called it a day."

"I did," Rhodes said. "But I just want to pull one final heist. One big beautiful job, as beautiful as a flawless solitaire diamond."

"Ah," Tallon said. "The last job. The big one. It's always the last one and it's always a big one and it's very stupid because the last big one usually puts you inside for fifteen years."

"Fifteen million," Rhodes said.

"Francs?"

Rhodes shook his head.

"Dollars?"

Rhodes shook his head again.

"Pounds?"

Rhodes nodded.

Tallon whistled. "There's never been a diamond heist as big as that."

"There's never been *any* heist as big as that. Operation Solitaire. When the pound's forgotten and the dollar's worth a cent, they'll still be talking about those beautiful rocks that were stolen back in '74, and they'll be speculating as to where they are and who the guys were who got away with them." Rhodes leaned forward. "This will be a class job—the sort they used to pull before the two-bit hoods decided that the way to do it was to bust into a bank with three shotguns, blow the manager's head off, leap into a car, and find the starting motor's jammed."

"You sound like an old man remembering his youth," Tallon remarked. "It's not what it was like in my day, *mon fils*. Any minute now you'll be telling me about the price of cigarettes when you were a kid."

"They were cheap," Rhodes said. "And the robberies were good."

"There's more unsolved crime today than there ever was when we were operating. They can't be that bad."

"The mass-produced article," Rhodes said. "Just like everything else. You know, sheer weight of numbers. But they don't plan like we used to, Pierre."

"Sure I know," Tallon said. "The age of the craftsman is over." He paused. "You want something to eat?"

"As long as it isn't fattening."

From the refrigerator Tallon took some legs of cold chicken, potato salad, Manchega cheese, and a couple of bottles of San Miguel beer and put them on the kitchen table. "So tell me about this job, this solitaire, the big one, the last one." He picked up a chicken leg and began to gnaw at it.

"Are you interested?"

"No."

Rhodes hesitated over the potato salad and found strength to ignore it. "You surprise me," he said. "You know how long it took me to choose you? A month. A whole goddamned month. Out of all the talent in the world, I figured you were the one with the guts, the sophistication, and the brains to deal yourself in with me."

"Well you were wrong." Tallon spooned potato salad into his mouth and took a swig of beer from a bottle.

Rhodes switched tactics. "Nice place you have here."

Tallon waved a chicken leg.

"Cost a few pesetas?"

"A few."

"Don't you get bored?"

"Never."

"It's got a sort of unlived-in air about it."

Tallon grunted. "No one's asking you to stay."

"What do you do with yourself?"

"Screw," Tallon said.

"Not all the time. Not at your age."

"What do you mean, at my age? For Christ's sake, I'm only thirty-eight."

"But you're putting on weight," Rhodes said, taking a gulp of beer.

"Sure, and that's the way to get it off. Can you think of a better way?"

"Broads can get kind of boring. You know, one after the other, all much the same."

"Boy," Tallon exclaimed, "you certainly are a romantic."

"As a matter of fact," Rhodes said, "I figure you are. That's why I think you're getting bored. What do you do when you're not doing that? Kill off oranges?"

"And lemons," Tallon said. "I'm a mass murderer." He belched.

Rhodes said, "Do you know what I reckon?"

"I don't care what you reckon."

"I reckon it's fast approaching the time when you should settle down. You know, find a nice Spanish or French girl—not this other stuff—and have kids. But,"

60

Rhodes put up one hand to stop Tallon from interrupting, "not just yet. You've got to have something to settle down with, something to be proud of. All you've got at the moment is five years of sitting on your ass killing oranges. Think what it would be like to know that you'd pulled off the world's greatest crime. A crime," Rhodes said softly, "that I *know* can be pulled off."

"Yes," Tallon said, "that would be nice. To be able to dangle the kids on your knee and tell them about papa's last big robbery."

"Better than dying of boredom and overweight and not having any kids to dangle."

"You should write a column in a woman's magazine," Tallon said. "Are you married? Have you got kids? Come to think of it," Tallon said, "exactly what are you doing?"

"Selling antiques," Rhodes told him. "That's why I'm here; I'm buying antiques. That's why I was in Marseilles. That's why I was in Antwerp."

"Antwerp?"

"Sure, Antwerp."

"Did you ever steal anything else but diamonds?" Tallon asked, fetching himself another beer.

"Not that I can remember. I go for class, Pierre, you know that. I once had dreams of stealing a really big stone. Like the Koh-i-Nor, which the Moguls set in the Peacock Throne as one of the peacock's eyes, or the Cullinan, the biggest diamond ever found: three thousand one hundred six metric carats. Even when they had cut it into 105 stones, two of them were still the biggest polished diamonds in the world. They're in the Crown Jewels in the Tower of London. Or maybe the Tiffany, that canary cushion-shaped beauty on Fifth Avenue."

"You want to be careful," Tallon said. "There's a lot of bad luck attached to some stones—like the Hope diamond. One owner lost his fortune and another lost her child and all her money and then committed suicide. Don't you think you've chanced your luck long enough with diamonds?"

"You know as well as I do that there's no cure for diamond fever. You and I regard diamonds like other men regard women."

Tallon said, "You speak for yourself."

He made some coffee, took a La Belleza cheroot made on the Canaries from a cardboard box. "I prefer them to Havanas," he told Rhodes. "Want one?"

Rhodes shook his head. They went back to the fire and stared into its smouldering caverns. A clock struck in the town a mile away; a dog howled. Through the windows they could see the night sky scattered with stars and the outline of the mountain, long and hunched, like a sleeping lion.

"It must get lonely here," Rhodes observed after awhile.

"I like my own company."

"You're as bored as hell, aren't you, Pierre." Rhodes stood up and kicked the logs, sending sprays of sparks spiraling up the chimney. "Like me, you quit too soon, and it's taking its toll. Up here," Rhodes touched his own forehead, "and down here," Rhodes prodded his stomach.

Tallon opened the French windows leading onto a terrace. He could smell wild herbs and hear the sea. Denia was a cluster of green and yellow lights. He stood at the window and after awhile said, "You want to sleep here?"

"I don't have any other place to go."

"Okay," Tallon said. "You sleep here tonight and tomorrow you go. The answer's still the same— *Non, merci.*"

Rhodes shrugged. "I was only giving you first refusal. There are others."

"Like who?"

Rhodes recited a few names. Leopold Zimmerman,

who had staged a crude stick-up in Tel Aviv in 1966, a bumper year for diamonds in Israel. Jackie Robbins, a Chicago gunman, who had gotten itchy feet, flown to Hong Kong, and tried to lift some of the exhibits at the jewelry exhibition organized by the Jewelers' and Goldsmiths' Association in the City Hall. He had just been released on parole. Mario Gordini, who had gotten the Syndicate interested in a system, perfected in an American laboratory, for artificially coloring diamonds. By the early sixties, New York's diamond industry was in a panic because so many big stones, their true color camouflaged by a coating that neither chemicals nor X-rays could detect, were circulating as a result of Gordini's initiative. Ultimately, the experts resurrected the ancient technique of examining suspected stones under a microscope in reflected light, and the "Gordini Gambit," as it was known in the business, was beaten. Rhodes gave a few other names.

Tallon laughed. "You're—how do you say it?— putting me on. Zimmerman and Robbins were crude amateurs and you know it. If you use them you must be out of your mind."

"Gordini wasn't so dumb."

"Gordini was a con man. You never liked con men, Johnny."

"It depends. I don't like con men who hustle old ladies or sell kids who've just gotten married apartments that don't exist. But I like style, you know that. Gordini had style, you've got to admit that."

Tallon admitted it. "But what part does a man like Gordini play in a straight heist in Antwerp?"

Rhodes, who had no idea, grinned enigmatically. "It's my job, Pierre."

"Sure and you can keep it." Tallon shut the French windows. "I'm going to bed. If I'm not up in the morning cook yourself some breakfast. *Bon nuit,* Johnny."

"Good night, Pierre."

At 3:30 A.M. Tallon woke Rhodes by switching on the light and shaking him. "The job," he said, "tell me about it." And as Rhodes rubbed his eyes and sat up in bed he said, *"Tu m'emmerdes.* You win, you bastard. You knew you would, didn't you. I couldn't sleep. The fever's returned."

Rhodes grinned sleepily. "We're too much alike, you and me. If I was tired of retirement, then I knew as sure as hell you were."

"Just one more job, eh, Johnny? The big one? Solitaire?"

Rhodes nodded. "Just one. Then we really quit for keeps. We'll marry nice girls and settle down and have kids and grow fat and drink port." He paused. "And maybe grow oranges?"

Tallon grinned. "Maybe they need respect, those damned oranges. Perhaps if I've pulled the biggest heist the world has ever known, they'll respect me."

Rhodes said, "Make some coffee then."

He pulled on slacks and a sweater and went into the lounge, where he kicked some life into the fire. From the kitchen came the smell of coffee.

They sat opposite each other at the long oak table like bank manager and client.

"So what do we do?" Tallon asked. "Who do we use and how much do we spend?"

Rhodes told him that they'd need a lot of money because they would have to pay for perfection. "Maybe £500,000. Maybe more." And when Tallon exclaimed, he said, "We can raise that sort of money. What's half a million pounds when we're playing for fifteen million?"

"It's half a million pounds," Tallon replied. "It's a fortune."

"But we can raise it."

"Oh sure," Tallon said. "We can raise it."

Rhodes told him they needed one other partner. Tallon agreed. Rhodes said they also needed a good pilot—a crooked pilot in good physical condition. A pilot, Rhodes said, like Hans Muller from Hamburg. Muller had been sacked by a scheduled airline for smuggling gold from New Delhi in May 1959, and he had subsequently flown for Air Congo and air-lifted food and medical supplies into Biafra. Since then he had been flying arms to Ireland and Palestinian guerillas. "Flying is to Muller what diamonds are to us," Rhodes said, sipping his coffee.

Tallon lit a Gaulloise and placed it carefully on an earthenware ashtray. The smoke rose in a thin, straight stem. "Who else do we need, and how many? We don't want too many, Johnny. You and I always worked alone."

Rhodes said, "A job like this has to be staffed. We just have to be very careful who we pick. Anyway, we've got the time. You know, we can spend ten or eleven months planning."

"Go on," Tallon said, as the ash lengthened on his untouched cigarette.

Rhodes said the robbery would be divided into three operations. They would need some good drivers on the staff. Then he told Tallon about the Hawker Siddeley BH-125 jet that flew the diamonds from London to Antwerp.

Tallon said, "You've been doing your homework. What do we do, hijack it?"

Rhodes shook his head. "Too crude, too risky. Leave that to the nuts, the terrorists, the gangsters, the sort of guys who, a few years back, would have been blasting barbers' shops with Thompson subs. No," Rhodes said thoughtfully, "we'll use a little more finesse."

"Okay," Tallon said, "it's your idea. Tell me."

Rhodes told him about the security van that picked up the diamonds at Antwerp airport and took them, by a different route each time, to the Diamond Club on Pelikaanstraat. What they needed most, Rhodes said, was a reliable inside man who would tip them

65

off when a diamond consignment was on its way. They would pay him fifty thousand pounds in three payments.

Down in the harbor the engine of a fishing boat erupted into life like a burst of gunfire. The ash toppled from Tallon's cigarette.

Tallon made some more coffee as the boats trailed each other like glow-worms into the Mediterranean.

They talked till eight, when, as the sun was throwing its first shafts over the mountain, the Spanish cook and her husband returned from their cottage at Miraflor. The stubble was dark on Tallon's chin, Rhodes' mouth was as dry as the ash on the fire.

"So what happens next?" Tallon asked after the Spanish couple had gone to their quarters.

"I call you in about a month."

"I haven't a phone. You don't need phones when you're in retirement. You'd better write to me care of the post office."

"Oh sure," Rhodes said. "I'll write to you just like I'd sign a confession in the precinct." He stood up and stretched. "I'll cable you to fly to London and I'll sign the cable 'Solitaire.' Okay?"

"Okay, Johnny, Solitaire's the code word, but why don't we call the job Cullinan? You know, the biggest stone ever found?"

"Call it what you like," Rhodes said. "Call it the Moon of the Mountain if you like. That was a 120-carat beauty that disappeared some time after 1900. Me, I'm going to call it Solitaire."

Rhodes showered and shaved. Then he shook Tallon's hand and walked down the hill, past Tallon's dead orange trees, past clouds of almond blossoms and sleeping white villas, where retired Europeans lived. Spaniards were on their way to work to build more white villas with arches, patios, and bamboo-covered carports, and when he reached the town, the bars were already open for the workers to fuel themselves with coffee and cognac and tuna fish bocadillos. At the kiosk on the corner newspaper vendors were untying the newspapers, and the doves and old men were settling for the day in the square.

A good place to retire, Rhodes decided. In twelve months time?

Near the cinema, home of John Wayne and Boris Karloff, he climbed into a black Mercedes taxi and told the driver to take him to Alicante.

After Rhodes had left, Pierre Tallon wandered thoughtfully around his home until the cook brought him a tortilla with some bread, still warm from the bakery, fresh orange juice, and more coffee.

Then he went downstairs and locked himself in a big, stonewalled room that smelled faintly of oil. He unlocked an antique chest, removed some sacking and a couple of layers of old magazines, and looked at his guns: handguns—automatics and revolvers— rifles, submachine guns, shotguns, Colts, Remingtons, Brownings, Smith & Wessons, Pythons.

From the top of his private armory he took a new Colt CMG-2 light machine gun, which could be fired from the hip or lying prone. It was gas-operated with a belt feed and was designed to be fired under the worst conditions of war. It was also stolen.

First Tallon field-stripped the gun. Then he stripped it fully, handling each part with love. Soon, he thought, he might have to use just such a gun.

By the time Tallon had fully stripped the Colt, Rhodes was being driven across the water-logged plains that separate Alicante town from the airport. He was content with the night's work, and he didn't know that his knowledge of Tallon was flawed. He didn't know that Tallon had no objection to killing on a job, that, in fact, he enjoyed it.

Chapter 5

Fort Pierce, in St. Lucie County, Florida, is fish—sailfish, dolphin, kingfish, tarpon, amberjack, barracuda—everything from the tigers of the Atlantic to humble croakers, grunts, and drums. Its fifty thousand or so inhabitants talk, catch, and eat fish. Within minutes of introduction they recall the world-record sea trout, caught with cut mullet in January 1949 by Clinton Hubbard. It weighed fifteen pounds three ounces. This weight is imprinted indelibly on your mind by the time you leave Fort Pierce so that whenever you're asked any other statistical question you always reply, "Fifteen three."

The main part of the town lies on the west side of the Indian River, which is part of the inland coastal waterway. To reach the Atlantic and its "tigers," you cross the waterway by one of two bridges. From both bridges people fish. There is a jungle torpor about the inland waterway; its waters are deep, and the air smells of luxuriant vegetation and boats and discarded bait; some days this is salted by a wind coming in from the ocean.

Next to fishing, the inhabitants like boating followed by the usual priorities of man. Then, not too far down the list, they enjoy going to church. Most interpretations of worship are catered to, including Baptist, Methodist, Roman Catholic, Lutheran, Jewish, Greek-Orthodox, and Seventh Day Adventists.

It was the churches that attracted Moses Ferguson to Fort Pierce after the Algonquin robbery. He sold his house on Long Island, rented the Manhattan apartment, and moved south to spread the word of God. He bought himself a luxurious villa at Palm Beach and used it as a base. Month after month, year after year, he toured the Deep South, whipping up congregations of blacks into religious frenzies. Soon he became accepted as a sort of Black Messiah and was treated with suspicion by some authorities; but he was careful never to preach violence, so mostly they let him alone. He also attracted the hostility of black militants because he was too pacifist; but such was his popularity that they, too, shied away as he brandished the Bible in their faces and slipped the occasional fifty-dollar bill in their pockets.

In Fort Pierce, Moses Ferguson was particularly well known because he was fond of fishing. He had also heard rumors that a couple of miles out to sea, the shifting sands of the Atlantic had moved to reveal the wreck of a Spanish galleon weighed down to the sea bed with gold.

The thought of the gold disturbed Moses. In 1964 Treasure Salvors Incorporated had recovered more than a million dollars worth of coins and jewelry from a wreck south of the Fort Pierce inlet. How much more might there be in this wreck, if it existed? But the rumors did more than merely whet the appetite of a born treasure-seeker; they alerted the instincts of a born crook. Gold is a magnet to any thief; but, to a man who has felt the cold touch of diamonds, it is second-grade, heavy and cumbersome, bearing no comparison to the aristocrat diamond with its icy dignity, its imperious fires and, of course, its viability.

The feel of the diamonds from the Algonquin had left a permanent itch in Moses Ferguson's hands. He usually managed to dispel it by communion with God (after all, the proceeds of the heist had recruited a lot of worshippers to the Baptist church); but these days, since he had come to Fort Pierce, the itch had become more persistent. It was only rumored that there

69

was a fortune lying out there beneath the basking turtles and the flying fish; but there was no doubt about the diamonds lying in vaults and safes while the owners paraded around the world's playgrounds wearing replicas.

Moses liked to spend the day fishing for *Istiophorus americanus*—or sailfish, as it is more familiarly known —and the evening preaching at an open-air meeting in the town, which already boasted thirteen Baptist churches. But these days he found his concentration was slipping.

Arms outstretched, he implored at the top of his voice, "Who do we love?"

Back came the responses from a sea of black faces: they loved God. With a passion and devotion that made Moses Ferguson want to weep with compassion for mankind.

Then he looked up at the velvet skies and saw them embedded with diamonds.

Johnny Rhodes left London Airport for New York on a Pan Am flight on Thursday, January 30. When he landed at Kennedy Airport, sleet was falling and the cab drivers were scowling about the weather and the fuel crisis. He asked his driver about Watergate and was told tersely that it had become a way of life, like mugging. A truck swept past, throwing brown slush onto the windows of the cab. When it cleared, Rhodes saw Manhattan floating in front of him like a mirage and was assailed by a pleasant excitement. Despite its pollution and corruption, it was still a great city, and you could feel this as you entered its portals. London and Paris might have more dignity, but they lacked the raw vigor of New York, or so it seemed to Rhodes on the outskirts of his home town. He thought he would like to visit his birthplace in downtown Manhattan, but first he had to find a man called Moses Ferguson.

It was noon, and the streets were crowded with pedestrians, their heads tucked into the sleet. It had been five years since Rhodes had been here. The skyscrapers seemed to have grown, the yellow cabs multiplied, the people became more preoccupied. To Rhodes, luxury was once any hotel with an awning over the sidewalk. With his last few cents he would buy a Coke and a hot dog and watch the rich (anyone who hired a cab was a millionaire) alight beside those awnings and stride with the assurance of the wealthy into the hotels. Today, many years later, he tipped the driver and wondered if there was a boy across the street drinking Coke, eating a hot dog, and watching him.

In his room he washed and changed and went down to the bar for a Bloody Mary. Then, a rich man in an expensive camel-hair coat, he walked onto Forty-fourth Street, turned into Fifth Avenue, and cut down East Forty-second, past the Daily News Building to Tudor City, with the sleet coming off the East River pasting him with icy sludge. No one at Tudor City remembered anyone called Moses Ferguson, not even when they saw the bills in Rhodes' wallet.

He hailed a cab, and told the driver to take him to the address on Forty-seventh Street. It was an unobtrusive sort of building, with a janitor and an armed guard wearing a uniform like a movie usher. As Rhodes approached, the guard's hand moved to his gun. Rhodes produced his wallet and the hand fell away. No, he didn't remember any particularly elegant spook who came here to sell diamonds a few years back; he had been here ten years and he'd seen many blacks coming and going, and they all looked pretty much the same to him. For twenty dollars he frowned his way back through the years; for fifty he reckoned an elegant spook with diamonds to sell might have done business with a guy called Anderson in Room 24 on the second floor.

Anderson was elegant, too. A thin, fragile man with silver hair and a skull that looked as if you could crush it between your hands. He had never heard of anyone with a name like Moses Ferguson. He laughed at the thought and opened the drawer of his desk where he kept a Beretta M-90.

Rhodes, who was sitting on the other side of the desk, said, "Please don't, Mr. Anderson."

The drawer stayed open. Anderson said in his thin voice, "Just who the hell are you?" A vein throbbed on his temple.

"It doesn't matter who I am, it's what I know."

"What do you know?" Anderson's voice sounded as as if it might break, like a boy's voice in puberty. "What the hell is this, some sort of amateurish attempt at blackmail?"

"Only if you've done something I can blackmail you about."

"Then you're out of luck," Anderson said, relaxing a little. "If you don't get the hell out of here, I'll call the police." He put one hand on the cream telephone on his desk.

"Go ahead, Mr. Anderson. Call the cops and I'll tell them you're one of the biggest diamond fences in New York."

Anderson laughed; the laugh reminded Rhodes of ice cubes chinking in a glass. "In that case I'll call your bluff, Mr. . . . ?"

Rhodes stared at him.

With slender fingers, Anderson picked up the phone, as though it offended him. He hesitated.

Rhodes said, "Go ahead, Mr. Anderson."

"You're very sure of yourself."

"Sure I am," Rhodes said. "Just as sure as the guy who sold you the diamonds from the Algonquin heist back in the sixties."

The slender fingers tightened on the receiver, the

knuckles gleamed. Anderson replaced the receiver, eyes glancing at the open drawer.

With one foot Rhodes kicked the desk. It hit Anderson in the chest and he fell backwards off his chair, lying motionless on the floor like an insect feigning death. Rhodes picked him up by his lapels and said, "Where can I find Moses Ferguson, Mr. Anderson?"

At 12:15 P.M. the next day, Rhodes caught the National Airlines DC-10 Sun King flight to West Palm Beach. Within two hours of arrival he had learned that Ferguson was on a tour of the Southeast spreading the good word. It took the blacks at the Baptist church at the back of the town a further half hour to convince Rhodes that the man he had seen walking coolly out of the Algonquin with a fortune in diamonds in his pocket was currently representing God. No one knew exactly where he was, but they thought Daytona Beach was a good bet.

Rhodes hired a blue Cougar and headed north, wishing he'd brought clothes with Florida sunshine in mind. At Dayonta Beach he booked into a motel overlooking the hard sands, which cars use as a road. Then he drove across the bridge spanning the inland waterway and headed for the churches in the black quarter. Churches! Rhodes shook his head in wonderment as he drove. He was told that the Black Messiah had left the previous night, bound for Fort Pierce.

The next day, Rhodes drove south again along Highway 1. On February 7 he sighted his quarry.

The white face stood out like a beacon. Moses Ferguson—leading his congregation in song, hands clapping, body swaying, sweat pouring down his face and neck into his expensive Palm Beach shirt, faltered for a moment. A white face in a black congregation could only mean one thing: trouble. Maybe there were other white faces creeping through the darkness outside the lamp-lit arena on the outskirts of Fort

Pierce. So far, he had found the locals tolerant. But it needed one nut only to start a riot, only one phoney call for help from that white face to swivel the shotguns toward the happy worshippers in front of him.

Ferguson decided to conclude the service. He whispered to the black playing the old portable organ with keys like yellow teeth to cut short the hymn. The music stopped abruptly, and the puzzled congregation was called upon to join their preacher in a last prayer. They left shaking their heads but content to do the Black Messiah's bidding. A few glanced curiously at the white man in their midst; he was jostled a little but he stood fast.

Toweling his face and neck, Ferguson stared at the white man speculatively, old instincts of self-preservation awakened. He had been in retirement a long time, and he knew it was easy to get lulled into a false state of security. Only this week, British police had flown to Rio de Janeiro and busted Ronald Biggs, one of Britain's Great Train Robbers, who had been living the sweet life since breaking out of jail.

Ferguson's mind went back over the years. What mistakes had he made? The most impulsive and risky job had been the last diamond job in Manhattan. But all these years later. . . . Ferguson wished he had a gun with him, but guns don't become preachers.

The white man was coming toward him, a grin on his face. A dangerous face, despite its humorous lines. Ferguson looked for the bulge at chest or hip but saw nothing. Vaguely, he wondered why anyone in Florida would be wearing a tweed jacket. He stopped toweling himself and waited.

Johnny Rhodes put out his hand and said, "Good evening, Moses."

Cautiously Ferguson took the hand and shook it, noting the powerful grip. "I don't think I've had the pleasure," he said.

"You haven't," Rhodes agreed. "I thought it was time you did."

"I'm afraid I don't understand."

Moses began to wonder if he *was* a nut; he met many of them in his work.

Rhodes went on. "I saw you once but you didn't notice me. You were in a hurry."

"Really? Where was that?"

"At the Algonquin hotel on West Forty-fourth Street, Manhattan," Rhodes said.

Moses Ferguson sat in one of the seats amidships on the Wellcraft twenty-four-foot Airshot Fisherman with a Nemrod Galleon II compressed air spear gun beside him. Rhodes sat in the stern beside the 245-horsepower LOMC engine. They had been angling for sailfish.

Ferguson said, "So what do you want, friend. Blackmail?"

"You're the second person who's asked me that in a week."

"And what did you tell the first?"

"I said I wanted to know where you were."

Ferguson stared at him. He didn't look evangelical, brown eyes wary, muscles hard in his jaw. He touched the spear gun with his foot. "Obviously that person knew."

"Obviously."

Rhodes trailed one hand in the water as they drifted across the deep, calm water. They both wore jeans and sweat shirts. It was 10:00 A.M. and the day was warm, with a haze on the horizon and a thin line of foam on the shore two miles away. A formation of pelicans flew above them, flying fish took off trying to join them.

"So what's all this stuff about the Algonquin?"

The previous night Rhodes had moved into Ferguson's motel on Seaway Drive, and they had agreed to talk out at sea, where only the birds and fish could listen.

Rhodes said, "It was a neat job. I couldn't have done better myself."

"Really?" Ferguson turned to look at the fishing line. "Are you just out of the funny farm, mister?"

Rhodes said, "I admire your style, Moses, particularly at Echternach." He grinned. "That was quite a firework display."

This time Ferguson reacted with a slight tautening of facial muscles that made his scalp move. "Echternach? Where the hell's Echternach?"

"The Grand Duchy of Luxembourg. You know that, Moses, because you went there after you moved to Europe when things got too hot for you in New York."

"You aiming to write my biography?" Ferguson had dropped the extravagant speech of the Deep-South preacher; he spoke with the cultured accents he had been taught at elocution classes, with occasional excursions into ghetto slang.

The spear gun was angled so that he only had to make one quick movement to dispatch its arrow into Rhodes' chest with a force that would throw Rhodes overboard as shark bait. Rhodes said, "I know all about you, Moses, and I have a proposition to make." He held up one hand. "Hear me out before you fire that goddamned thing."

"Okay, shoot."

Rhodes told him about himself, Pierre Tallon, and Solitaire. Then he trolled his bait—$40 million worth of it.

Ferguson was thoughtful. He peered over the side of the motorboat before asking, "You interested in gold?"

Rhodes shrugged.

"They reckon there's a lot of it down there. It seems a Spanish galleon strayed away from the Keys in 1773 and sank in a storm. Or so they reckon. Me, I'm a bit doubtful, although they've fished up a million bucks of loot from another wreck. Maybe if we had the capital, you know, we could get a salvage operation going and make ourselves a legal fortune."

"You've got a fortune already," Rhodes said.

"I'm not complaining. But I spend a lot, too, spreading the word." Ferguson looked at Rhodes quizzically. "But you didn't answer my question. Gold. Does it interest you?"

"Diamonds interest me, Moses. And they interest you, too. Diamond fever's like malaria: you never get rid of it. And I figure you're just about to have another bout."

"Maybe you're right, I don't know, but tell me one thing, Mr. Johnny Rhodes. Tell me why you chose me?"

Rhodes told him what he had told Tallon: that he was chosen because he was the best and had never committed the cardinal crime of getting caught. "You're a professional, and the cops haven't got a thing on you."

Above them a pelican hovered as though listening. Ferguson was silent for a moment, a frown on his flat, handsome face. "Maybe I don't have any record," he said after a while. "You're right there, I'm clean as far as the fuzz is concerned. But I'm also black."

"I'm not color-blind," Rhodes said.

"It can be a drag when you're pulling a heist. You know, the sort of heist you got in mind, not a ten-dollar mugging on the West Side. In a smart place like Antwerp, the first guy they'd pull in would be a spook. Do you ever see any blacks in the diamond area?"

"It's getting so they're everywhere," Rhodes said, adding, "in any case it never seemed to hinder you."

Ferguson shrugged. "I always had an angle."

"So have I," Rhodes replied. "That's why I'm basing you in Amsterdam. It's not too far from Antwerp, and there are plenty of blacks in Amsterdam from the old Dutch colonies. They've hit that place like the Jamaicans hit London. And in any case," Rhodes grinned easily at Ferguson, "Haarlem is just down the road."

A quarter of a mile away a black fin broke the surface, then another. Ferguson pointed to the sharks. "The fuzz have arrived already," he said.

"Are you in?"

"I'll think about it. In the first place I don't see why I should believe a goddamned word you say; in the second I'm in retirement."

"Sure," Rhodes said. "I know all about that. I was in retirement, so was Tallon, and we both got the itch, just like you. Don't kid me, Moses, I know all the symptoms of the fever. And I know all the symptoms of premature retirement," Rhodes said, pointing at Ferguson's waist. "We're all going to have to do some workouts, Moses. We have to be in peak condition."

"Man," Ferguson said, "I just knew a white face in my congregation was trouble."

"Salvation," Rhodes corrected him.

Ferguson said, "Give me time. I need to check out a few things—including you."

"Check me out here," Rhodes said, fishing a pocket book from his jeans and handing Ferguson his business card with the Mayfair address. "While you're at it, check out a job in Brussels in August 1964, when a black Citroen was stopped beside the Statue of Godfrey of Bouillon, and a leather bag containing two hundred thousand dollars worth of cut diamonds was lifted by a police motorcyclist."

Ferguson looked impressed. "You?"

Rhodes, who was proud of that particular snatch, nodded.

"The papers went to town on it, huh? Right outside the Palace of Justice." Ferguson chuckled. " 'Belgium's Most Audacious Robbery.' Man, if that was yours, I like your style."

"You followed it closely?"

"I follow all crime closely. It's my hobby."

"Then you remember the stones involved?"

Ferguson thought about it. "Some beautiful pieces," he recalled, and Rhodes noted with satisfaction that he was beginning to drool. "Not brilliants, as I remember it. Pendeloque and marquise, weren't they? And one was a fancy color I think. Pink was it?"

"Full marks," Rhodes said. "I kept the pinky." He reached into his pocket. "Here it is." He handed it to Ferguson.

"Jesus," exclaimed the preacher. He held it away from the sun. "It's a beauty. Artificially colored?"

Rhodes was pleased he had asked. It was difficult to detect artificial colors these days, especially since heat treatments and gamma irridation had been introduced —even Britain's Atomic Energy Authority was in on the act. Ferguson hadn't been naive enough to accept it, nor had he been too proud to ask.

Rhodes said, "No it's a natural fancy. Keep it while you check me out."

"Okay, it's up to you. But the stone doesn't prove a thing except that you've had access to the loot. For all I know you're a fence." Ferguson slipped the pink diamond into his pocket. "I presume it was Anderson who put you on to me."

"It doesn't matter who put me on to you. All that matters is I found you."

"I guess so." Ferguson nodded wisely. "I guess that's all that matters. And, of course, that I might tell the bulls a guy named Rhodes staying on Seaway has given me a diamond and they might just take you inside for a few questions."

"Sure," Rhodes said, "and they just might check out the history of a Bible-puncher sought out by a diamond thief in Fort Pierce."

"Smart ass," Ferguson said.

Rhodes said, "You can also check out a couple of

jobs in Chicago and Los Angeles. I'll give you details no one else could know. Okay?"

Ferguson said it was okay. He glanced at the business card. "I'll be in touch."

Ferguson returned to the wheel and the Wellcraft took off trolling mullet bait behind. When the line jerked, Ferguson shouted, "Here we go, it's a big bastard." Then the line went slack. "Shit," said the man who spread the good word. "Do you know what that was? A kingfish, king mackerel, black salmon. The bastards can judge the end of a hook like you and I can judge the grain in a gem diamond. They take the end of the bait and then they're gone."

"Let's hope there's no kingfish in Antwerp," Rhodes said.

The next day Rhodes drove the Cougar to Miami, left it at the airport, and at 6:05 P.M. caught the National DC-10 flight to London. He arrived at 7:20 the following morning wondering how to explain to Marie that the big antique deal in New York had fallen through.

Chapter 6

At 11:35 A.M. on Friday, February 1, 1974, a tall man going elegantly to seed hailed a taxi outside his apartment in Gray's Inn Road, London, the long street that links Holborn with the twin railway stations of King's Cross and St. Pancras, and told the driver to take him to the races at Sandown Park.

"It'll cost you, mate," the driver said, "what with the shortage of diesel and everything."

"It doesn't matter," the man said impatiently. If you were going to make a killing at the races, what did ten quid, even twenty, matter?

He settled himself in the back of the taxi, lit a cigarette, and began to read the papers. The miners' wage demands, the three-day work week, Janie Jones, another massacre in Northern Ireland.

Having dutifully glanced at the headlines, the man turned to the racing pages, then opened the *Sporting Life* and his form book. He became so engrossed that they reached the Scilly Isles near Sandown Park, in the Surrey fringes of London, before he looked up.

He folded the papers and closed the form book, happy that he had found nothing to deter him from his bet, a treble involving L'Escargot in the 2:30 Gainsborough Chase. The betting forecast was 11 to 4, which he thought was a generous assessment for a horse that had already won the Cheltenham Gold Cup twice. Another prize for the American owner, Raymond Guest, owner of the 1968 Derby winner Sir Ivor, the final jackpot for himself before he quit punting and the other despicable profession he was following.

He paid the taxi driver and headed for the gates, a distinguished figure, plumage slightly moulting, among the punters, tipsters, and bookies. He wore a light tweed suit with finely rolled lapels and the vaguest shine to the seat of the pants; suede shoes by Church's, slightly stained; a brown Derby a little too small, as all brown Derbies should be; binoculars in a leather case bearing initials that weren't his; and an Old Etonian tie just beginning to fray. His face was noble, and his sleek hair, touched with grey at the temples, just covered the tops of his ears. There was about him the hint of shabbiness that only breeding can carry off. And yet there was an intangible air about the man that made bookies check his money for counterfeit; bank cashiers check his credit-card number on the black list; shop assistants check with the floor manager before accepting his checks. Perhaps it was the slight odor of stale whisky; the unsolicited tales of his career in the Guards; a wetness of the eyes; an unspoken plea for acceptance behind the mannered assurance. No one was quite sure what it was. He was like a peer in full regalia with his fly open.

Inside the enclosure he headed for the bar, ordered himself a large whisky and soda, and listened with indulgence to a well-known actor suggesting that Royal Toss might beat L'Escargot to the post. He ordered himself another large whisky. The bar was filling up, and the runners in the first race, the February Novices Hurdle, were making their way to the starting post.

He sauntered outside to enjoy the brilliance of the scene: the bright jockey silks; the green river of the course; the sinewed grace of the horses. High above, a jet bisected the sky with a white pencil mark. Confidence flowed warmly in his veins. He made his way to a telephone and called his bookmaker in the West End.

The cockney voice at the other end of the line was doubtful. "Five hundred pounds on a bet like this? That's a lot of bread. . . ."

The man interrupted him. "My credit's good."

"For the first time in nine months." There was a pause. "Your credit's good to the tune of £50."

"Then the bet's covered."

"I suppose so."

"Then you've got to take it."

"We haven't *got* to take anything." Another pause. "All right then, you're on." The line went dead.

His mood slightly spoiled, the man returned to the bar and ordered himself another whisky. At 1:48, with studied nonchalance, he went to the stands to watch the first leg of his treble, the Park Handicap Chase, in which his selection, Black Andrew, had shortened to 7 to 4 favorite.

He watched through his binoculars as the five horses

galloped toward the last furlong of the 2-mile 18-yard race, observing the intensity on the jockeys' faces as they called for a last effort from their mounts, man and horse an entity. Only a flicker of muscle on his jaw betrayed his emotion. First past the post was Black Andrew. Smiling a little, the man made his way back to the bar as the loudspeaker announcement confirmed the win.

One up, two to go, not that there was any real doubt in his mind. In fact, he was surprised to find, when he returned to the stands for the 2:30 race, that Kulvulgan had been made joint favorite at 5 to 2 with L'Escargot.

They were off at 2:33 P.M. Ten minutes later it was all over. L'Escargot was a game fourth. The man stayed on the stands for a few minutes, staring above the heads of the crowd.

A little man in a peaked cap and hacking jacket nudged him and said, "Cheer up, guv, you can't win 'em all."

"No," said the man in the light tweed suit. "You can't, can you." His lips trembled slightly as he made his way back to the bar and ordered a beer.

He returned to London by train, arriving at Waterloo at 5:45. He went to the bar overlooking the main hall, ordered himself a pint of bitter, and watched the crowds of commuters clustered around the indicators waiting for news of their trains, which had been disrupted by the work-to-rule.

He finished his beer and hesitated outside the station before deciding to walk home since it took up time and there was nothing to do at the flat. He set out across Waterloo Bridge. It was dusk, and the lights were fusing on the waters of the Thames. There was loneliness in the winter air. A smell of mud, the tide bearing dark, anonymous flotsam to the sea. He stared over the parapet, considering the deep, swift-moving water, then straightened up and walked briskly across the bridge.

He turned up Aldwych, cutting down Kingsway and Theobalds Road. There was only one light in his small apartment building.

The elderly porter looked up from his desk. "No luck?"

The man shook his head and smiled, the financier returning from an indifferent day on the Stock Exchange. "You can't win 'em all," he said.

The porter, who thought punting was a mug's game, nodded and returned to his evening paper.

Inside the flat—furnished, like its tenant, with shabby dignity—the man sank into an armchair and stared at the blank eye of the broken TV. After a while he brightened up, as he always did, because there was always a next time. But first he would have to return to his despicable profession, because he needed a very large sum of money for the final big killing at the races. A *really* big sum of money, he thought; one straight bet on the nose and no fancy trebles.

The man, named Nigel Lawson, whom Johnny Rhodes had struck off his short list of potential accomplices, decided to consult his dossier in Hatton Garden, which had helped him foil so many big diamond robberies.

The essence of diamond security is its discreet approach, especially in London, with its unarmed police. In Hatton Garden, one of the great diamond centers of the world, discretion is taken to its limit: it is invisible.

Like Pelikaanstraat, Hatton Garden is a dingy thoroughfare, a dirty bandage wrapped around a glittering storehouse. It links Clerkenwell Road and Holborn and comprises two rows of undistinguished buildings lining a narrow street. At the Clerkenwell

84

end stands the building where Sir Hiram Maxim (1840–1916) designed and manufactured the Maxim gun; at the Holborn end stands a statue of Albert, Prince Consort (1819–1861).

Although security is unobtrusive, it is elaborate. De Beers, for instance—the giant of the rough diamond industry, with its headquarters in a handsome building on the corner of Charterhouse Street opposite Hambros Bank—have one of the most comprehensive closed-circuit TV systems in the world, and the electronically operated doors can trap a thief within a second. The deep vaults, encased in amor plate, are programed to open and shut at specific times, and the whole Aladdin's cave is laced with inescapable electronic beams that trigger burglar alarms.

The wealthiest companies in Hatton Garden are identifiable by the Bentleys, XK-12s, and Rolls Royces outside. Unlike the diamond barons of Belgium and Holland, the British are compelled to convert riches into internal combustion machines. These companies —with dignified limousines parked incongruously outside small, sooty buildings—have alarm systems directly linked to the Snow Hill police station, just across Holborn Viaduct south of St. Paul's. When these systems work successfully, their instigators can stroll down the road at a later date and see the thieves dispatched to jail by a bewigged judge at the Central Criminal Court, better known as the Old Bailey.

The trouble with Hatton Garden's security set-up, however, is that it cannot confine its precautions to British criminals. Diamonds are an international currency, and, therefore, the world's criminals set their sights on Hatton Garden. Other diamond centers—Antwerp, Amsterdam, New York, Tel Aviv, Johannesburg—encounter the same difficulty, and, therefore, an international security system has been developed in which information about the activities of criminals specializing in diamonds—stealing them, imitating them, coloring them, smuggling them—is exchanged. It works in similar fashion to Interpol, with an intricate system of spies and informers.

It was for this bureau, with its headquarters in London, that Nigel Lawson worked.

Lawson was so good at his job that the bureau would have liked to have him on the staff. But you can't employ a man with a suspected criminal past in the middle of Hatton Garden, where so much depends on integrity. Nothing was really known about Lawson's past; certainly there were no convictions recorded against him. But his encyclopedic knowledge of the underworld and the vaguely dishonorable aura that surrounded him convinced everyone that his past was "murky." So the bureau treated him as an elite informer: they paid him a proportion of the expenses he submitted; dished out bonuses calculated on the value of the diamonds he recovered, and allowed him the use of a Dickensian office, where he kept his secrets in a green safe.

The morning of February 4 was cold, and Lawson plunged his hands deep in the pockets of his British Warm overcoat. He walked up Gray's Inn Road, turned down Clerkenwell, and entered Hatton Garden at Hiram Maxim's end. As always, he assimilated the whole scene: the slightest incongruity and his criminal instincts, now perverted to the side of the law, were alerted. Once upon a time, the presence of a post office van with a team of burly engineers repairing telephone wires would have warned him: Flying Squad. These days the presence of such a team cried: A heist. And, perhaps, a bonus.

This morning there was nothing unusual, only a few harassed pedestrians with faces mottled by the cold (and, probably, small fortunes inside their jackets); a maroon Rolls 28FS BB 150 parked at the side of the road; four Orthodox Jews talking intently outside the

Diamond House; a young couple holding hands and gazing into the sign window of Alberts of Hatton Garden: 40 Percent Off All New Rings; a few pigeons pecking in the gutter, where Lawson had once spotted a tiny industrial diamond.

He hesitated outside the Mecca Bookmakers, sniffed the breath of Ye Old Mitre public house, and finally mounted the worn wooden stairs that led to his garret. In the ouside offices he was greeted by the staff, mostly retired CID, with a patronizing air that was close to contempt. The usual attitude of the law to a grass. The grass who was indispensable to them, Lawson thought. Which was worse, a bent copper or a straightened villain?

He hung his coat on a twisted wire hanger, lit the gas fire, and called out to the girl in the mini-skirt and goose-pimpled thighs to bring him a cup of tea. When she brought the tea it was milky and tepid; he drank it in one draught, pulling a face as though it were medicine.

Then he closed the door and locked it, switched on the electric light inside a charred plastic shade, and pulled the curtains. He warmed his hands in front of the broken teeth of the fire before kneeling in front of the safe. After a minute's manipulation, the heavy door swung open.

Lawson took out a file made of pink cardboard and opened it. This was the dossier that would one day earn a bonus big enough to enable him to quit; this was the dossier in which Lawson tracked the movements of diamond thieves who had never been convicted.

As always self-disgust enveloped him as he began to read.

Nigel Lawson was born on August 8, 1928, in Tunbridge Wells, the son of a leading stockbroker in the city and a former debutante. It wasn't until his second year at Eton that his parents realized he was genuinely delinquent. By his fourth year he was showing a predilection for liquor, cards, and girls. But because he was a fine off-spin bowler, capable of wrecking Harrow on the right wicket, and a flamboyant number five in the batting, his extracurricular activities were overlooked. When £8 10s was stolen from a pair of trousers hanging in the changing room, the investigation was not pressed home, because suspicion pointed at Lawson and the Eton v. Harrow match was only a fortnight away.

When he was on vacation in Tunbridge Wells, prior to going to Cambridge, some diamond rings and brooches were stolen one night from a country mansion, the home of a girl Lawson was taking out. No one would have suspected Lawson, if a barmaid hadn't accused him of making her pregnant. When Lawson's girl friend heard about the accusation, she told her parents that Lawson had asked to see the stolen jewelry because he was thinking of taking a job in Hatton Garden after he finished school. At the same time it was discovered that Lawson had settled a pressing bookmaker's bill four days after the jewel robbery. Two days after the police called, making routine inquiries, Lawson's father consulted a business acquaintance in Hatton Garden and dispatched his son to South Africa to make his fortune.

This Lawson accomplished with little difficulty. He caught the diamond fever endemic to South Africa since the first authenticated discovery of a diamond in 1867 on the De Kalk farm in the Hope Town area in Cape Colony. A fifteen-year-old boy named Erasmus Jacobs brought home a glittering stone some children had been using to play five-stones. It turned out to be a 21¼-carat diamond—known, subsequently, as Eureka —and the great diamond trek was on, luring the world's adventurers and crooks, making and breaking men, creating a colossus such as Cecil Rhodes, the founder of De Beers; dispatching prospectors scrabbling across deserts and dried-out river beds, spanning the continent from the mouth of the Orange River to Kimberley, where, in the mine known as the Big Hole, it had been estimated that three tons of diamonds were recovered from 25 millions tons of ground, until digging stopped in 1914.

In Kimberley and Johannesburg, Nigel Lawson learned as much as he could about diamonds. Then, after serving a compulsory two years in the Guards, he set out for the wild desert coasts of South West Africa, where, in 1908, a colored laborer named Zacharias Lewala found diamonds while shoveling sand. When the wind shifted the sands, more diamonds were found lying on the surface. Another diamond rush was under way. When the Germans were thrown out of the territory, Ernest Oppenheimer, later chairman of De Beers, formed the Consolidated Diamond Mines of South West Africa Ltd., and took over most of the prospecting. In 1935, sometime after the discovery of deposits of diamonds in the mouth of the Orange, the diamond town of Oranjemund was built by C.D.M.

Today, some of the world's prime gem diamonds still come from a bedrock lying parallel to the coast of South West Africa. There are several theories about the presence of diamonds there; but it is generally accepted that they were swept there by the Orange River. For awhile, diamonds were sucked up from the bed of the ocean, but this has since been abandoned. Most of the sand is now excavated by giant diesel scrapers, which need two bulldozers to push them while they clear sand at the rate of 450 cubic meters an hour.

Nigel Lawson went there to smuggle diamonds. It seemed to be his vocation.

He had been assured in Johannesburg that gem

stones could no longer be found lying on the surface. He was disappointed to find this was true.

But the challenge of the security precautions ("as tight as a hyena's asshole") titillated him. Jet planes combing the lonely beaches; radar screens to detect intruders by sea or air; X-rays applied to anyone leaving the territory. Many smugglers still tried to hide diamonds in their rectums; but this didn't appeal to the Old Etonian Lawson, and he was one of the pioneers of the system of stitching diamonds inside wounds—not his wounds, though.

Finally, he decided that the most profitable move would be to join the diamond security staff. References from London and his Etonian background got him the job, and while chasing suspected smugglers across the border, he was able to acquire his own hoard worth about £200,000.

The tension made him drink heavily. And when this was noticed by the authorities, he quit and moved to the Belgian Congo, where the diamond fields shared with Angola are some 150,000 square miles in size. From Leopoldville he crossed the Congo at night, braving crocodiles and guns, to the accepted sorting house of illicit diamonds, Brazzaville, in the French Congo.

In Leopoldville he fortified himself with Bols gin; in Brazzaville he celebrated with cognac. At the age of thirty-four, after smuggling ventures in other parts of Africa, when he was worth about £500,000, he returned to Britain to embark upon a more refined career. He became a diamond thief.

From his house overlooking Dulwich College, he planned three ambitious diamond heists, two of which were successful. One of these was a classic and there were many imitations—just as there were after the French movie *Rififfi*, when a gang of thieves bored a hole through a ceiling, using an umbrella to catch the falling plaster. It was, like many great works of art, so simple: a security van was hit *before* it picked up its cargo; the crew was relaxed—who would want to steal an empty van?—and the vehicle was driven away with a minimum of fuss. Uniformed gangsters in possession of the password then drove the van into Hatton Garden and picked up £200,000 worth of cut gem stones destined for Paris and West Berlin jewelers.

Immediately before and after the snatch, Nigel Lawson was drinking about a bottle of scotch a day.

The second heist was pulled with the help of an inside man at a dealer's near the Clerkenwell end of the Garden. The inside man substituted strontium titanate for the gem stones in his care. The simulant is detectable, but it passes muster when a trusted employee, before disappearing with the genuine articles, hands it over to be locked in the vaults.

During that period Nigel Lawson found that one bottle of scotch wasn't quite enough.

The third heist was set, after months of planning, for London Airport, the second busiest center of criminal activity in Britain after London and its suburbs. This time the diamonds were arriving on an Air India flight, and with a considerable amount of connivance at the airport, the haul was to be driven straight off the runway, out of the airport, and onto the main road—a feat that has since been accomplished with other merchandise.

But with his brain fuzzy with alcohol, Lawson got his timing wrong. Two accomplices received long jail sentences at the Old Bailey, and Nigel Lawson knew it was all over.

He began gambling heavily, and within four years he was broke. In desperation he crossed over from Hatton Garden to the other side of the law, giving them the benefit of all his knowledge and experience. He acknowledged his weakness and duplicity just as a corrupt policeman acknowledges his.

On any given day, some sort of diamond robbery or swindle is being planned somewhere in the world. Nigel Lawson couldn't hope to anticipate all of them; but with his elaborate system of cross-references, his underworld informants—and, in particular, his personal files on the top diamond thieves in or out of jail—he could occasionally thwart a spectacular coup.

Lawson's successes were founded largely on his knowledge of diamond fever: like malaria it reoccurred.

On this February morning he spent a couple of hours perusing his records, studying the movements of criminals as an ornithologist studies the migration of birds to establish a pattern. But no semblance of a pattern emerged; his birds either were caged or hibernating. Nevertheless, according to the laws of diamond criminology, there had to be a big snatch soon.

Nigel Lawson decided, for the time being, to invent one. He presented himself to the head of security, a retired detective superintendent from the Flying Squad named Carmichael, and asked for one hundred pounds for expenses in advance.

Sitting at a desk in his sparsely furnished office, a replica of his old room at Scotland Yard, Carmichael regarded Lawson with distaste. "A hundred quid," he said. "What the hell do you want that for?"

"I'm onto something," Lawson said.

"What?" Carmichael was a big man, running to fat, a lifetime's association with human greed and treachery written on his face.

"A big one. I can't tell you any more at the moment."

All his life Carmichael had employed snouts and despised them. Lawson was a snout, one of the elite, but a snout just the same. Carmichael said, "I'd have to know more than that before handing over a ton."

Lawson shrugged, lighting a cigarette with hands that shook a little. "Depends on whether you want to save a million." He blew smoke across the desk. "Maybe more."

"A million?"

Lawson nodded, his thoughts beginning to expand as they had in the old days when he was planning a job. He knew of a way in which a fortune unrecorded in the annals of crime could be stolen. On the Antwerp run. He was surprised it hadn't occurred to any of the names in his files. Suppose he were to tip off one of them about the possibilities and then set into motion the machinery by which they would be caught. His bonus would be a fortune in itself. Could he, Nigel Lawson, aristocrat of diamond thieves, be quite such a shit?

Carmichael said, "I'm not handing over a hundred nicker without knowing more. That's final."

Lawson gazed at him with his moist eyes. A big, dumb copper. It was thanks to men like this that he and the retired villains had stayed free. But Lawson did have respect for some policemen—those with the brains and acumen to personally outwit a good villain; those who would have made first-class villains themselves.

If only, Lawson thought, I could organize a heist on the Antwerp run myself. Wishful thinking. Those days were over, and what he needed at the moment was a drink.

Lawson told Carmichael that, if he didn't hand over one hundred pounds, he would lodge a sealed letter with a solicitor, to be opened when the next diamond robbery took place. The letter would state that the missing million could have been saved if Carmichael had handed over one hundred pounds. A measly hundred quid!

"Did you ever dabble in blackmail?" Carmichael asked.

"I didn't dabble in anything," Lawson said, exaggerating his Etonian accent because he knew it infuriated Carmichael. "I made my money in the diamond fields of Africa. You know that."

"One of these days," Carmichael said, "I'll get something on you, matey."

"And lose the best grass you've ever had? Come off it."

"Is this on the level?" Carmichael asked, acknowledging defeat.

"Yes."

"You haven't come up with anything for over six months."

"Then now is the time to invest in the future."

"I'll give you fifty."

"Seventy-five," Lawson said.

Carmichael opened a battered safe, which Lawson reckoned he could open with a knife and fork, and handed over seventy-five pounds in soiled fivers and tenners. Everything connected with diamonds, except the product themselves, seemed to be grubby, Lawson thought.

"You'd better come up with a big one."

"Don't fret," Lawson said.

When he got back to his office, Lawson found three letters lying on his desk. One was a final demand from his tailor; the second was a suggestion from Barclays Bank that he should attend to his overdrawn account; the third was a vague anonymous tip that a robbery *was* being planned in Antwerp.

Lawson frowned. Such tips were commonplace. The informant waited until some minor theft took place, pointed out that he had issued a warning, and tried to sell information about another robbery.

But Antwerp! Not New York, Tel Aviv, or Tokyo. Bloody Antwerp. Lawson shrugged; there was nothing he could do about anything so nebulous. In any case it was probably coincidence. Nevertheless. . . .

He picked up the preceding day's Sunday paper, which bore the imprint of his teacup, and made his way to the Globe for a drink. He ordered a large scotch and soda and stood at the bar with the newspaper in front of him.

Now, with seventy-five pounds fraudulently obtained, he had to come up with something big.

He ordered another large scotch and glanced at the sports pages. England had lost the Calcutta Cup to Scotland with the last kick of the game; England was once again in a tight spot in the Test Match against the West Indies.

He turned the pages, lingering over a gossip column. One name leaped out at him. "Mr. John Rhodes, the American antique dealer living in London. . . ." Nigel Lawson knew better. Mr. John Rhodes, retired diamond thief living in London.

The columnist recalled that Rhodes had recently given evidence in the lower court against three men accused of a diamond robbery near Covent Garden and described how he had thrown a paperweight at a gunman. The story recorded Rhodes' departure to New York to finalize a big antique deal.

Lawson drummed his fingers on the bar. That had been the ultimate in ironies: Johnny Rhodes, of all people, helping to bring diamond thieves to justice. At the time of the Covent Garden affair, he had checked out Rhodes; but Rhodes had been going straight for years and was making such a fat living out of Messrs. Chippendale and Sheraton that he had no need to revert to old habits.

Just the same, diamond fever was incurable. Which copper had been on the Covent Garden case? Lawson ordered a third whisky. Willis, wasn't it? Now, Willis was a copper Lawson admired; he thought he might have a word with Willis, just to see if there were any angles.

He finished his drink; invested a fiver with Mecca Bookmakers; took a bus to the West End to see the movie *Sleuth;* and snoozed in the stalls until opening time.

Part 2
REHEARSALS

Chapter 7

Rhodes sent one cable signed "Solitaire" from the post office in Fleet Street opposite Fetter Lane on March 20. That was the cable for Tallon in Denia. To avoid arousing any curiosity, he sent the second, to Ferguson in Palm Beach, from a cable office in Piccadilly.

The following morning—a daffodil morning with blue skies and the scents of spring in the air—he went jogging in Kensington Gardens, his mind turning over the burgeoning plan.

The two immediate problems were: how to allay Marie's suspicions, and where to discuss developments with Ferguson and Tallon. He postponed the first problem and concentrated on the second.

He rejected London with its criminal population and police, who might dig into their memories and find a coincidence in the presence of an elegant black American, a tough Frenchman who looked like a bandit, and an antique dealer. Where could three such oddly assorted characters meet without raising suspicion? Rhodes frowned and the other grim joggers frowned back. Then he had it; wherever movie people met—stars, directors, extras, stunt men—a kaleidoscope of characters. Rhodes chose Shepperton; they didn't make too many films there any more, but in the three pubs in the square—the Anchor, the King's Head, and the Rose and Crown—the characters still gathered.

Happily, he jogged past the tip of the Serpentine by the fountains and headed for home. When he let himself into the apartment, blowing a little, Marie was packing.

"Where are you going?" he asked.

Marie, who had taken a part-time modeling job, said, "Out."

"Like out where?"

"Paris, France," she said.

"You didn't tell me."

"You don't tell me anything, I'm going to treat you the same way."

Rhodes, steaming in his maroon track suit, thought she looked very chic in her Lanvin, hip-length cardigan jacket and pleated skirt.

He asked, "What don't I tell you?"

"A lot. You're up to something, Johnny, and you can't hide it from someone, not when they love you. Tell me the truth, what are you planning?"

"A big coup in the cross-Atlantic trade in antiques."

"Is that why you went to Spain?"

"You know why I went to Spain: to buy up some old rocking chairs before the New York dealers clean out the Iberian Peninsula."

"Don't lie to me, Johnny."

"What the hell do you *think* I'm up to?"

"I think you're breaking your word."

"What's that supposed to mean?"

"Are you planning . . . a job? Answer me truthfully, Johnny." She stared at him, tears forming in the corners of her eyes.

Rhodes considered telling her the truth. But by doing so, he risked both losing her and establishing an unnecessary flaw in the armor of Operation Solitaire. "No," he said, "no job. As a matter of fact, I'm thinking of writing a book about investment, with a lot of stuff about diamonds in it."

"You're lying."

He moved to kiss her but she backed away saying, "Why, Johnny, for God's sake why? We've got everything. Money, a future, each other. . . ."

He walked past her into the kitchen and began to make coffee. "How long will you be away?" he called out.

"I don't know. A few days. A week maybe."

"Stay longer if you want. Not much point in staying with a guy you don't trust."

"I trust you," she said. "Like I trust a dressmaker who can get me into movies."

The door slammed, leaving behind a thick silence.

Moses Ferguson received his cable after catching a barracuda a mile off the Atlantic coastline at Fort Pierce. It was phoned to him from his headquarters in Palm Beach.

"Who the hell's this Solitaire?" his secretary asked. "A chick?"

Ferguson, who had told his congregation that he would soon be going to Africa to carry out some missionary work, said that no, it was the name of a Nigerian official working for the organization in London.

He hung up and returned to the barracuda lying on the wooden jetty outside the motel on Seaway. The fish lay on its side, ugly uneven teeth in its projecting jaw bared in the fury of defeat. The barracuda had given Moses a good fight, diving and leaping, feigning death and then sprinting away like a champion. It seemed a good omen to Moses that he had won the fight.

That night he carried out a test he had been planning for weeks. Many of his European spectaculars had been cat burglaries, using the agility, timing, and nerve that he had acquired in the ghetto. How much had these skills been affected by time? Did a cat burglar ever come back?

At the back of Fort Pierce he had found two half-finished apartment buildings abandoned by a building company that had gone bankrupt. They were only two stories high, with an alley eight feet wide between them, Not a particularly ambitious jump; but at the age of forty, out of condition, in the dark. . . . Would his nerve fail?

Blending with the night, his fine black skin the ally it had always been, Moses climbed the inside of the shell of the building without difficulty. He could feel his heart pumping, the old exhilaration upon him. He saw again the moonlit bedroom of a chateau in Provence with a heap of jewelry gleaming frostily on a dressing table and a beautiful woman, breasts bared, lying asleep on a four-poster bed. He saw again a jewel case lying on a window sill, with a black cat asleep beside it, and heard the cat meow with a voice like a tiger as he approached. . . .

Poised on the edge of the unfinished wall, he gazed across the alley at the wall on the other side. It looked about ten feet away. Never look down, they said. Moses looked down and it was like looking down a precipice. The sweat froze on his body and he bit the inside of his mouth, drawing blood.

Then he leaped, swayed backwards, jerked forward —and was safe. It was on his way down that he tripped and pulled a cartilage in his leg.

On March 22 the Black Messiah limped out of Florida on his way to London.

Pierre Tallon received the cable after a day in the harsh, olive-green mountains behind Denia while he was practicing with the stolen Colt CMG-2. They were blasting a new road to one of the villages tucked in the folds of the mountains protecting the coastal strip of orange groves, and no one took any notice of a few more explosions cannoning around the crags. Tallon had taken with him two bottles of Spanish champagne, two hunks of bread, a slice of Manchega cheese, two oranges, and 150 rounds of 68-grain Colt.

From the branches of an acebuche, a wild olive, he hung a life-size cut-out of a man with a St. Valentine's heart painted red. He withdrew to the maximum range for accuracy and first fired the gun, designed for a Vietnam-type operation, from the hip. He blew one of the cardboard man's legs off. Tallon swore softly with Marseilles invectives, pulled the cork from one of the bottles, and drank the bubbling wine as if it were beer. Then he fitted the bipod, lay prone beside a clump of prickly oak, and squeezed the trigger once more. This time he chopped the target in half across the lower ribs. He punched his hand into the bushes, drawing blood on his knuckles. At the third try he cut out the heart.

But it wasn't good enough. He stood up and gazed toward the sea in the distance. It seemed hazy this bright, gusty day. Was it hazy or was it his eyes? Did he need glasses at thirty-eight?

He field-stripped the gun into six parts, packed it in the boot beneath a tarpaulin, and drove back to Denia too fast, scaring the old men with their donkeys and the workers in the vineyards spending siesta in the sun with leather bottles of wine.

At 4:00 P.M., as the shops were opening, he called at an optician's near the harbor. By 4:30 he had their verdict: nothing to worry about. . . . Your eyes are going through the usual process of aging—normal astigmatism, mild myopia.

Did he need glasses?

If he was doing a job that needed accuracy, yes.

Tallon decided that he might have to shoot a man dead with one shot—and that needed accuracy. He told them he would come back the next day to be fitted for glasses. No, he thought, contact lenses. Whoever heard of a gunman wearing glasses?

Then he called at the post office, at the other end of the town, where he was handed a slip telling him a cable was waiting for him at the telegraph office. He picked it up. The summons to London. The job was on.

Next day he took the CMG-2, an Armelite rifle, and three hand guns—a Python, a big .44 Magnum, and a Sterling; packed them in the boot of the Interceptor; and drove to Altea, where he handed the guns over to the skipper of a fishing boat, with 27,000 pesetas and instructions to hand them over to the owner of a yacht called *The Happy Virgin* anchored at Marseilles.

Two days later Tallon headed north, through Valencia and Barcelona, crossing the French border south of Perpignan. Thirty-six hours after leaving Denia he was in Marseilles. There, in Le Paradou bar, he met his twenty-year-old illegitimate son, already an established criminal. Together they caught an Air France flight from Marignane Airport to Paris, where they picked up a British Airways flight to London.

The guns came by sea.

They met in the Warren Lodge, a comfortable hotel with balconies overlooking a mossy backwater of the Thames, and a period bar where you expect to find old gentlemen drinking Madeira, and, instead, find film stars with vodka and tonics. The hotel stands in a corner of Shepperton's square opposite a church. Either Mr. Pickwick or David Bowie, you feel, would be equally at home in it.

They took three rooms adjoining each other at the

end of a corridor so that no one could eavesdrop. The rooms each possessed a TV and an electric waiter called a bell captain, which dispensed anything from scotch to toasted rolls.

After an hour in the bar, establishing the movie-world identities of Ferguson and Tallon, they adjourned to the last room in the upstairs corridor.

Rhodes said, "We have a lot to discuss, gentlemen."

They settled down with drinks, switching on the radio so that a disc jockey and his music would blur their voices if anyone became inquisitive.

Tallon said, "The first thing we have to establish is who's in charge of this operation?" Tallon lay on one of the two single beds in his shirt sleeves, the knot of his tie pulled down his chest, smoking a dark Burma cheroot.

Rhodes said, "That's already established. I am." He sat in an easy chair, wearing slacks and brass-buttoned blazer, assessing the mood of his partners. "I thought that was understood," he said, looking at Ferguson.

Ferguson was the dude. He wore a blue suit with wide lapels and, instead of a clerical collar, a trendy striped shirt and a bright tie with a big, loose knot.

Tallon and Rhodes waited for him to speak.

The Black Messiah sipped a neat scotch, gazed reflectively at his partners, sensing the power of his pronouncement, and finally said, "That's the way I understood it. Johnny's in charge."

Rhodes took a gin and tonic from the bell captain and sat down again. "Is that all right by you, Pierre?"

"*D'accord.*" Tallon blew a jet of acrid smoke across the room. "It's the way it always was. The guy with the idea is the boss. But"—he smiled at the other two—"I do have some reservations."

"Such as?" Rhodes asked.

"You are not dealing with two amateurs. You told me you picked the best."

"So?"

"Then we cannot be treated as little boys. We cannot be treated as you would treat a getaway driver, a messenger boy to be paid off with a couple of rolls of notes and forgotten. Agreed?"

Rhodes said it was agreed.

"Then this is the way I see it," Tallon said. "There are several stages in this job, right?"

Ferguson said, "Why don't you get to the point?"

Tallon stared at him. "That's just what I am doing, *Monsieur* Ferguson. Each of us must be in complete charge of his part of the heist. You see," he said to Rhodes, "we must have our pride. Each of us has class, eh?"

"The best in the world," Rhodes said.

Tallon shrugged. "Maybe—a few years ago."

"I haven't heard of any better since we were in business."

Tallon said, "I want to talk about that later. Do you agree that each of us should be in control of his own operation?"

Rhodes and Ferguson exchanged glances. "Agreed," Rhodes said.

"*Ca va.*" Tallon relaxed with his hands behind his head. "That's all I wanted to know at the moment."

Rhodes said, "I'll be in charge of the final stage, the getaway. I'll also be in overall command of the whole thing. And I'll arrange for the disposal of the goods before we split the loot. Okay?"

They said it was. But Tallon still had another reservation. "I'm responsible for hitting the security van somewhere between Antwerp airport and the center of the city. Correct?"

Rhodes nodded.

"Then I do it my own way," Tallon said with finality.

Rhodes went to the bell captain, who served him with another gin and tonic. He opened the door to the balcony to get rid of some of the smoke from

Tallon's cheroot. It was a dark, misty night, and they smelled water and boats. Rhodes closed the window and said, "No killing, Pierre."

Tallon raised his hands dramatically. "Why should we kill? We are artists. All I am demanding"—not asking, Rhodes noted—"is that I'm in sole command of my bit of the action. All that need concern you and Ferguson is timing so you can take over. Any objections?"

Ferguson said, "None, as long as my action slots in with Tallon's."

"Okay," Rhodes said, "do your own thing. I think we should tackle Solitaire like a play, a Broadway production, giving ourselves as much time as we need to make it work perfectly. I've done the casting of the principals but we still need a supporting cast. Any time now we should start rehearsals, then the premiere, then the finale—the way jobs used to be planned."

"What we need most," Ferguson said, "is the tip-off guy. Without one we could stake out Antwerp airport until 1980."

Rhodes spread out a Geographia map on the empty twin bed. "This is the building from which they dispatch the stones." With a red ball-point pen, he made a cross at one end of Hatton Garden. "The communications set-up is across the road. That's where the message is telexed to Antwerp in code, and that's where we need to have our man. I've been making some inquiries, and the BH-125 never leaves Heathrow at the same time. And another thing," Rhodes said, jabbing the ball-point toward Tallon, "the message isn't telexed to Antwerp until the jet has started take-off procedure, so you won't have all that much time. In fact, you'll have just the same time to play with as the guards going out to collect the goods in the security van."

"Don't worry about me," Tallon said, stretching.

"I'll make it. You get the message to me and I'll make the time."

Ferguson got himself a can of Heineken beer and said, "You've been a busy boy, Johnny. How did you get all this stuff about the way they ship the stuff?"

"I found a tip-off man," Rhodes said. And when they both looked suitably impressed he said, "It wasn't so difficult. Not for fifty thousand pounds. Any trade that makes such a thing about its honesty and trust has to have loopholes. You know, honesty and corruptibility are good bedfellows; they attract each other like torturer and victim."

"Johnny," Ferguson said, "you should have been a psychiatrist. How did you find him?"

Rhodes told them.

The communications staff is small, and Rhodes had followed a few of them across Holborn and down Shoe Lane to a new pub called the Cartoonist, where Fleet Street journalists and PRO's drink. The communications people were celebrating a birthday, and after five of them had left to catch their trains, one remained. Rhodes watched him write a check for five pounds, and noticed the barman examine it with distaste before showing it to the manager, who authorized him to cash it. Intuitively, Rhodes knew then that this was his man: white-haired, ruddy-faced, upright, and, if the price was right, as bent as a fiddler's elbow.

After two more drinks, the red-faced man left the Cartoonist, with its wall lined with sketches by famous names, and made his way to the corner of Ludgate Circus, where he hesitated, gazing down New Bridge Street in the direction of Blackfriars Station. Then he turned into the Albion, a pub used by a lot of sports writers, and ordered himself a whisky, frequently glancing at his wristwatch. Rhodes, who had followed him into the pub, guessed he was making sure he didn't have enough time to catch his train. Ex-Army, Rhodes reckoned; an expert in communications with a good service record proving that he had never been caught.

Rhodes contemplated joining him, knocking over his whisky and getting into conversation. But there was something more to the man's indecision than a reluctance to go home to the suburbs to an over-cooked dinner and a nagging wife. Rhodes held back. Now all his instincts cried sex; an old swordsman drinking the courage for one more foray.

Suddenly, the man downed his drink, turned abruptly, and plunged out of the bar. He turned up Fleet Street and waited at the bus stop. Rhodes called a cab and waited on the corner of Ludgate Circus. The man jumped onto a number 9, and Rhodes guessed Shepherd Market, where the girls still operated in small bedrooms above entrances with open doors and illuminated doorbells. Rhodes was right.

The red-faced man pressed a bell and vanished up the stairs two at a time. Half an hour later he re-emerged, looking furtively about him, before heading for Piccadilly and a ruined dinner in the suburbs.

Rhodes climbed the stairs without ringing the bell. It was 8:00 P.M., a slack time in the profession. The maid, an old crone with a bright slit of mouth in her powdered face, greeted him enthusiastically.

Madam, she said, would be ready in a minute. What did he want? Something special?

Rhodes said, "I want information."

The expression on the greedy old face changed. "Are you the law?"

Rhodes took twenty-five pounds in five-pound notes from his wallet. "What was the name of the man who just left?"

"We don't know. . . ."

Rhodes interrupted. "It's your job to go through the pockets of any man who comes here."

Her tongue slid around her lips, and Rhodes knew she was thinking that anyone who was willing to produce twenty-five pounds for openers had more to offer.

He said, "Another twenty-five pounds, no more questions—except the address if you've got it—and you'll never see or hear from me again. Come on, quick, before Madam wants a cut."

"All I know is that his name's Masters and he comes here once a week, 7:30 on the dot, and he lives at Mitcham."

Rhodes gave her the other twenty-five pounds.

She said, "And he likes. . . ."

Rhodes—who didn't want to know what private desires unfulfilled in Mitcham kept a man for half an hour every week in Shepherd Market—said, "Thanks, Lilly." He turned and started down the stairs.

"How did you know my name was Lilly?" She stood at the top of the stairs holding the notes in her hand.

"Do you ladies ever have any other name?" he asked, as the door on the landing opened and Madam appeared just as the maid was stuffing the money down her blouse.

One week later Rhodes knocked over Masters' glass in a pub in Holborn and offered to buy him a replacement.

Two days later—after an indefinite suggestion that neither Hatton Garden nor Mitcham would take kindly to his weekly excursions to Shepherd Market, and a definite offer of £25,000 then and £25,000 in January 1975—Rhodes had established a tip-off man in the communications center.

Both Tallon and Ferguson were impressed. But they both thought it was a lot of money.

Letting some cheroot smoke out of the room, and some Thames-side air in, Rhodes said, "Are you crazy? For £15 million?"

"I guess you're right," Ferguson said. "Think big, huh?" He pulled at the large knot in his tie. "I guess no one ever thought as big as this."

Tallon rolled off the bed and replenished his glass from the bell captain. He returned to the bed, propped the pillow behind his head, and said, "I presume we split three ways?"

"Of course." Rhodes shrugged. "None of us is short anyway. It's the job that counts."

"Sure it's the job that counts," Ferguson said. "But a little extra bread never hurt anyone. Let's say fifteen million split three ways before the fence cuts it down to size. That's five million English pounds. Jesus! I could build a hundred churches with money like that. Even if we invested a million each—would you believe? —we'd still end up having the edge on Howard Hughes. Shit," said the Black Messiah, "it's unbelievable." He paused. "But there are a couple of angles we should explore."

"Like what?" Rhodes asked.

"Like," Ferguson said, "none of us is getting any younger."

There was a silence for a moment; Tallon examined the smoking tip of his cheroot, Rhodes closed the window and stood staring at the black water outside.

Finally Tallon said, "I know what you mean, I need contact lenses." He pointed the cheroot at Rhodes. "How are you keeping these days?"

Rhodes grinned sheepishly. "I'm doing exercises," he confessed. "At our age you have to, I guess."

Tallon said, "Moses is right. We have to remember our age. It might still be all right here"—Tallon pointed at his crotch—"but not up here and here"— he pointed at his head and heart. "I wonder if we're capable of it," he said thoughtfully.

"We have the experience," Rhodes said. "We've got the brains. We know more about pulling a heist than any kid operating today. Sure, we've got to get fit. Didn't we always?"

"So what do we do?" Rhodes asked.

"Maybe we should take lessons," Ferguson said. "Maybe we should have a look at the way the kids work today. Maybe we should stop talking about the good old days and think about what goes on inside the cops' skulls these days."

Rhodes said, "So even crooks have a problem with the generation gap. So what do we do, go to night school? Take a refresher course?"

Tallon stood up and yawned. "I'm tired," he said. "Old men need their sleep. But I tell you this, Johnny, Moses is right, we can't run as fast these days."

"Speak for yourself," Rhodes said. "I'm known as the Hyde Park Flyer."

Tallon said, "I have a suggestion." He hesitated. "You may not like this, Johnny."

"You got hardening of the arteries?"

"I brought my son over," Tallon said.

"So?"

"He's a good boy. In the business, you know." Tallon paused. "I think we should deal him in."

There was a pause while, on the radio, the disc jockey played an old Nat King Cole number. In the parking lot outside a motorcycle took off.

Rhodes broke the silence. "I thought we agreed it was going to be just the three of us," he said. "The Three Musketeers, the Unholy Trinity."

"Listen," Tallon said, "three of us can't pull a job like this. We've got to have a pilot, drivers. Already we've got a tip-off man."

Rhodes said, "Just the three of us knowing what it's all about."

Ferguson examined the deep shine on his black shoes. "You're a bit of a dreamer, huh, Johnny? Since when could you kid a getaway driver that he was taking your shirts to the laundry?"

Tallon squashed his cheroot into an ashtray. *"Nom d'bleu!* You've got to face facts, Johnny. We worked alone and we were good. Right? But the scene has changed. We'd be like . . . like a Viscount pilot stepping straight into the cockpit of the Concord." He held up his hand as Rhodes began to speak. "I know, I know. I was the one who said we should keep the numbers down, but, you know, that was before I found I needed glasses. *Merde!* Pierre Tallon putting on glasses to blow a safe. Crime has changed, and we've got to know how it works and how the cops operate. The only way we can do that is to consult some of the best operators working today; and I think that if we keep it in the family, we're playing safer than if we consulted some bandit from London or Paris or New York who would double-cross you for the takings of one lousy bank raid, let alone £15 million."

Ferguson said, "He's right, Johnny. Okay, so maybe we know how to plan a job better than any of the kids today, but we don't know the scene. Tallon's kid could fill us in."

"I guess you're right," Rhodes said. "Okay, deal him in."

Tallon said, "Thanks, Johnny. But he'll have to know what it's all about, otherwise he won't play. You know what we Tallons are like."

"I know," Rhodes said. "But I don't like too many people to know what's going on." He glanced at Ferguson. "What do you think?"

"He doesn't have to know everything."

Tallon said, "He'll want to."

Rhodes said, "Just tell him it's a diamond heist and leave it like that. Is that all right by you, Pierre?"

"What's the matter anyway?" Tallon asked. "Do you think my own son would double-cross us?"

Ferguson said, "Let Pierre tell his boy what he thinks he should know. Anyway, I figure he'll know the score before we're through."

Rhodes shrugged. "Okay, Pierre knows the score." He switched off the radio. "Now let's go downstairs and drink to Solitaire."

"Just one," Tallon said. "I've got a fitting for my contacts in the morning. I don't want them to think I need red lenses."

Chapter 8

At a set of lights controlling the flow of vehicles onto a traffic circle—one of the many that interrupt the A3 before it finds its own way to London just outside Waterlooville, in Hampshire—the lights changed to green, and a silver truck bearing the words "Thomson and Figgis, Long Distance Transport" moved forward. An empty truck behind, which had cut across the traffic to get into the near lane and now lay diagonally across the road, stalled. By the time the driver had started the engine, the lights had changed to red again, and the silver truck was off with a cargo of fifty tea chests.

When the green Granada 2.5 liter rented car took off, there was hardly any traffic in sight. Two men, each wearing stockings over their faces and black leather gloves, leaped out of the car. One of them leveled a shotgun at the truck driver's head, left hand on the pump action. "You," he said, "out. Move."

The driver climbed down slowly. "Is tea *that* short?" he asked.

"Shut up," said the man with the shotgun.

On the other side of the cab, another man with a shotgun had got the driver's mate onto the roadside.

The first man snapped his fingers. "The keys!"

"Are you crazy?" the driver asked.

"The keys." The man jabbed the shotgun into his chest.

"All right, mate," the driver said. "But there must be easier ways of getting a cup of tea."

The second gunman said to the driver's mate, "Turn around." The driver's mate turned around and the second gunman hit him just below the ear with the butt of the gun, not too hard. The driver's mate collapsed on the side of the road.

The driver climbed onto a step on the back of the truck and opened the heavy steel doors. They dumped the unconscious body of the driver's mate on top of the tea chests.

The first gunman said, "Which ones?"

The driver pointed at two chests marked with small crosses in pink chalk. So far the operation had taken thirty seconds; in the distance the traffic held up at the circle was beginning to pour onto the main road.

The two gunmen rested their shotguns on the side of the truck, picked up one chest and put it onto the tailboard of the Granada's trunk, where the driver waited with a rubber strap. They placed the second chest beside the first, and the driver secured them with the strap.

The gunmen turned to the driver, who was still standing on the tailboard of the truck. The driver said, "Is it really necessary? I know we agreed. . . ."

The first gunman said, "It's necessary if you don't want the fuzz to suspect you. Now get moving—the traffic's piling up."

"Sorry," said the second gunman, as he brought the butt of the shotgun onto the back of the driver's head.

They slammed the doors and jumped into the Granada as it took off, the driver slamming the stick through the gears.

The gunmen ripped off their stockings, stuffed them in their pockets, and hid the shotguns under a tartan traveling rug.

"Not too fast," said Pierre Tallon's son, Daniel, the first gunman. "We don't want to be stopped for speeding."

At Havant they drove into a yard, where they packed the two chests into the back of a battered Morris van, spattered with mud and straw, and drove to a farm near Horndean. After dark, they unloaded the chests. Nestling in the tea were two bags containing thousands of industrial diamonds, many of them as small as grains of sand.

The robbery didn't attract much attention in the press, neither tea nor industrial diamonds having much charisma; and in any case, gem diamonds, the aristocrats, were having a lot of exposure these days. A shotgun gang had just held up an armored car—collecting diamonds from Hambros Bank in Charterhouse Street, adjoining Hatton Garden—and escaped in a bronze Triumph with £350,000 worth of stones. And in Kimberley, on April 17, they had just found the mine's biggest stone ever—a 616-carat yellow octahedron, a good shape but not the best quality. It was also the eighth largest to be found in the world, sandwiched between the Reitz stone (650.25 carats), found in South Africa in 1895, and the Baumgold Rough (609.25), found in 1923, also in South Africa.

Nigel Lawson wasn't too concerned with the Hambros heist—"a highly professional raid that was timed perfectly," according to a Hambros spokesman—because it was over, and there was no money to be collected, only a lot of lip from Carmichael for missing it. But he was vaguely interested in the industrial diamond robbery; although to his way of thinking, any importer stupid enough to try and beat organized crime by hiding diamonds in a consignment of tea instead of using a security service deserved to have them stolen.

Sitting with his feet on his desk, sipping a cup of weak tea, Lawson wondered about the destination of the industrial diamonds. These days, villains found a market before stealing anything; a member of the team toured Europe in search of outlets for watches, cigarettes, drugs, contraceptives, jewels—almost any commodity was viable in 1974. He guessed the industrial diamonds had been "ordered" by some crooked manufacturer in the North or the Midlands. Few industries could survive without them; nuclear missiles, computers, record players—they all needed their industrial diamonds.

Although comprising four-fifths of all diamond production, industrials, to men like Lawson, are a bore. They are a second-rate product, each rejected because it is too small; a poor color, such as strong yellow or a brown; or hopelessly flawed. At the bottom of the scale is boart, minute black and grey crystals used for polishing and grinding. The derivative of boart is said to be "bastard," a name Nigel Lawson considered appropriate.

He picked up the evening paper and reread the brief account of the robbery. The tea chests had arrived by sea at Southampton, having been shipped from Marseilles. And that was what interested Lawson.

Marseilles: the gangsters' paradise, the Chicago of Europe. When Lawson last paid a business visit there, the hoods were still playing their parts like the supporting cast in a George Raft movie: dark striped suits; white tie on black shirts; dark glasses; gunning each other down in the bistros with Thompson submachine guns. One day, Lawson thought, pushing away the cup of scummy tea, I shall return to Marseilles and drink champagne.

Marseilles had one other attraction for Lawson. It had once been the home of a man he admired: Pierre

Tallon, one of the best diamond thieves in the world. Odd that it should have been diamonds that were shipped from Marseilles straight into the hands of the hijackers outside Southampton.

Lawson unlocked the safe and took out the file on Tallon. He would be thirty-eight now, and his son would be twenty. Following in his father's footsteps?

Lawson shook his head and smiled. No son of Pierre Tallon would stoop to stealing industrials, those undistinguished little bastards. He put the file away and shut the safe. He glanced at his watch—5:15 P.M. He took his British Warm off the wire hanger and left the office to meet Detective Chief Inspector Willis in a pub near Scotland Yard.

The briefing was held in a fifty-foot blue-and-white fiberglass motorboat moored at Sunbury, near Shepperton, at 8:30 P.M. on April 24. Rhodes hired the boat in case another meeting at the Warren Lodge attracted attention.

They sat around a table in the wood-paneled cabin, optimistically called a stateroom. It was furnished in mauve and blue, and it led directly into the galley.

Daniel Tallon was in a chair. He was a slighter, sleeker version of his father but lacked his flamboyance. He wore glasses, and he talked quietly and intensely, a young executive on the way up.

As he sat sipping coffee, he told Rhodes, Pierre Tallon, and Ferguson not to deride the industrial diamond robbery. It had probably netted about fifty thousand pounds or less, but that was the way the gangs operated today.

He smiled indulgently at the three older men drinking scotch and gin. He never drank liquor because it blurred the reflexes. Were these three really the greatest diamond thieves of the fifties and sixties?

He coughed as a jet of smoke reached him from his father's cheroot and said in immaculate English,

"Crime is an organized business these days. It's all worked out on paper weeks beforehand. First we find a customer, then we find the goods, then. . . ." Daniel Tallon gestured expressively.

Rhodes said, "But there must be a few individualists still operating."

Daniel nodded. "And they're all in prison." He poured himself more coffee, wondering what sort of job these three middle-aged men hoped to pull. "Rule number one these days is never to operate in your own territory, not even in your own country if you can help it. After all, we are supposed to be members of the Common Market." He smiled slightly. "For instance, it won't occur to the British police for a long time—perhaps never—that the industrial diamonds was a French job."

His father interrupted him. "I think you underestimate the British police, *mon fils*. After all, the diamonds did come from Marseilles."

Daniel shrugged. "Perhaps. But these days we move from one country to another, just as you used to move from city to city. And as for Interpol, it's just a joke, despite what you see on television."

Ferguson said, "Never underestimate the fuzz."

Daniel thought, Who the hell is supposed to be giving this briefing? "We don't" he said. "We pay them well."

"And never trust a crooked cop either," Rhodes said.

Daniel said carefully, "I thought I was supposed to be helping you gentlemen with modern methods."

Rhodes grinned. "Sorry," he said.

"Right. Now, not only must you operate away from your home ground, but you've got to live like a businessman, not like a bandit with a blonde on one arm and a bottle of scotch in the other." He gazed steadily at his father. "It's best to have a house in the country and commute to the city you're operating from. When one member of an organization returns from a shopping expedition in Europe, then we assemble the team for that particular project. We might need four men, as we did with the industrial diamonds—three of us here and an inside man in Marseilles. Or we may need a safeblower—and they're in short supply these days. We may even have to spring one from jail. The blower, like the other leading members of the team, always gets a share of the loot, not a fixed wage. That way there's no trouble."

Rhodes asked, "What would you expect to pick up from a heist—sorry, a project—netting say £200,000?"

"Difficult to say," Daniel told him. "It depends on what sort of project it is. Let's say it's a jewel robbery. They were your specialty, I believe." He poured himself more coffee. "Well, for a start, the fence is going to take more than half. Then you've got to pay for the blower's gear, guns, and documents—say one thousand pounds."

"Guns?" Rhodes raised his eyebrows.

Pierre Tallon said, "I've already told Daniel we won't be using them."

Daniel wondered what they would use instead—crutches? He went on, "You can still hire a gun in Paddington, if the project's in England, for about fifty pounds, but they want a deposit as well. You can't blame them. The old-timers"—Daniel looked at his audience apologetically—"still have a habit of throwing their guns into rivers. Then you've got to pay for your information, a doctor, and many other smaller items. If this £200,000 is shared by a four-man team, then I suppose each would finish up with about fifteen thousand pounds. The whole essence of successful crime today is the business approach. Regular, organized robberies—say eight a year, netting perhaps £1 million—would provide about £100,000 a year for the executives."

"You're doing better than I thought," Pierre Tallon told his son. "I'm proud of you. I note you used a rented car for the industrial diamonds. What's the matter with stealing one?"

"It's an unnecessary complication. In the first place, there might be something wrong with it. In the second, the owner might report the theft to the police before you've even started the project, and they would be out looking for you. You can hire a car within five minutes; all you need is a forged licence, and they're very cheap these days. And always keep your documents up to date," he warned his audience. "It's amazing the number of second-rate crooks who get picked up because their papers are out of date."

Outside, the water slapped against the hull of the boat. Downstream, a bigger ship sounded its horn, making the river a lonely place.

Rhodes asked, "What's the best place to buy documents these days?"

"In England?"

Rhodes nodded.

"Birmingham's still about the best. It's best for cars, too, if you want to buy a really fast one. They specialize in ordinary cars with souped-up engines. In France, Lyons has the best service; and Marseilles, of course, for guns. Amsterdam is excellent for forged documents."

"And fences?" Ferguson asked.

Daniel looked wary. "I can always find an outlet for you." He took off his glasses; without them he looked even younger and more vulnerable. "I understand you're after gem diamonds."

Rhodes nodded.

"It's tricky these days. The police get good information. A man named Lawson—he was operating in your day—helps them. He thinks like a crook, and that's bad for business. He even managed to stop a team of four getting away with a consignment of diamonds,

Sauer design, in West Berlin six months ago. I think he should be killed," said the young man with the earnest, vulnerable features. "Or maybe you should shoot his kneecaps off."

"No violence," Rhodes said. "Which reminds me—you talk about the young criminals of today as if they were business executives. What about the mobsters terrorizing Paris these days? Ten bank holdups a day this winter. Most of them kids taking hostages and shooting anyone in sight."

Daniel nodded. "True. In 1966 there were six bank holdups in Paris; in 1973 there were six hundred. And the police caught less than half of them. They're mostly Colt-.45 kids who come in from the suburbs, steal a motorcycle, and storm into the first bank they see. But they're all amateurs, and I don't deal with amateurs."

"But you do use guns?"

"Sometimes, if it's that kind of job. We used them with the industrial diamonds. You can't threaten a man with a peashooter."

"Maybe you shouldn't put yourself in a position where you have to threaten."

"Maybe." Daniel poured more coffee. "But it's the quick way, the businesslike way. You see, we don't regard ourselves as artists; we're not interested in a good write-up—we just want the money and everything that goes with it."

Ferguson said, "Have you ever killed a man?"

"A few." He ran his fingers through his hair, which was softer than his father's virile growth.

"You won't on this job," Rhodes said.

"Just as you please. It's your job, I'm just the consultant. In any case I'm only here because my father asked me." He leaned forward. "But what I don't understand is why any of you want to make a comeback. You've got the money, the good life. Why risk it all?"

His father said, "You don't think we can do it?"

"I didn't say that. But times have changed. . . . Let's face it, none of you are as young as you were." He stared at his father. "What's wrong with your eyes?"

Pierre Tallon pressed his fingertips against his bloodshot eyes. "The second fitting for my contact lenses. They weren't a good fit."

"And he's limping." Daniel pointed at Ferguson who had gone to fill a jug of water in the galley.

Rhodes said, "And you might as well know I have a weight problem."

Daniel Tallon said, "Look, I know you were all great in your day. You probably planned a job better than anyone operating now. But that isn't the point."

"The point," Rhodes said, "is that we've asked you to help. Leave the planning to us. And don't worry, you'll get your corner."

"I never doubted that," Daniel said stiffly. "I always get paid."

After he had gone Ferguson said, "He's gotten too tough too soon."

"Marseilles is a tough school," Pierre Tallon said.

Rhodes said, "Is there any danger of him turning violent on us?"

Pierre shook his head. "He'll do what he's told."

"He'd better," Rhodes said.

Ferguson said, "Anyway, what the hell did we learn from all that?"

"Pierre learned a lot," Rhodes said. "He learned that he mustn't go around with a bottle of scotch in one hand and a blonde on the other."

Some days later Rhodes read the De Beers annual report in the *Financial Times*. It pleased him. According to the chairman, Mr. Harry Oppenheimer, 1974 sales of diamonds were expected to attain the same record level as 1973, if present conditions were maintained.

The report said:

> The recovery in the rough-diamond trade from the difficulties in the last quarter of the year is occurring more rapidly than had been expected. The Israeli cutting industry is nearing full capacity, and there are signs of renewed demand for polished stones in Europe and in some Far Eastern markets.
>
> Demand for all sizes of diamonds is good, though one must recognise that buying in anticipation of inflation and depreciation of currencies is to an extent responsible for the improvement.

All being well, Rhodes thought, Mr. Oppenheimer's calculations may be off by about £15 million.

Chapter 9

Pierre Tallon was determined to carry out his end of the operation in his own way, and on May 6 he took an El Al flight to Tel Aviv to find out about antitank guided missiles.

The man he went to see was Joseph Kaplan, an expert on diamonds and armaments. During the Yom Kippur War, launched by the Egyptians and Syrians in October 1973, when sophisticated Soviet weapons savaged the Israeli Army, Kaplan left his diamond office at Ramat Gan and, with the rank of colonel, applied himself to methods of combating the Russian missiles.

By the time the Israelis had counterattacked successfully across the Suez Canal, Colonel Kaplan had acquired a sizeable armory of Russian hardware.

Tallon read about his exploits in *France-Soir*. It

seemed that fate was assembling its forces on his side. First, a portable antitank guided missile was a foolproof method of knocking out a security van. Second, he knew Kaplan in the fifties, when he bought gem diamonds without asking where they had come from.

Tallon booked into the Dan Hotel, overlooking the Mediterranean, after making a date with the Israeli girl who had sat next to him on the plane. The next morning he arose at 7 A.M. A khamsin wind was blowing in from the desert, and the sky was yellowish-red; but it didn't deter the elderly Americans from doing their exercises on the beach in front of him.

Tallon dressed in a yellow shirt and flared slacks and hung a star of David on a gold chain around his neck. He ate a kosher breakfast before strolling down Dizengoff—the Champs Elysée and Via Venito of Israel—seeing everything with new clarity through his contact lenses, enjoying the swaggering virility of the place.

Nom d' bleu, he thought, they're all film stars— the strapping soldiers with submachine guns on their shoulders; the soldier and civilian girls, each with an individual beauty brought back to the Promised Land from the far-flung nations of the diaspora. He had been here many years ago, but he had forgotten.

Here, too, were the Orthodox Jews, with their black hats and luxuriant beards, and other older Jews with suffering indelibly recorded on their faces, some with numbers printed on their arms by the Nazis. The street—with its boulevard cafés at one end and its dusky shops crammed with sausages, matzos, and dried fish at the other—was the same vital, sexually aware thoroughfare that he remembered. And yet it seemed to him that there was a new thoughtfulness abroad, another notch of responsibility and maturity from a nation that had come so close to being driven into the sea. Israeli and Syrian forces were still shelling each other, and every family had experienced a direct or indirect bereavement from those cataclysmic weeks when the biggest tank battle since El Alamein was fought in the Sinai Desert. And it showed.

He found Kaplan playing chess in a café near the banks of the muddy little Yarkon River. He was a big man with a paunch, close-cropped, pepper-and-salt hair and a face with fierce creases in it. He was dressed in baggy trousers and an open-neck white shirt. He pointed to a chair and continued to sit, head between his hands, staring at the black-and-white oilcloth squares on the table. Three moves later his opponent resigned, and Kaplan said, "Come, let's go to my car."

In the battered Chevrolet, Kaplan said, "Well?"

"I need your help," Tallon said, lighting a Gaulloise.

"Trouble?"

"Not for you."

"I think so. Why else would you come to see me?"

"Old time's sake," Tallon said.

Kaplan grunted. "I was right. Trouble. In that case we'll drive while we talk." He let in the clutch, and they took off through the suburbs of Tel Aviv.

"I want some information about guided missiles," Tallon said.

"Shit," Kaplan said. "You've grown up, eh? It used to be Thompson subs. What do you want to steal—a Sam missile?"

"I didn't say I wanted to steal anything."

"Since when did you beg, borrow, or buy anything?"

"I'm respectable these days. Like you."

"Sure. And you want to know about missiles. What do you want to do? Take on De Beers?"

"Look," Tallon said, as Kaplan turned onto the Jerusalem road, "I told you, there's no trouble in it for you. I just want information. You won't be involved."

"You're so right," Kaplan said. He kept the car at a gas-saving fifty miles an hour. "And why should I help you?"

"I helped you once," Tallon said.

"Am I never to be allowed to forget it?"

"I've never asked you for anything since. But let's not forget that, if it wasn't for me, you'd have done five years in a French prison, and maybe you wouldn't have that fine office in the diamond exchange; and maybe you wouldn't be one of the saviours of Israel." Tallon squeezed Kaplan's arm feeling a surprisingly hard bunch of muscle for a man with such a belly. "After all, I did kill the man who was going to inform on you."

"And you enjoyed it," Kaplan said. They passed a group of soldiers thumbing lifts, and Kaplan said, "I don't like to pass them. Those kids. . . . You've no idea what they've been through."

"Tell me about missiles," Tallon said.

"What missiles? What do you want to 'buy'? A Russian SS-19 Intercontinental with multiple nuclear warheads? Or an American Minuteman III, maybe? Or just a Soviet SA-6. They've got ten thousand launchers for those, and I'm sure they wouldn't miss one."

Tallon grinned. "Nothing quite so ambitious." He stubbed out his cigarette, wondering how much to tell Kaplan. "I read about the smaller hardware, the stuff they knocked out a lot of your tanks with."

"We knocked out a hell of a lot of theirs," Kaplan said sourly.

"I know," Tallon said patiently. "I read the newspapers. I know you nearly won the war. So you must have captured a few little missiles, eh, Joseph?"

They passed orange groves and fields planted with sunflowers; the gentle hills flanking Jerusalem lay ahead of them.

Kaplan said, "What are you interested in, my friend —Snappers, Swatters, Saggers?"

"You tell me," Tallon said.

"Then you tell me what you want one for."

"I collect armaments."

"And my name's Henry Kissinger."

Tallon sighed. "A job."

"A bit old for that, aren't you?"

"And you're a bit old for charging around the desert capturing rockets."

"So you want to hit a security van, eh?"

Tallon was startled. "How. . . ."

"I can't think of any other reason why a Marseilles gangster would want an antitank missile."

"All right," Tallon said, "something like that." He hurried on. "Just supposing you were right, what would I need?"

"Your brains tested," Kaplan said.

"And then?"

"Maybe a Soviet RPG-7, which fires rocket-propelled grenades. But I suppose a Sagger would be the answer. That's the baby you read about: a wire-guided missile. The launcher sends the signals along a wire as fine as a hair unreeling behind the bastard. They're small and compact, and one soldier can operate them. In the West they've got the AS-11, which is a version of Nord's SS-11 antitank missile, adopted by eighteen countries. You mount them on the gun barrel of a tank, and they take off at 360 miles an hour, pierce armored plate half an inch thick at a two-mile range, and explode seven feet inside it."

"Joseph," Tallon said, "you're showing off. I don't have a tank."

They were climbing now, with the first disappointing view of Jerusalem ahead: a wall of modern blocks.

"Or the British Vigilant may be your answer. Very small and maneuverable and will penetrate twenty-two inches of armor plate at one mile." Kaplan changed gear half way up the hill. "The point is, do you want to wreck the van or get something out of it?"

"What do you think?"

"Diamonds?"

"You've got a criminal mind," Tallon said.

"Diamonds?"

"Maybe."

"Well, just make sure they aren't diamonds meant for Israel."

"All right," Tallon said. "Now just tell me what I need."

"Buy British," Kaplan told him. "Buy yourself a nice little Blowpipe manufactured by Short Brothers and Harland of Belfast. You wouldn't like to think you'd collaborated with the Russians, would you, Pierre?"

From the roadside near the Intercontinental Hotel they gazed across the old city of Jerusalem, its mosques and towers glittering in the sunlight against the hot blue sky. Kaplan pointed across the jumbled rooftops and said, "Jews, Persians, Egyptians, Romans, Mongols, British, Arabs—they all took it, the Holy City. And now it's ours again." He turned to Tallon. "And we'll never give it up. No matter how far our 'friends' sell us down the river of Arab oil." The big man with the paunch straining the buttons of his crumpled white shirt had suddenly assumed dignity. Three Phantom jets screamed overhead; north, south, or east, Tallon thought, and they were heading toward enemies. He felt a little ashamed that he was wearing the star of David catching the sunlight on his Gentile breast. "Come on, Joseph," he said, "let's get back to Tel Aviv and have a drink."

Before Pierre flew back to London, Kaplan gave him a pamphlet about the Blowpipe. It was developed in 1966 as a portable antiaircraft weapon for the Army and the Marines. The idea was to produce a missile that one man could carry and fire at a low-flying aircraft traveling at supersonic speed. In 1972, after exhautive tests, it became operational.

Blowpipe comprises three main parts: missile, launching canister, and aiming unit. In a matter of seconds you can fit the aiming device to the canister, rest the weapon on your shoulder, and track the target through a monocular sight. Finger pressure on the trigger closes an electric circuit supplying power to missile and canister. The operator issues commands to the missile by radio.

Blowpipe even has an identification friend-or-foe safety unit, which can kill the firing sequence if the marksman discovers he is about to blast a friendly aircraft out of the sky. It can also be used against armored vehicles and small ships, and has a range of three thousand meters with supersonic speeds.

The challenge of stealing a rocket launcher and missiles, however small, appealed to Pierre Tallon. Perhaps one day he'd try and hijack an SS-9 Intercontinental missile from Red Square. But first Monsieur Blowpipe. He thought about it all the way back to London in the El Al jet. Finally, he decided, regretfully, to designate responsibility to his son; one robbery was enough for a man in his dotage.

At Heathrow he phoned Daniel and told him to meet him at the Skyways Hotel. The girl he had met on the plane worked in the Israeli Embassy in London; they had returned together and booked into the Skyways. He bought her a couple of drinks in the bar, and when she said she had to catch up on some sleep, he didn't protest, just watched her admiringly as she made her way to reception, a slender girl with green eyes and soft hair that smelled of lemons. She was also a judo expert and a parachutist—a distinct challenge and a stimulating improvement over the plastic beauties he imported into Spain.

When Daniel arrived he moved to a table in the corner of the bar. There weren't many customers around: a few passengers stranded by "technical difficulties"; a few crew members celebrating the enforced stopover. He ordered himself a Chivas Regal and his son a pineapple juice.

"So," Pierre asked, "how's big business?"

Daniel polished his glasses. "Fine." He looked around the bar. "Furs from Iceland. Mink."

His father nodded approvingly. "Times have changed since my day, eh?"

Daniel smiled politely.

"You say you always find the customer first?"

"That's right. Then we supply the goods."

"The goods. That's what they call diamonds in the business. Did you know that?"

Daniel said he didn't.

"So if I found you a customer, you'd guarantee delivery?"

"Of course."

"For anything?"

"Within reason."

"What's outside reason?"

"I don't deal in drugs," Daniel said.

"Good boy." Pierre paused to light a cheroot; Daniel moved his chair back. Pierre went on, "Supposing I was to tell you that I have found you a customer."

"Does he have money?"

"Enough."

"Then maybe we can do a deal."

"The customer," Pierre said, "is me." He sipped his whisky and watched his son.

"What do you want?"

Pierre wished his son would show emotion sometimes; his mother hadn't been a particularly placid woman.

Pierre said, "A Blowpipe."

"A what?"

Pierre lowered his voice and told his son about the guided missile.

"Es tu fou? Where the hell am I supposed to find one?"

Pierre shook his head. "You disappoint me. Here I am testing the generation gap, and you fail me first time. In my day we wouldn't have let a problem like that bother us. The missiles exist; therefore, they can be located and stolen. You know, perhaps you'd better leave a job like this to your seniors."

Daniel knocked back his juice as though it were vodka. "All right," he said, "tell me about these Blowpipes. How much do they weigh for instance?"

"Eighteen kilograms, with missile. I want three missiles."

"You want a lot," Daniel said. "How much?"

"Ten thousand pounds?"

"I wasn't asking for my pocket money," Daniel said. "Fifteen?"

"I'll take twenty because it's in the family. And that's on top of my corner of the job itself."

"You're a greedy boy," Pierre murmured. "Still, like father like son. When can you deliver?"

"When I've found the bastards," his son told him.

They were interrupted by Raquel. She was wearing a navy blouse and a white linen skirt. "I couldn't sleep," she explained. She sat down and added, "You didn't tell me you were meeting a friend here."

"Friend?" Daniel took off his glasses and looked vulnerable and boyish. Then he smiled and his young face looked radiant. "Didn't my father tell you he was meeting his son?"

Merde, Pierre thought, it comes to something when your own son cuts you up.

Chapter 10

The tank, an old Centurion that had last seen active service with the Sixth Royal Tank Regiment in Suez in 1956, was cornered and couldn't even make a flight of it.

She was a beautiful, brutal old lady past her prime. Conceived in 1943 with a seventeen-pounder gun and armor strong enough to withstand the German eighty-eight millimeter cannon, the first model didn't become operational until 1945, by which time the war was over. She finally came into her own during the Korean War, when the King's Royal Irish Hussars went into action with the Mark III, fitted with a twenty-pounder, a .30 Browning machine gun, and bomb throwers. After that, she saw duty in many parts of the world, including Vietnam. In the Six-Day War, between the Israelis and Arabs, she proved more than a match for the hundred-millimeter guns of the Russian T.54 tanks. Centurions, which netted Britain £200 million in exports, are still in use, but the upstart Chieftan is poised to take over their glory.

Today the enemy of the cornered Centurion was France. An Alouette III antitank helicopter had risen from behind a ridge of dunes, its blades throwing up clouds of sand, and was circling the tank. After a couple of minutes taunting her, one of the crew of the helicopter fired a Very light; it exploded in the blue sky like a bottle of red ink thrown against a wall.

The turret of the tank opened, and three British soldiers, a sergeant, and an officer made a break for it. The pilot of the Alouette gave them four minutes before banking, hovering above a cluster of silver birch trees and loosing off one SS-11 wire-guided missile. The old lady disintegrated in a sheet of flame.

"Bastards," exclaimed the young British officer crouching with a sergeant and one soldier in a slit trench five hundred yards away.

"Don't worry, sir," his sergeant said. "Our turn will come. And in any case it's not a proper war," he added.

"We've got to treat it like one," the young officer said, "or else there's no point." He was twenty-one years old, on the plump side, and he took life seriously.

The battle, part of an Anglo-French exercise, was being staged on the heathland surrounding Bovington Camp, in Dorset. The gorse and heather there is constantly being chewed up by the treads of tanks, wheeling and maneuvering like prehistoric reptiles. And in the camp itself there is a tank museum, where war veterans gather with their sons to show them "what it was like."

The object of the battle was to exchange ideas "in view of the lessons learned in the recent Mideast Conflict." (On this particular day—Monday, May 13, 1974—the indefatigable Dr. Henry Kissinger had just arrived in Jerusalem from Damascus for another attempt at settling the aftermath of the conflict: the Israeli-Syrian hostilities.) But the "battle" had become more intense than the authorities had expected; all the combatants were bored with inaction, and the spirit of Waterloo was abroad.

It was a lazy spring day, the puffs of gunsmoke on the heath like cocoons. Most of the staff officers and armaments experts sat on a central observation platform; a few wandered around the safety areas.

The Alouette settled on the ground, and the pilot and two soldiers in combat uniforms climbed out to inspect the flaming wreckage of the Centurion.

"Just one burst with a machine gun," the young British officer said. "That's all it would take."

"Steady on, sir," the sergeant said. "They're supposed to be our allies." He was a calm, resourceful man of thirty, suffering from a hangover following an Anglo-French celebration in the sergeants' mess.

"Or just one blast with that"—the officer pointed at the Blowpipe missile the soldier squatting beside them was balancing on his shoulder—"and bang, no helicopter."

"And no commission, sir, if you'll beg my pardon. We're only supposed to be knocking out obsolete vehicles, not spanking new choppers."

"I wish to God we could see some real action," the officer exclaimed.

The sergeant, who had seen plenty, didn't reply.

The officer glanced at his watch. "Still, we'll be able to have a crack at the enemy in ten minutes. At eleven hundred hours we're expected to knock out an old AMX-13." He turned to the soldier, a young cockney. "And we don't want any mistakes, Anderson."

"No, sir."

"There's not much chance of that, sir," the sergeant said. "Not with a Blowpipe."

The helicopter rose into the air, hovered for a moment over its burning victim, and then whirred away in search of other prey. The staff officers and civilians, who had been watching from an area pegged off with yellow flags, moved on.

The officer said, "I suppose they're not even going to bother to stay for our moment of glory."

"Don't worry, sir," the sergeant said. "They'll be back." He paused. "Mind if I have a smoke, sir?"

"A good idea," the officer said. He took a packet of Benson and Hedges from his combat jacket and offered it to the sergeant and the soldier. They had smoked about half their cigarettes when the Land Rover pulled up behind them and three men in

French combat uniforms, carrying shotguns, got out. Two jumped into either end of the slit trench; the third stood on the edge pointing a shotgun at the officer's head.

The sergeant said, "Can't you buggers run to anything better than toy rifles?"

The man standing on the edge of the trench said, "The Blowpipe, we want it. Tell that soldier to pass it up to me. No tricks. Now—move!" His features beneath his helmet were made unrecognizable by daubs of mud.

The officer stood up, plump cheeks flushed. "Just what the hell do you think you're playing at?"

"We're not playing," Daniel Tallon said.

"For God's sake, it's only a bloody game. The Napoleonic Wars are all over, or perhaps someone forgot to tell you."

Tallon snapped, "The Blowpipe, please."

"Like bloody hell," the officer said. "In any case, what's the good of threatening us with blanks?"

"Blanks?" Tallon smiled one of his rare smiles. "No blanks, *monsieur*. I told you, we're not playing games. One barrel of his shotgun would blow your head off."

The sergeant said, "I think the silly bugger means it, sir."

"I don't care what he means," the officer said, his hand straying toward the pistol at his hip.

Tallon said, "Don't touch it. I'm warning you for the last time."

The officer's hand reached the holster.

Tallon fired one barrel of the shotgun to the right of the officer so that only a handful of shot sprayed his leg. "The second barrel takes your head off," Tallon said.

The officer gazed at the blood seeping through his combat trousers. "You're mad," he said.

"The Blowpipe, *monsieur*."

"Better do as he says, sir," the sergeant said. "They must be on LSD or something. You can't risk young Anderson's life. Or mine, come to think of it."

The officer stared up at the young man with the glasses and soft hair stirring in the breeze. "You realize you'll be court-martialed for this?"

"I doubt it," Tallon said. "But you will. Dereliction of duty, isn't it? By the way," he added, "are you allowed to smoke on duty?"

"You cheeky frog bastard," the officer said, watching the blood drip on to his boot.

"The Blowpipe!"

"Hand it up to him, Anderson," the officer said.

"Sir." The soldier handed up the Blowpipe with alacrity.

"And three missiles, please."

The soldier handed three vicious-looking pointed missiles, each containing two-stage solid rocket fuel, guiding devices, and high explosive warheads.

"*Merci, monsieur.*" Tallon jerked his head at the other two Frenchmen. "*Allons.*" They climbed out of the trench, picked up the missiles, and took them with the Blowpipe, to the Land Rover while Tallon kept the shotgun leveled at the officer's head. Then Tallon backed toward the Land Rover still pointing the shotgun. Just before the Land Rover took off, tires spitting dust, Tallon smiled for the second time and shouted, "*C'est la guerre.*"

With the French pennant fluttering on the hood, the Land Rover sped along the A352 to Wareham, where the three Frenchmen were staying at the Black Bear. They had told the landlord they were taking part in the exercise but, being French, couldn't stand the thought of the food in the British mess. Already a few hopeful girls had assembled.

The Frenchmen went up to their rooms, changed into civilian clothes, and told the landlord they were bored with the exercise and were driving into Bourne-mouth for the afternoon. Three girls sitting at the bar smiled; their afternoon, the smiles said, was free, and there was nowhere they would rather spend it than in Bournemouth.

Tallon, who had registered under the name of Captain Paul Bouffard, paid the bill, and the three Frenchmen departed without speaking to the girls.

Just outside Poole, they pulled into a side road and parked beside a Ford shooting brake. They unclipped the aiming unit from the canister of the Blowpipe, hidden under camouflaged tarpaulin; heaved the whole weapon into the back of the shooting brake; and covered it with sections of drainpiping.

Then they picked up the A31 and headed for London. The time was just 12:30 P.M.

By that time the young officer had made an oral report to his commanding officer and had reported to the hospital for treatment of his leg. They dug the shot out, bandaged him up, and sent him back to his unit.

The commanding officer, fortyish with a fierce moustache, issued half-hearted instructions to apprehend a Land Rover with three French soldiers in it. He didn't hold out much hope.

He returned to the central platform and watched a French tank being annihilated by a British tank without much interest. There were, he mused, one or two explanations. Either the French had pulled a stroke of genius and got away with it, in which case the British would look like bloody fools if they made a formal complaint; or some villains had dressed up as French soldiers and had pulled a stroke of genius, in which case the British still looked like bloody fools.

After lunch the commanding officer visited the wounded officer, the sergeant, and Anderson. It was, he told them, highly irregular, but he had decided to write off the loss of the Blowpipe with minimum fuss. He would be obliged if they said nothing more about it.

Two days later all three men were posted to the Far East.

Chapter 11

By the time the Blowpipe had been stolen, Pierre Tallon was in Antwerp. He took the ferry from Dover to Ostend because no one seems to bother about hijacking ferries, and, with no frisking, they are one of the best modes of transport if you're taking a gun into a country. Risky, but Tallon liked risks, and he took the Python with him.

At Ostend he hired a Citroen GS and took the highway to Brussels, turning left at Ghent onto the road that dives under the Schelde through the J.F. Kennedy Tunnel into Antwerp. At 6 P.M. he booked into the Waldorf on Belgielei, a hotel popular with diamond people. He used a passport forged in Lyons: he was Albert Lavaud, diamond merchant.

Rhodes' idea was to study two dry runs. The first one, in late May or June, would be to check whether the information of the inside man, Frederick Masters, was good. The second, in August or September, would be to make an exhaustive check on the arrival procedure after the BH-125 touched down with the diamonds on board.

At 8:00 A.M. on Friday, May 24, Tallon received a telephone call from London in his room. Rhodes said, "About Solitaire. . . ."

The hotel operator, who figured he knew just about

every term used in diamonds, yawned and left them to it.

"Is it good?" Tallon asked.

"We think so. Nine carats from Messrs. Heath and Row."

"Fine," Tallon said. "I'll buy."

He hung up the receiver. If the executive jet was leaving Heathrow at nine he would have to get to Duerne pretty quickly.

He put on the sort of drab grey suit Monsieur Lavaud would favor and drove to the airport. He stopped in the parking lot outside the main entrance and waited. Half an hour later a dark green security van drove up and stopped at the taxi stand. The driver stayed at the wheel while his partner went into the rental office; three minutes later he returned carrying a packet of Gitanes and a girlie magazine. He wore a pistol, a Smith & Wesson by the look of it, at his hip. The two guards wore helmets and dark green uniforms. He wondered what reinforcements they had in the back of the van.

The driver let in the clutch and the van headed toward the control tower. Tallon strolled to the edge of the airfield. The driver's mate went into the building, stayed five minutes, and emerged with a new alertness about him. Tallon searched the sky and saw a black dot approaching from the direction of the North Sea. Five minutes later the executive jet touched down smoothly, its two Rolls Royce Bristol Viper turbojets whistling happily. Tallon saw the security van, followed by a Fiat, speed out to the end of the runway. So diamonds had VIP treatment. So they should, Tallon thought; all aristocrats should get the treatment.

He wandered back to the Citroen. Ten minutes later the green security van came past, turning right into the wide road lined with small square buildings. Tallon picked up the map marked by Rhodes. The security van carried on for a mile before making the turn across the E3 highway into the city. Tallon let it go; he had decided the hit would have to be made between the airport and the highway before the van burrowed into small, complicated streets crawling with cops.

He drove back to the airport looking for a suitable site from which to fire a guided missile launcher no bigger than a bazooka. Half way back he noticed a half-finished three-story apartment building.

At 11:30 that night, with light rain polishing the cobblestones, Tallon returned and parked the Citroen at the end of the road. He had to establish whether he could guide the Blowpipe's missile onto the security van from the apartment at a range of a quarter of a mile. He thrust his hands into the pockets of his blue raincoat, the butt of the Python nestling in one palm.

There was no one around. But the rain was thickening, blowing in from the sea across the Schelde, trying to swamp the city, take over the lowlands. Tallon paused in the doorway of the building. He took a flat torch with a microscopic beam from his pocket and began to climb the improvised stairs.

He went up to the first floor, gingerly making his way along a passage to a doorway leading into the uncompleted lobby of the apartment. Rain was sweeping in through the arch that would be the window. Tallon knelt just beyond the range of the rain, put the Python on the floor, and switched off the torch.

In front of him, in the light of the street lamps, the road lay deserted, washed clean by the rain. It was the perfect spot for the hit. Tallon thought he heard a faint noise; but he was tracking an imaginary van through a monocular sight, seeing the burst of flame as the warhead exploded on impact. His breathing was quicker; this was what he had missed all those years.

The voice from the doorway said, in Flemish, "Stand up. No tricks—I've got a gun."

Tallon didn't know much Flemish, but he understood the message. He fired the Python from the floor at the silhouette in the doorway, the explosion muted by the silencer. The man grunted as the bullet hit him in the chest and stumbled back, dropping his pistol.

Tallon went after him, But as he dived across the room, the man slid to the floor. Tallon stepped back, Python in hand, not wanting blood on his clothes. With one foot he found the pistol and kicked it away. The man's breathing grew slower, then stopped.

Tallon stuck the Python in his raincoat pocket and retrieved the torch. The tiny beam found the widening pool of blood on the floor; Tallon stepped around it and played the beam on the man's face. It was a hard old face with grey bristles on the chin. Tallon shrugged; he had no business to be wandering around half-built apartment buildings with a pistol.

Tallon examined the man's wristwatch. It was still ticking and the hands pointed to 11:56. Tallon turned them to 12:50, then smashed the glass with the butt of the pistol. He could almost hear the police: "We estimate the time of death to be 12:50 A.M., the moment he smashed his watch as he fell mortally wounded by the gunman's bullet." If the body wasn't found until daylight, no pathologist would disagree.

By 12:30 A.M. Tallon was in a dockside bar—drawn there as any good Marseilles gangster should be—drinking a foaming Stella Artois with a blonde whore named Françoise. By 12:35 he was involved in a brawl with an out-of-work docker living off the girl. By 12:50, having clubbed the docker unconscious with the Stella Artois bottle, he was in bed with the whore, making love with a passion not unconnected to the killing.

The next morning he reported the attack by the

docker to the police. Painstakingly, they recorded Monsieur Albert Lavaud's complaint. Later in the day they checked it out, then dropped it. What was another dockside brawl when, at the very time Lavaud had been filing his complaint, a man had been murdered on the other side of town?

Chapter 12

April is a time for meeting a girl under trees dripping with rain after a shower. May is a time for flirtation, with blossoms falling and couples entwined in the parks. June is the time for love. It was June, still young and green beneath warm skies, and Johnny Rhodes knew now that he was deeply and irrevocably in love with Marie Tellier.

Should he tell her about Solitaire and lose her? Should he keep up the pretense and lose her?

Marie made her views clear as the E-type pushed its aristocratic nose through the South Downs. "Either you tell me what you're up to or I leave tomorrow. This time for good. I'll fly to Montreal on a one-way ticket."

He wanted to stop the car, to kiss, to confess. But he had been a professional too long. Women—however sincere, however loyal, however deep their love—wanted to reform you. They could even tip off the police "for your own good." "I'll be waiting for you when you come out," they said. Not that Marie would do that, but you never knew what she might let slip. These days Chief Detective Inspector Willis was paying far too much attention to him and Marie. It was a friendship encouraged by Marie as a discouragement to whatever she thought he was up to. No, Rhodes decided, he couldn't tell her, not with the climax of a long and honorable career at stake.

"Well?" She plucked a cigarette lighter out of its holder and lit a long filter-tipped cigarette.

"Like I told you, there's nothing. Just a few important business deals."

"New York? Florida? Marseilles? Spain? Weekends in the country with God knows who." She blew two thin jets of smoke from her nostrils. "Have you got another girl, Johnny?"

Rhodes laughed. At times like this it was always good when you could tell the truth. He took one hand from the steering wheel and touched her knee. "No girls," he told her.

"I mean it, Johnny, if you don't level with me, I'm flying to Montreal tomorrow."

"Maybe," he said carefully, "that wouldn't be such a bad idea. You know, we've been at each other's throats for awhile, and maybe if you took a vacation with your people in Canada things would sort themselves out. You know, with all this work, I've been getting a little hard to live with."

Marie said, "So you want me out of the way while you get on with whatever you're doing?"

"I didn't say that."

"You meant it. I can read you like a book. What is it, Johnny? Diamonds? The old fever?"

"I was cured a long time ago," Rhodes said, thinking that this serene day, with curls of clouds in the sky and the cushions of the South Downs printed with flowers, was going sour. "What about a drink?" he suggested.

She shrugged. "If you like."

Rhodes drove into Lewes and parked the car. He loved these old towns curled up in the countryside; they seemed to be supported by oak beams and soaked in cider. Maybe he would spend Christmas here, after Solitaire. He saw the town covered with snow, church bells chiming, carolers making their way through the snow-muffled streets. But without Marie, it would be nothing, just another place to sleep.

They went into the White Hart and drank Bloody Marys, savoring the sharp edge of the vodka in the tomato juice.

He raised his glass. "To us."

She drank without replying. The farmers and businessmen in the old-fashioned bar eyed her. As well they might, Rhodes thought, because she looked very desirable in a daisy-print crepe-de-Chine dress that revealed the gentle swell of her breasts.

They ate a light meal and drove into Brighton, the dormitory home of London actors, businessmen, and villains. They coasted slowly along the sea front, listening to the waves on the shingle, glancing at the Regency squares. Somehow Brighton managed successfully to encompass everything from vulgarity as loud as a belch to dignity as restrained as the court circular in the *Times*.

When he looked at Marie she was crying.

He stopped the car. "What's the matter?"

"You know what's the matter."

"Tell me," he said gently.

"Everything. This." Gesturing at a terrace of Georgian houses, families sitting on the beach, children playing in the waves. "The sharing. Because that's what it's all about, isn't it, Johnny? The sharing."

He leaned over and kissed her.

When he awoke the next morning she had gone.

So Frederick Masters' information was good. Rhodes paced the empty apartment, which still smelled of Marie's perfume, pausing to empty an ash tray containing butts with her lipstick on them. If she didn't return, he would fly to Montreal when it was all over and fetch her.

So, Masters was reliable. Rhodes forced his thoughts back to Solitaire. The call had come on the telephone, manned in shifts by Rhodes and Ferguson, five minutes after the coded Telex message had been sent from Hatton Garden to Antwerp.

But there were complications. How could Masters tip them off in December when they were in Belgium and Holland? A direct call to Antwerp? Rhodes rejected it. There might be delays; and if Masters was absent for a long time, it might alert security in Hatton Garden.

No, after the ninth consignment of diamonds for 1974 had been dispatched in September or November, someone would have to man the telephone twenty-four hours a day. He decided that Daniel Tallon and a couple of his "business associates" would have to take over the Park Lane apartment. It was hardly likely, Rhodes thought, that such prosperous professionals would attempt a double-cross. You didn't carve up your own father. . . .

Who else did he have to recruit? Muller, the pilot, was already on the staff, carrying out trials near Munster. They also needed a getaway driver with experience on Continental roads; Daniel Tallon should be able to provide one.

But the factor that worried Rhodes most was violence. Could Solitaire be accomplished without it? The Great Train Robbers had almost managed it; the driver needn't have been injured. So why not the Great Diamond Robbers? Gas grenades, he decided, were the answer.

He picked up a newspaper and read that train robber Ronald Biggs seemed to be getting away with it; although he had been arrested in Rio, the British police hadn't yet managed to extradite him.

Rhodes stripped off his dressing gown and pajamas and put on track suit and running shoes. He was much fitter now, although there was still a slight bulge to his belly and he had developed a lust for spaghetti bolognaise.

He glanced at his watch. Five past eleven—late for jogging. He let himself out of the apartment and made for the park across Park Lane. At first, as he headed for Kensington Gardens at a steady pace, his thoughts returned to Marie. The sharing. . . . Then, once again, he forced his mind back to diamonds, his first love. The diamonds he would steal were probably being mined now. Rhodes imagined them surfacing like currants from the earth's crust.

The diamonds Rhodes planned to steal were being mined in June 1974 in two of the great sources of gem stones in the world: South Africa and South West Africa.

But the process that was to provide the loot started millennia ago. According to recent theories, diamonds were formed 120 miles or more below the earth's crust and forced to the surface by explosions of gas. The crystals, formed from carbon during intense heat and pressure, came spouting up in rock called kimberlite—blue or yellow ground—which is found in pipes and fissures where it pierced the surface. Kimberlite also contains scores of other minerals; even coal, human bones, and ostrich eggs have been found in it.

The diamonds of South West Africa are alluvial. It is presumed they were thrown up in kimberlite pipes, washed downstream by the Orange River to the coast, and distributed by the movements of the sea. On January 14, 1927, Dr. Hans Merensky, a German South African, proved his theory that diamonds would be found on the oyster line (where fossilized oyster shells lie) at Alexander Bay, Namaqualand. A vast treasury of stones was found, and they are still being churned out of the old marine terraces beneath the beaches.

It has been estimated that since diamonds were discovered, more than two thousand years ago, only 130 tons of them have been taken from 3 million tons of rock.

As Rhodes jogged past the nannies out with their babies in Kensington Gardens, his prospective loot was being brought up by various methods from the deep mines of South Africa; and, in South West Africa, it was being bulldozed from ancient beaches uncovered by fleets of sand-shifting machines.

But it was the processing that whetted Rhodes' appetite—the crushing and milling of the rock and alluvial deposit to nuggets; the shaking and sifting and rotating, when diamonds and other heavy stones drop to the bottom of containers; the journey of these stones across tables and belts covered with thick yellow grease. It is on these grease beds that diamonds first display their magic: they stick to the grease and reject water, so the residue of ordinary stones is swept away, leaving the rough diamonds stuck in the grease. The process for alluvial diamonds is a little different because mineral salts have coated them, counteracting their water-repellant quality; so chemicals are added to bring back the magic.

Rhodes pictured the rough stones embedded in the grease, and his mouth watered: some transparent; some with regular shapes; some like pieces of opaque quartz with blunt surfaces, cold and greasy to the touch. Colorless or slightly yellow for the gem trade; occasional blues, greens, pinks, violets and reds, fancies, as they called them. Each with its superlative ability to scatter light, which the cutters and polishers have to encourage as they convert pebbles into jewels.

This conversion would take place after Rhodes had disposed of the rough stones—he had agreed to shift them for Ferguson and Tallon—in New York and Tel Aviv. They would be cleaved or sawed, according to their characteristics. If you cleave you split the stone with the grain; if you saw you cut against it.

Rhodes imagined a saw whirring against a prize gem, a thin disc of phosphorated bronze covered with oil and diamond powder rotating 4,500 to 6,500 revolutions a minute. To saw a one-carat stone might take as long as a day, and in some workshops they had batteries of saws working.

Then the bruting is done to round off the stones, and finally the grinding of the facets—fifty-eight for a brilliant—on a horizontal wheel. Then the gem is polished with diamond powder mixed with olive oil or—according to the whim of the craftsman—egg white, detergent, or even spit.

In every process they needed diamond to cut diamond.

Rhodes jogged on determinedly, the incurable fever upon him.

Diamond. Even the word had power. It came from the Old French *diamant,* derived from the Greek and Latin *adamas,* 'unconquerable.' Long ago diamonds were thought to cure illness and combat evil spirits; Plato thought they were alive. Diamonds were said by some sages to reveal the presence of poison and, when sucked, to purge a liar. Others believed diamond powder to be poison, and throughout history, attempts were made to kill with them. The magic of diamonds was also supposed to banish nightmares, send ghosts packing, and protect crops against pests and storms.

Automatically, Rhodes' thoughts turned to the famous crooks who had been lured by the hypnotic fires of gem stones. Men like the Frenchman Henri Lemoine, who, in 1905, informed Sir Julius Wernher, a South African financier and a governor of De Beers, that he could manufacture gem stones. Sir Julius watched a crucible containing a mixture placed into an electric furnace for thirty minutes. When the crucible was taken out, it contained twenty-five small diamonds. Sir Julius paid up, and for a few years Lemoine sent him diamonds. When it was discovered that these diamonds were identical to crystals recovered from a mine in the Orange Free State, Lemoine was arrested for fraud and jailed for six years. And, of course, there was also the founder of the movement, Captain Blood, who had tried to steal the crown jewels.

Rhodes passed a pretty girl wearing an engagement ring, the June sunshine splintering on its diamonds. As he jogged along in his track suit, he smiled at her. The girl, who had been warned about the nuts in the park, looked the other way.

When Rhodes got back to the apartment, it was full of echoes. He showered and dressed, waiting for the phone or doorbell to ring. Neither obliged. He poured himself a beer, drinking it slowly. So you wait all your life for one girl, he thought, and then you throw her out. He left the apartment and walked down Park Lane. The sky was hot. There were memories of youth on the breeze, and the pavements seemed to be occupied by lovers walking hand in hand. He turned into the Inn on the Park and ordered lunch in the Vintage Room. Opposite him, a young couple sat engrossed with each other, heads almost touching across the red and white checkered tablecloth. Rhodes ate without appetite, lonely for the first time in his life.

Chapter 13

Johnny Rhodes carried out his first diamond robbery when he was seventeen and still living with his parents in a tenement in downtown Manhattan.

His father was a night watchman in a warehouse

on the docks, and his mother took in laundry. His father drank, his mother grumbled; both were grieved at having produced a son who wanted to improve himself.

Rhodes never discovered the source of his aspirations, but in later years, he liked to think that perhaps there was a line connecting him with Cecil Rhodes. He did odd jobs around the piers—which protrude like the teeth of a comb into the Hudson—without upsetting the unions, and he went to night school.

Then his father fell sick, and his mother had to sell the only family heirloom—a brooch fashioned from a pendeloque diamond set in sapphires. She got four hundred dollars for it, and later Rhodes saw it on sale for three thousand. He had no particular love for his parents, certainly no respect, but he didn't like injustice and he didn't like crooks who robbed the poor.

So Johnny Rhodes, already tough and smart, with disconcerting blue eyes, had his first affair—with a sophisticated blonde of twenty-two who worked for the jeweler who had bought the heirloom.

He followed her to Battery Park, where she ate a picnic lunch; sat beside her; and tried to impress her with his knowledge of Castle Clinton (Lafayette spoke there and Jenny Lind sang), which he had culled from a guidebook on a newsstand half an hour earlier. She wasn't impressed by his recitation, but she was attracted to him.

They made love in the office behind the jeweler's shop, and on the third occasion, Johnny Rhodes, confident of his appeal, made certain propositions to her. As a result, he obtained the combination of the wall safe and a duplicate key to the premises. The next day the girl immobilized the burglar alarm, and at 2:10 A.M., Rhodes successfully carried out the first venture of his criminal career.

He sold the brooch for two thousand dollars and

gave the money to his parents. Having taken the precaution of helping himself to a few brilliant cuts and one exquisite marquise, he was able to rent a studio apartment in uptown Manhattan and set up home with the blonde, who was already envisaging a Bonnie-and-Clyde relationship.

The affair lasted two months. By that time, Rhodes—already hooked on diamonds after his first heist—was working as a clerk on Forty-seventh Street and taking a course on minerology at night school. Through his work, he was able to make contact with some professional thieves. In return for information, they taught him their trade.

A brunette, who worked as a temporary maid in some of the mansions in New Jersey and upstate New York, replaced the blonde. On his nineteenth birthday Rhodes broke into a big house, owned by a Wall Street financier, two miles off the Palisades Parkway. The brunette was working there; and, with her plan of the house in his pocket, he climbed into two bedrooms while a swimming-pool party was taking place and pocketed jewelry worth twenty thousand dollars.

The brunette laid on two other lucrative robberies before allowing herself to be seduced by a movie director who thought he could fix her up with something in Los Angeles. This turned out to be a job as a hat-check girl in a club on the Strip. By the time she returned to New York to continue the partnership with Rhodes, he had left for Europe. He was twenty-two and determined to make enough money to retire at thirty-five. To do this, he had to travel, staging robberies in cities where he wasn't known and moving on before his presence could arouse suspicion.

He rejoiced in the sophistication of the great European capitals, and liked to sip Pernod on the terraces of dignified old hotels, where, perhaps, Hemingway and Scott Fitzgerald had once lingered. About every six months or so he returned to New York, staying in Manhattan and pulling an occasional job in Chicago or Texas, where women like to convert their husband's oil into compressed carbon. As he fled into the night, he drooled at the cold touch of diamonds and grinned stupidly when, later, he gazed at their fire, their luster—or *adamantine* as it is known in the trade.

When his mother died, Rhodes bought his father a house next to a bar in Miami.

He made a few mistakes—such as trying to sell a doctored gem to Toni Ludi, the leading New York diamond fence—but not many. By the age of thirty he was the best diamond thief in the world. He had his quota of narrow escapes but was only trapped once—by a nineteen-year-old airline stewardess named Marie Tellier.

He was waiting at the Salisbury, Rhodesia, airport for a flight to Nairobi in the days before air travel between the two cities was stopped. He had just relieved a Cape Town financier of uncut Wesselton stones worth about thirty thousand pounds, and, en route to Brazzaville to sell them, had decided to stop over in Salisbury to case the residence of a tobacco baron who was sensibly investing his profits in diamonds.

It was early Sunday morning; the East African Airways Fokker Friendship, which flew in once a week, was waiting on the runway. A delayed flight from London had just landed, and the airport was full of pale businessmen, already beginning to sweat in their crumpled clothes; children coming home for the summer vacation; and African porters.

While he was getting on line to check in, Rhodes noticed a broad-shouldered man with a crew cut heading for a phone booth. He wore a light-weight fawn suit taut across his shoulders, a striped tie, which had worked loose, and socks of different colors. Give this man two thousand pounds to spend in Savile Row and he would still emerge as if he had just walked out of a brawl in a seamen's pub. In fact, his clothes were expensive, and it was this combination of affluence and untidiness that jogged Rhodes' memory. Where had he seen the man before?

Rhodes worried about it until he reached the check-in desk. As the clerk noted the weight of his baggage, Rhodes turned and looked for the badly dressed man. He saw the broad back in a phone booth; he had the sort of physique you would expect a rugby player to have. Then Rhodes had it: he had seen the man in the company of the financier he had fleeced in Cape Town. Was he a detective, bodyguard, or both? Thoughtfully, Rhodes picked up his hand baggage and went upstairs to the restaurant, where he ordered an orange squash.

Obviously, the man had followed him. But why hadn't he made a move? Perhaps he was on the phone to Cape Town checking some detail. What would *I* do now? Rhodes wondered. Make another call and tip off customs at Nairobi?

It was then that Rhodes noticed a small tartan suitcase identical to his own. It belonged to an East African Airways stewardess drinking coffee with another stewardess and a first officer at the next table. As the Fokker outside was the only East African aircraft at the airport, it followed that the stewardess was on the Nairobi flight. He glanced at her face; delicate features, green eyes—a French face, he decided, with shadows under the eyes as if she had spent a late night at Brett's club. He stared out through the window with the panoramic view of the airfield and, with his left foot, gently eased his suitcase toward the next table.

He stretched, yawned, and stood, picking up the stewardess' bag and leaving her with his bag containing four Wesselton diamonds concealed in a large tube of Palmolive shaving cream.

If she discovered the switch before Nairobi, he would "discover" his mistake and change bags. But it was unusual for customs to search crew baggage—except when there was a tipoff, as there had been at Rome recently when a stewardess was caught with diamonds and rubies in the false bottom of her hand luggage. If she was stopped, there would be considerable hilarity at her possessions—shaving gear, socks, underpants—but probably nothing more serious. If the diamonds were found, Rhodes would intercede.

Ten minutes later he saw her walk across the apron to the Fokker, tartan bag on her shoulder. He went to the toilet with her bag and ditched cosmetics, perfume and wisp of handkerchief bearing the initials M. T. In the lobby he bought a couple of paperbacks and some new shaving gear and put them in the bag.

Twenty minutes later the flight was called, and Rhodes and forty other passengers boarded the neat little aircraft. The girl served him a scotch, showing no hint of concern. Obviously, she hadn't bothered to use any cosmetics in the past two hours, but with her complexion, Rhodes noted, it wasn't really necessary. He hoped she didn't try to erase the evidence of her late night for the benefit of a boyfriend in Nairobi, where East African Airways were based. He thought she was an extremely desirable girl, but, as he had a big thing going with an excitable Italian girl in London, he decided not to make any moves.

The untidy South African sat five rows behind Rhodes. Rhodes read a magazine, gazed down at lion-colored plains, dotted with game and mosslike bushes, and pretended to doze.

At Nairobi Airport the heat was bouncing off the runway. The passengers straggled into the arrival lounge to have their passports stamped. After a ten-minute wait, Rhodes was fatalistically making his way to customs.

"Mr. Rhodes?"

Rhodes nodded.

"Would you come this way please."

It took an hour, and they searched everything, testing the heels of his shoes, feeling the lining of his suits, squeezing his new tubes of toothpaste and shaving cream.

Then they apologized for the delay.

Rhodes was magnanimous. "You've got a job to do," he told them, "just like me."

He picked up his case and the stewardess' bag and walked into the main concourse of the airport. He was on the threshold of the Africa of popular fiction: white hunters meeting their clients, bearers carrying guns, dignified Africans; and, outside, lions, ostrich, zebra, roaming the game park under a hot blue sky.

Rhodes spotted the broad back heading for the exit doors. He caught up with the man, tapped him on the shoulder, and said, "Haven't we met somewhere before?"

The man turned and stared at Rhodes malevolently. "I don't think so," he said. Sweat was staining his suit at the armpits, making him more unkempt than before.

"I've got it," Rhodes exclaimed. "Cape Town. Weren't you there on Thursday?"

The man said, "I've never seen you before in my life. Now please excuse me, I've got an appointment in the town."

"How did you get on with customs?" Rhodes asked, walking beside the man toward the taxi rank.

"I don't know what you're talking about."

"I had a lot of trouble. I thought you might have."

The man couldn't resist it. "What happened?" he asked.

"Nothing. I was clean." Rhodes grinned. "And by the way, you've got odd socks on."

The crew of the Fokker Friendship were boarding a mini-bus. They had come through a different customs check; the stewardess was there, laughing with the other girls, her thirty thousand pounds worth of hand baggage slung over her shoulder. Everything was all right.

One problem remained: getting the bag back. He reached the mini-bus just as the African driver started the engine. He knocked on the window to attract the girl's attention. When she noticed him, he pointed at his suitcase and to hers, indicating in sign language that there had been a mistake.

The girl came to the door. "What do you want?" He was right; she was French, Canadian variety.

Rhodes explained that they must have accidentally picked up each other's bags.

The girl shook her head. "No, this is mine."

Rhodes frowned. "It can't be. . . ."

"It is," the girl said.

The rest of the crew stared at him with hostility. A steward leaned forward, tapped the driver on the shoulder, and said, "Come on, let's go."

Rhodes said, "There's been a mistake."

The girl smiled. "No mistake, Mr. Rhodes. Have a good day."

The mini-bus took off leaving Rhodes holding one pigskin suitcase and a tartan bag that smelled faintly of perfume. And he didn't even know her name.

Thoughtfully, Rhodes went to a phone booth and called the personnel manager of East African Airways. Smoothing the American accent from his voice, he said he was Griffiths from immigration. "With reference to the French Canadian airline stewardess on your staff. . . ." He paused.

The woman's voice on the other end of the phone was bored. "You mean Marie Tellier?"

"Yes, Miss Tellier."

"What about her?"

Rhodes didn't know what about her. He hung up.

He took a cab into Nairobi and booked into the Norfolk Hotel, a gracious old place that was part of the history of Kenya. Here you can stay in cottages on the grounds, have cocktails on the terrace listening to the evening breeze in the eucalyptus trees, and eat curries beside the swimming pool.

He showered, put on a blue mohair suit, and headed for the Thorn Tree, the open-air restaurant outside the New Stanley Hotel, where, like the Strand in London, you usually meet someone you know.

Rhodes didn't meet anyone he knew. But he saw two girls in colored blouses drinking coffee and eating toasted cheese sandwiches. They were unmistakeably air stewardesses, just as cops in plainclothes are unmistakeably policemen.

Rhodes sat at their table, ordered coffee, and introduced himself. "Paul Tellier from Montreal."

The girls greeted the announcement without enthusiasm and went on talking about the dresses they were having made from silk bought in Bombay.

"Perhaps you could help me," Rhodes said, thinking what a bastard the French-Canadian accent was to imitate. "I've flown in from Salisbury to meet my sister, Marie, and I've lost her address."

"Why should we be able to help you?" one of the girls asked. She had been working on her tan and her teeth seemed very white.

"You are stewardesses, aren't you?"

"Does it show that much?"

"Afraid so. I can always spot a stewardess and I can always spot a model." Rhodes tried one of his smiles; the girls seemed to thaw a little.

The other girl said, "What did you say your name was?"

"Tellier," he told her.

"You don't look much like Marie's brother. How long has she worked for East African?"

Rhodes thought quickly. Marie Tellier was only about eighteen or nineteen and therefore hadn't been in the job long; nor did she have a tan. He said, "She started about six weeks ago. I was supposed to meet her in Salisbury on Saturday night at Brett's. She was on the Friendship flight I believe."

The first girl said, "That's right, she was on the Salisbury flight." She shrugged. "I suppose you must be her brother." She took a green address book from her handbag and gave Rhodes an address in Muthaiga.

His first instinct was to burgle her room, but there were snags. In the first place it seemed likely that she had found the diamonds. Why else would she want to hang on to the bag? Secondly, she shared the house with two other girls, and they probably had a guard dog. He could fix the dog with doctored meat, but that would take time, which he didn't have because he had to be in Brazzaville in three days' time.

Rhodes slid lower down in the bathtub, rested his feet on the taps, and stretched out a hand for his martini. This little indiscretion, he thought, is going to cost me one diamond in blackmail, one third of the retail value of the loot. Ah well, you can't win 'em all. He climbed out of the bath, wrapped a large white towel around himself, and walked into the bedroom, where Marie Tellier was waiting for him.

"What the hell. . . ."

"I thought I'd save you the trouble of coming to my place."

Rhodes sipped his drink, gaining time. "What makes you think I had any intention of coming to your place?"

She was sitting on the edge of the bed, legs crossed; good legs, Rhodes noticed. She was wearing a flimsy

159

pink and mauve blouse and a grey skirt. She seemed to have recovered from her fatigue.

She said, "Come on, Mr. Rhodes, let's not play games."

"Why not? Here I am in my bath towel. Why not play games?"

She raised her eyes to the ceiling. "I don't play games with men who steal girls' handbags." She giggled. "Men who walk around with lipstick and perfume and heaven knows what in their hand baggage."

"I tossed those out," Rhodes said.

"That was good perfume."

"It just wasn't me."

"You'll buy me some more?"

I shall have to do whatever you ask, Rhodes thought, saying, "I'll even buy you dinner."

"You know the way to a girl's heart, I'll give you that."

"You like good food?"

She gazed at him steadily. "I like all the good things of life, including diamonds. A girl's best friend, I believe."

"So they say," Rhodes said warily, watching her unclip her ostrich-skin handbag.

She tossed the Wesseltons onto the bedside table. "Yours, I believe, Mr. Rhodes."

"It's what they call a fair cop, huh?"

"Nairobi warned us on the radio that you might be a diamond smuggler."

Smuggler? That was interesting, Rhodes thought, confirming his suspicion that the diamonds had been stolen by the financier in the first place. He wouldn't want to be involved in inquiries about theft. So the untidy South African had merely been an anonymous informant carrying out an act of revenge.

"So you realized why I switched the bags?"

"Of course. But it took me quite a long time to find them in the shaving cream." She lit a cigarette and smoked it without inhaling; Rhodes guessed she had only recently started smoking. "How on earth do you get the cream back into the tube?"

"You don't," Rhodes said, sitting down opposite her. "You open the tube from the bottom and seal it up again with a serrated grip." He fixed the towel so that it didn't slip down and asked, "Why didn't you stop me?"

She shrugged. "It's none of my business, I suppose. I wouldn't like to think I'd helped put anyone behind bars. And you don't look the sort of man who goes around hurting people."

"Thanks. You make me sound as tough as a chocolate éclair."

"You look tough enough," she said, squashing out the cigarette when it was half smoked. "But you don't look vicious."

"Ah so. And now what are you going to do?"

"Nothing," she said. "But if you get dressed, you can take me to dinner."

"You don't want one of these?" Rhodes picked up the diamonds.

"No, Mr. Rhodes. . . ."

"Johnny," he interrupted.

"If men give me diamonds, I like to think they've bought them."

"So be it." Rhodes stood up, crossed the room, and slipped the stones into the breast pocket of his jacket. "Maybe one day. Now perhaps I can have my bag back."

They dined in the grill room of the New Stanley. They ate oysters, followed by steak and green salad. In between courses, they danced on the small floor.

Over coffee and liqueurs, Marie showed Rhodes her diamond ring. "What do you think of it?" She slipped it off her finger.

Rhodes examined it and told her, "It's pretty."

161

"It's very valuable."

"It's pretty."

"Are you trying to tell me something?"

Rhodes sipped his cointreau. "Diamond people can usually tell a diamond at a glance. But sometimes they make a mistake. You know, if there's some new fake on the market or if the light's not so hot."

"And?"

"The first thing we notice is the luster, the adamantine. This, with the flat facets and the reflectivity, makes for good reflections. If you tilt a good stone you should be able to see a good reflection of say that electric light over there." Rhodes tilted the stone and grimaced.

Marie said, "But surely that doesn't apply to a stone in a setting?"

Rhodes inclined his head. "Not just a pretty face, eh?"

"Please continue the lecture," Marie said.

"There are ways of identifying a stone in a setting. For instance, if you look into it, it should look shallower than it really is. You don't get that impression so much with simulants. But, of course, it's easier to identify a diamond that hasn't been set. You won't get the same transparency as you will with some simulants. You can see the letters on a printed page through synthetic spinel but not through a genuine diamond. Then, of course, there's the question of brilliance. In a really top-class stone, the brilliance looks almost black. Then there's the question of the temperature of the stone; the water test; twining, which only occurs in a diamond; and, ultimately, X-rays."

She took back the ring. "Do you need X-rays for this?"

"No, it's a fake and you know it."

She raised her eyebrows. "Quite correct, the original's in the vaults of the Bank of Montreal. You're a real professional, aren't you." She lit a cigarette. "But a professional what?"

"Thief," Rhodes said. "Shall we dance?"

"You say it as if you were a banker or a politician," she said as they moved slowly around the floor.

"Politician? Not much difference, is there?" He felt the warmth of her cheek against his. "How old are you?"

"Nineteen."

"Just?"

"Yesterday."

"Don't let this life get a hold of you," he said, hand touching the nape of her neck. "You know, don't spend your time visiting the swimming pools of the world. Don't ever settle for what the others are doing." He wanted to offer her more personal advice, but it was none of his business.

They went to the old Equator Club and danced again. He felt a tenderness for this girl that he had never experienced before. It alarmed him. Since when did a jewel thief have the right to be concerned about anyone's morals?

They took a cab back to Muthaiga and he kissed her on the porch like a teenager on his first date. He thought about making another date. But she was too young, too goddamed honest. But still. . . . He felt his resolve dissolving in the moonlight.

"Marie. . . ."

"Will you always be a thief?"

"I guess so." The steely resolve of every woman to convert and reform reached him. He kissed her again, gently, and said, "Good night, Marie. Remember what I said—or tried to say. I guess we'll meet again soon."

But they didn't meet again for nine years, by which time Marie had worked for two other airlines, survived one disastrous marriage, and Rhodes had gone into retirement. Then he gave her the diamond he had promised her in the cottage at the Norfolk Hotel, omitting to tell her that it was stolen, not bought.

Chapter 14

The crime rate in Amsterdam is high, so Rhodes and Ferguson felt at home. Their cab driver warned them about being mugged at night ("The safest place is the porn area"), and Rhodes remembered that New York was once New Amsterdam.

They arrived by DC-8 on the 10:05 KLM flight from Heathrow on June 19, and spent two hours checking out Schiphol Airport: the position of the bar; snack bar; the big tax-free shopping complex; the three exit gates, A, B, and C.

Then, with an airport map obtained through contacts at Heathrow—where most commodities can be bought for a price—and a pair of Zeiss binoculars, they checked the runways and perimeter of the airport that handles some 3½ million passengers a year.

"It's a hell of a big airport," Ferguson said, gazing at the blue-and-white Dutch jets scattered around like toys. "We're going to need some help here, especially with the new security since they forced that VC-10 down here and burned it."

"You're in charge of Amsterdam," Rhodes told him.

The cab took them into town along the E10 highway, which links Rotterdam with Amsterdam. Half way there, they saw an exit to Haarlem. "Home from home." Ferguson grinned.

They passed a suburb, which looked as if it consisted of dolls' houses, before entering the city built on 90 islands and linked by 550 bridges across its 60 canals, although figures seem to differ according to the authority.

They booked into a medium-sized hotel called the Roode Leeuw—the Red Lion—on Damrak, around the corner from the Dam, the center of Amsterdam, where the Royal Palace stands. They took a pleasant twin-bedded room and began to unpack.

"So now what?" Ferguson asked.

"We're a couple of tourists, right? So we do what the tourists would do. We take a trip around the canals, look at Rembrandt's house—not to be confused with Rubens' house, which is in Antwerp. We eat at the Five Flies; drink too much Pilsener; and then, with the usual excuse that we're drunk, we head for the red-light area."

"It's the best job I was ever on," Ferguson said, rolling up his sleeves and washing his face.

"The porn is no different from Times Square," Rhodes told him. "And anyway, why would a man of God want to visit those places?"

Ferguson gave him a big white grin in the mirror. "It's no good preaching to the converted all the time. It's time I did some missionary work."

"Yeah." Rhodes took out his tourist's clothes—new lightweight suit, white raincoat and brogues, and a Pentax camera in a case containing three lenses, a light meter, and a couple of filters. "And at midnight we meet Daniel Tallon's contact at a bar on the corner of the Achterburgwal Canal, which, if I'm not mistaken, is in the middle of the porn area."

Ferguson glanced at him slyly. "You know it then?"

"I've done my homework," Rhodes said.

"Sure," Ferguson said.

"I'll stay a couple of days working out the routes, then it's all yours. But don't stay holed up here too long. Don't make yourself conspicuous."

"You seem to forget," Ferguson said, "I was in this

business too, and I never got busted." He opened the envelope of brochures the tourist board had given them and took out a blue-and-white card. "Hey," he said, "what does this mean, *pas op autodieven.*"

"Beware of car thieves," Rhodes told him.

"They must have known we were coming," Ferguson said.

Wearing their new raincoats and carrying their camera cases, they took a tour around the canals in a glass-roofed barge, photographing the gabled houses crowding the maze of mossy waterways. Then, with light rain falling, they visited the floating flower market; window shopped down Kalverstraat; found the old synagogues, which used to be packed before the Nazis arrived; and called at number 4 Jodenbreestraat, where Rembrandt once lived. They also took in a diamond-polishing factory, where Moses said, "Let's hope he finds himself short of supplies early next year."

At the Five Flies, a restaurant decorated in seventeenth-century style with Delft tiles, they ate Rijsttafel, washing it down with dark Munchner beer, followed by cheese flavored with pepper and caraway seeds. They drank a liqueur known as Bride's Tears in the bar of the luxury Krasnapolsky on the Dam, and then headed for the red-light district down the road.

From the shop windows in the alleyways, girls winked and smiled—fat girls; thin girls; bespectacled girls; dark girls with gypsy earrings; bored blondes reading books; busy girls knitting socks. It was all very cozy, almost domestic; and whenever the curtains were drawn, you knew a girl was earning her living.

Rhodes and Ferguson went into a couple of bookshops, one with an old lady in charge. Smiling at them, she pointed out the sections arranged public-library style, except that the headings were lesbianism, flagellation, rape, etc. The old lady, Rhodes thought, looked a little out of place among the color prints of genitalia and the sex aids.

They went past a couple of theaters with neon lights outside proclaiming Live, Hard Porn, crossed a bridge spanning a dark canal, and went into the bar to meet Daniel Tallon's contact.

No one looked up when they entered. It was 11:55. Two toughs sat at the bar reading sports papers. A plump girl served them two draught beers with good necks of foam on them and went on painting her fingernails. The records on the juke box changed and played the Rolling Stones instead of a girl incongruously singing "*Y Viva España.*"

Rhodes and Ferguson took their beers to a corner table overlooking the canal.

"What do we know about this guy?" Ferguson asked.

Rhodes shrugged. "Not a great deal. If Tallon says he's okay then I guess he is. In any case we don't tell him too much. You know, we don't even tell him who we are. Just give him the money, a quarter now and the rest in stages."

"This must be the biggest-spending heist ever pulled."

"It's the biggest heist ever pulled."

"Do we know what he looks like?"

"A crook," Rhodes said.

"That makes three of us, brother."

At one minute past twelve a man of about thirty wandered into the bar. He had a Mexican moustache, which looked too big for his face; long, lifeless hair; and a yellowish complexion. He was wearing faded blue Levis, a blue woolen shirt open at the neck, and a string of beads. As arranged, he was carrying *De Telegraaf* under one arm and a pack of Roxy cigarettes in one hand.

He sat down at their table. "Are you the guys?" He

spoke English with a slight Dutch accent and sounded very bored.

"What guys?" Ferguson asked.

He yawned. "Aw, shit. The guys Daniel Tallon told me to meet. Let's not be mysterious, man."

"Let's not be a smart-ass, either," Ferguson said. "Is your name de Gooyer?"

"As far as I know." But his tone was subtly different as he looked at the big black man sitting opposite him, as if he could see the muscle packed inside the raincoat.

"You a friend of Tallon?"

"We've done a few jobs together."

"You mean you've done a few jobs for Tallon."

De Gooyer shrugged. "Comes to the same thing, doesn't it?"

"It doesn't," Ferguson said. "Now listen, Pancho, we've got some business to talk with you and it's us who does the talking."

"I'm not sure. . . ."

"Ten thousand," Rhodes said.

De Gooyer wiped his moustache. "Guilders?"

"Pounds," Ferguson said. "Paid in guilders."

"Wow." De Gooyer subsided in the chair. "Are you on the level?"

"Two thousand five hundred pounds at the end of the week. The rest in installments, the balance on delivery."

"Delivery of what?" de Gooyer asked.

"An ambulance," Ferguson said.

A blue movie involving a transvestite voyeur was playing on a small screen. On a four-poster bed a couple were preparing to give an exhibition. At the far end of the club, a group of girls in tiny skirts were grouped around a horseshoe-shaped bar waiting for customers. Ferguson, Rhodes, and de Gooyer sat at a table well away from them. Half a dozen other men sat at tables with girls, their attention divided between the girls and the movie.

De Gooyer, whose attitude had changed considerably, apologized for bringing them there. He was minding one of the girls, he said, and he liked to vet her clients.

"Think nothing of it," Ferguson said. Every time he moved, the girls, attracted by his size and obvious affluence, nodded up and down at the bar like pigeons.

"But why an ambulance, for God's sake?" de Gooyer asked.

"That needn't bother you," Rhodes said. "Can you get one?"

"I can get anything. Didn't Tallon tell you?"

"Yeah," Ferguson said, looking at him doubtfully, "that's why we're here."

"But an ambulance?"

"Ask any more questions," Rhodes told him, "and the deal's off."

"So when do you want this ambulance delivered?"

"When we're good and ready," Ferguson said.

One of the girls caught Rhodes' eye; she came over and sat down at their table. "Are you a movie star?" she asked, eyes taking in the cut of his suit, searching for the bulge of his wallet.

Rhodes gave her a couple of small bills. "Beat it," he said. "Buy yourself a drink."

She snatched the notes and walked away, bottom waggling haughtily.

Ferguson said, "So how would you go about getting us this meat wagon?"

"I haven't thought about it," de Gooyer said. He sipped his Bols gin. "I suppose I'd dial 35-55-55, and when the ambulance came along, I'd hijack it."

"Listen," Rhodes said, "we're not playing cops and robbers. We don't want a nationwide alert for one hijacked ambulance."

"Okay, so give me time to think. Tallon will tell

you, I've never failed anyone yet. He's a hard man, that Tallon," de Gooyer added, thoughtfully.

Ferguson leaned across the table and grabbed de Gooyer's arm, his thumb finding the bone beneath the bicep and digging at it. "We're hard men, too, de Gooyer. Don't blow this one. Right?"

"Okay," de Gooyer said. "Don't get rough."

The movie finished, and an undernourished young couple began to make love, without enthusiasm, on the bed.

Ferguson said, "The same bar in four days' time, and you'd better have some ideas." He sighed. "Hijacking an ambulance, Jesus, man. . . ."

They walked out into an alleyway. It was still drizzling, and the rain made halos around the red lights of the girls' shop windows. Most of the tourists had disappeared, and a few solitary men slunk past, glancing into the windows with exaggerated disinterest.

Ferguson stopped in front of a window occupied by a fat-thighed girl in glasses. She smiled and beckoned, and Ferguson said, "I always did like chicks in glasses. Perhaps she needs converting."

As they walked back to the hotel, they saw the old lady in the book shop packing up some of her pink rubber merchandise for the night.

At the airport bar Ferguson said, "I'm not so sure about that de Gooyer."

Rhodes said, "See how he shapes up. We've got plenty of time. I'll see what Tallon has to say."

"Okay," Ferguson said, "we'll see how it goes."

"If he doesn't make out, then find someone else."

Rhodes stood up as his flight was called. "Good luck, Moses, and take my advice—don't play smart-asses with girls who wear glasses."

"And you take my advice," Ferguson said, standing up. "Get that girl of yours back. You're acting like a man who lost a five-carat diamond and found a marble."

It wasn't until two days later that Ferguson, checking his clothes and baggage, realized that he had lost the pink diamond Rhodes had given him at Fort Pierce.

Chapter 15

Nigel Lawson gazed at the pink diamond lying on Carmichael's desk with fear and puzzlement. It both strengthened and weakened his theory that was going to net him a fortune.

"Well?" Carmichael picked up the diamond and held it between thick fingers.

"About seven carats. Probably about seventeen before it was cut. A beautiful fancy."

"Worth stealing, eh?"

"I wouldn't know about that," Lawson said. He spoke mechanically because he was used to cracks about his past.

"Come off it," Carmichael said mildly. *"If* you were a thief, then would it be worth stealing? You know, could you get rid of it?"

"It would have to be recut," Lawson said. He took the diamond from Carmichael and examined it. It was flawless, fires burning in its roseate depths. It was unique. "If you tried to shift a stone like this, you'd be pinched before you got out of the shop."

Carmichael watched Lawson suspiciously, as if he might pull a sleight-of-hand trick with the diamond. "And has this stone been recut?"

"How the hell should I know?" Lawson said, knowing that it hadn't.

"It shouldn't be difficult to tell."

"Does it matter?"

"Of course it matters," Carmichael said patiently. "If this was stolen, it was the work of a top-class pro. Right?"

Lawson said, "I suppose so."

"And if it hasn't been recut, it means he hasn't tried to dispose of it. Kept it to give to a bird maybe."

"No bird's worth a diamond like that."

"So that means," Carmichael went on, "that it was your actual thief who lost it in Amsterdam."

Lawson handed him back the pinky. "Perhaps."

"So this is what you've got to do, and this is why we employ you," Carmichael said. "It won't be difficult to find out where the diamond was stolen from. Then you, with your *special* knowledge, will be able to tell me who stole it. If he's still in Amsterdam, I might even go over there myself and help the Dutch police."

The theory that had been taking shape in Lawson's mind was simple: he suspected an attempt was going to be made to steal a consignment of diamonds in Antwerp. The idea had taken root when he met Detective Chief Inspector Willis, the sort of policeman he almost admired—not bent but sensible when it came to dealing with villains; not adverse to doing a deal in the interest of law enforcement.

They met on a bench in St. James' Park on a warm evening in June; and while they talked, they watched the ducks and the girls in mini-skirts. Behind them, a military band was playing a selection from *Rosemarie*.

Willis, elegant in a grey lightweight suit and Pierre Cardin tie, was smoking a small cigar. "Well?" he said, waving the cigar.

Instinctively, Lawson looked around, but they had the seat to themselves. "I thought you might be able to help me," Lawson said.

"Oh yes," Willis said. "How much?"

"I want help, not money."

"Did you back a winner?"

"I backed three, including the winner of the Derby."

"Then the beer's on you for a change," Willis said. "How can I help you?" He stared appreciatively at a Scandinavian-looking girl with a suede mini high around her thighs.

"It was something you said about Rhodes last time we met."

"That he must have wiped the paperweight clean?"

Lawson shook his head. "He may have been wearing gloves."

"He may have been," Willis said. "None of the boys who interviewed him afterward could remember whether he was."

"God help your neighbors when you retire," Lawson said. "Do you suspect everyone?"

"Unfortunately, yes," Willis said. "I think my wife's fiddling with the housekeeping money and my son's stealing apples. What was it I said about Rhodes?"

"You said the second time you went to his flat he'd just come back from Antwerp."

"Did I?" Willis tossed his cigar butt to the ducks, who swam away in disgust. "Oh yes, I happened to see the used part of his ticket lying on a table."

"Happened?" Lawson loosened the knot of his Guards tie and unbuttoned his blazer with the tarnished buttons.

Lawson grinned. "All right, I looked at it when he went to the loo. Anyway, what if he did go to Antwerp? He's in the antique business after all."

"Bit like the scrap-metal business, isn't it?"

"A bit higher on the scale. But I checked out Rhodes and he's straight."

As the three-card trick, Lawson thought. "Is Antwerp famous for its antiques?"

Willis shrugged. "It's famous for diamonds, isn't

173

it?" He looked at Lawson quizzically. "You're not trying to say our Mr. Rhodes has a sideline, are you?"

Lawson cadged a cigar and said, "I'm not saying anything. I'm just interested. As far as I know, Rhodes is straight," he lied. "But I may be onto something."

"And you don't want paying?"

"Not yet."

The ducks had returned, and a small boy was throwing hard crusts to them. The band was half way through *Rosemarie,* and Willis began to hum, "Dead or alive. . . ."

"Are you interested or not?"

"Of course I'm interested—as long as whatever you're onto happens before I retire."

"And when's that?"

"End of December," Willis said.

"It could be the greatest coup of your honorable career."

"Then tell me about it," Willis said, glancing at his watch and adding, "Soon be time for you to buy me a dirty great pint."

"I can't tell you about it. Not yet."

Willis sighed. "I wish I was a bit younger," he said, as another mini-skirt passed by. "Why can't you?"

"It's just a hunch."

"One of those, eh?"

"I'm not asking for any lolly."

"But you will."

"If I'm right."

"What do you want me to do then?"

"I want to know more about Rhodes' movements."

"You're not suggesting I put a tail on him."

"You're supposed to be a friend of his, aren't you?"

"In a manner of speaking. Funny"—Willis looked thoughtful—"but I get the impression that it's his girl who wants me around."

"Perhaps she thinks you're like Clint Eastwood—you know, the tough lone cop."

"But I'm not," Willis said, "am I? No, she's not interested in me. She's in love with Rhodes, the lucky sod. It's almost as if she's seeking protection for him."

Lawson thought about it, wondering if she wanted Willis around to discourage Rhodes from coming out of retirement. It all added up; whichever way he looked, it added up to a great big hunch, from the first anonymous tip from Antwerp to the report on the murder just outside Deuvre Airport.

Willis said, "Has it got anything to do with that shooting?"

Lawson was astonished. "What shooting?"

"The one in Antwerp."

"How the hell did you hear about a small-time murder like that?"

"Interpol," Willis said briefly. "The dead man had an English wife. I just happened to read the report. He was a small-time thief with an unpleasant history of crimes against children. The murderer did a good job."

"You're always 'happening' to do things," Lawson said. A terrible thirst was coming upon him. "No, it's got nothing to do with that. Not as far as I know."

"So what do you want me to do, ask Rhodes to account for his movements over the past six months?"

"No," Lawson said, "just 'happen' to find out."

Their third meeting took place at Madame Tussaud's waxwork exhibition in Marylebone Road.

Willis said, "Our friend Rhodes gets around."

"You just 'happened' to find out?"

"That's right," said Willis, pausing to look at the scene of the Battle of Trafalgar.

"Where's he been?" Lawson's voice was eager.

"Don't you want to know how I found out?"

"Not particularly," Lawson said. "But if you want to show me what a good detective you are. . . ."

"I went to the travel agent's nearest his apartment."

"Very astute," Lawson remarked.

"He went to Marseilles."

Lawson stopped walking, fingers combing his silver hair. "Are you sure?"

"He booked a ticket there. Funny," Willis mused, "because when he came back from that trip, he brought his girlfriend a present. But it wasn't the sort of present you'd buy in Marseilles. You know, it was one of those wickerwork donkeys—the sort of thing you buy in Spain."

Lawson moved on, his mind racing. Was Rhodes recruiting? He knew of only one man worth recruiting in Marseilles, but he had retired. But where to? His files would tell him.

Willis paused opposite Brigitte Bardot and Twiggy. "Does it mean anything to you—Marseilles or Spain?"

"Perhaps. Has he been anywhere else?"

"As a matter of fact he has. He flew to New York." Christ, Lawson thought, he's recruiting the Godfather.

"But he didn't stay there," Willis said.

"Ah."

"No," Willis went on, "he used his credit card for an internal flight."

"How the hell do you know that?"

"I checked with the credit-card company."

"Are they supposed to hand out information like that?"

"I doubt it," Willis said.

"So where did he go?" Lawson asked, thinking: Rhodes is slipping, poor bastard, he's out of touch. "Florida," Willis said. "And he flew back to England from Miami on National Airlines."

Now what operator had moved from New York to Florida? Lawson tried to concentrate, but he found it difficult at this time in the morning, before the pubs opened.

"And that's all I know," Willis said, as they passed

176

astronauts Armstrong and Aldrin. "Except that Rhodes made one more trip somewhere, but I don't know where it was because he must have paid cash and didn't use a travel agent—almost as if he sensed someone was checking on him."

"With you as a friend," Lawson said, "I'd think twice about buying a bus ticket." He had to get back to the office in Hatton Garden, so he said, "Well, thanks anyway. I'll be in touch."

"You'd better be," Willis said. "I'm not doing this because I want to go into the travel business."

"There's just one thing," Lawson said.

"How much?"

"A fiver?"

"Fast women and slow horses?"

"Just horses," Lawson said, taking the £5 note.

Back in his office he unlocked the safe and spread his files across his desk. First he looked at the file on Pierre Tallon, who had once used Marseilles as his headquarters. And, when he quit, had retired to Denia, in Spain! Lawson's hands trembled.

Now who the hell might have left New York for Florida? As an ex-jewel thief himself, Lawson tried to read Rhodes' mind. It would have to be a top-class professional who had never been caught. Mafia apart, that narrowed it down to half a dozen men in New York who had specialized in diamonds.

Lawson cleared the desk of all the rejected files. He lit a cigarette and studied seven files, tapping his ash into a cup of cold tea. Twenty-five minutes later, only one file remained on his desk: Moses Ferguson. The entry was written in shaky handwriting, as if Lawson had been recovering from a hangover at the time: "Believed to have gone out to grass in Florida."

Lawson lit another cigarette and leaned back in his chair, staring out of the dirty window, a great balloon of excitement expanding inside him. So three of the best diamond thieves in the world were coming out of retirement to pull a heist.

He knew how they had reached their decision; he would eventually have done the same if things had been different. He knew they were planning the biggest diamond robbery in history, and he knew it had to be Antwerp.

If he could forestall a robbery involving anything from £12 million to £15 million, his reward would be a fortune in itself. If, on the other hand, he collaborated with Rhodes, Tallon, and Ferguson—using his knowledge as a threat—he could become a millionaire.

And now the pink diamond had turned up in Amsterdam, confirming his theory about Rhodes and challenging his theory about Antwerp.

There was no doubt about the diamond. It was part of the haul from a classic snatch in Brussels in August 1964, when a Citroen was stopped outside the Palace of Justice and eighty thousand pounds worth of diamonds were stolen by a thief posing as a police motorcyclist. Lawson knew the policeman had been Johnny Rhodes.

But what the hell was he doing in Amsterdam? Lawson wondered. Could I be wrong about Antwerp? Certainly there was a valuable haul to be lifted from Amsterdam, but nothing like the goods transported to Antwerp ten times a year. Perhaps they were using Amsterdam as an escape route. Yes, that was it, Lawson decided. They would move the loot by road from Antwerp and put it on a plane at Schiphol.

The pink diamond had been found in the bedroom of a small hotel near the Central Station in Amsterdam and been taken to the police by the hotelier. Lawson shook his head in despair at such honesty.

The police had taken it to the Diamond Exchange

on Weesperplein and it had been flown back to London for examination by the security bureau.

Lawson scanned the report by the Dutch police. The room had been vacated about three hours before the diamond was found. It had been occupied by a man traveling under a United States passport: Henry Ballantine, aged thirty-eight, from Detroit. Forged, of course.

Lawson went back to Carmichael. "I want to make a call to Amsterdam," he said.

"Don't you trust the Dutch police?"

"I don't trust any police," Lawson said. "Do you want something done about this stone or not?"

"Can you speak Dutch?"

"Every Dutchman I've ever known can speak English."

"All right, go ahead."

"And keep your hands off the extension," Lawson said.

Within five minutes he was through to the hotel. He told the hotel owner he wanted a description of Henry Ballantine.

"Well, he was black of course. . . ." And when he heard Lawson exclaim, he said, "Didn't you know?"

Lawson said he didn't and listened with growing agitation to an exact description of the man he knew as Moses Ferguson.

Lawson made himself a cheese sandwich, brewed a pot of tea, and sat in front of the blank TV. Bachelor apartments seemed lonelier in the summer. In the winter you could convince yourself that you were escaping from the rain and cold; in summer you had to face the truth that you had nowhere else to go.

But a rich man always has somewhere to go, and someone to go with. So what was he to do about Messrs. Rhodes, Ferguson, and Tallon?

I've got two choices, Lawson decided, walking to

the window and watching the traffic, each driver with a destination, a purpose, a home. Either I deal myself in with Rhodes or I find out when the job's going to be pulled, delay the tipoff until the last moment—because Carmichael's methods of criminal detection would alert a corpse—and then collect the reward.

But first things first. When and where? Lawson poured himself some tea and tried to take a firm grip on his straying thoughts. *If I were in charge of the heist, what would I do? The consignments to Antwerp have no pattern about them; therefore, I would have to employ an inside man.* He was pleased with himself; his mind was beginning to function as it had in the old days. *And where would I find that inside man? Surely it had to be in the communications department, which transmitted details of the diamond consignments to Antwerp.* Lawson snapped his fingers.

The next day he got out the bureau's list of Hatton Garden employees with their security ratings. Communications. . . . The screening was less stringent here because the staff didn't come into direct contact with diamonds. *Typical,* Lawson thought. *Just because they haven't got temptation glaring them in the face, they're considered a lower risk than sorters.*

He ran his finger down the list and stopped at Masters, Frederick—Ex-regimental sergeant major, excellent record, decorated for bravery in the D-Day landings, married with wife and two children, living in Mitlham. No record of dishonesty, but, according to his commanding officer, had a weakness for women.

And still has, I'll bet. Lawson grinned to himself. *Wasn't it bloody marvelous? Any rank above corporal who had served king and country and got a gong was above suspicion.* But Lawson knew the Army mind and he could imagine the commanding officer giving his rating. Masters had been one of his men and, therefore, you couldn't knock him. "Had a weakness for women" probably meant that he was a rapist, but, most probably, he only raped enemy wives.

Lawson studied the credentials of the rest of the communications staff. Not a sniff of corrupt potential. Tonight, Lawson decided, I shall have words with Frederick Masters.

Chapter 16

On Thursday, August 15, they held the dress rehearsal. The call came from Frederick Masters at 9:38 A.M. Daniel Tallon was eating a croissant in Rhodes' apartment, which had begun to smell very French with the aromas of Gaulloise and coffee. Tallon immediately put a call into Amsterdam 73-06-22, the number of the Amsterdam Hilton (on the actual day Rhodes intended to use a smaller hotel). He was through to Rhodes at 9:44.

Rhodes made a direct call to Pierre Tallon at the Florida Hotel on De Keyserlei, in Antwerp, and to a private number near Munster.

By 9:40 A.M. Masters had also called Nigel Lawson at his apartment. Lawson, shaving with an unsteady hand, put down the razor and stared at his mottled face in the mirror. Every professional instinct told him this was a rehearsal; this was the way he would have planned it. But what if it wasn't? What if the heist was pulled today and he had failed to take precautions?

Lawson didn't want to alert Carmichael yet because Carmichael would balls it up. No, he'd have to leave Carmichael with the false leads he'd given him about the pink diamond.

What about Willis? Willis would have to tip off the Belgian police. If nothing happened, Willis would presume he was being taken for a ride. What's more, Rhodes, Tallon, and Ferguson might be scared off by police activity.

Lawson continued shaving, drawing blood from his chin. No, this was the rehearsal. I've picked a winner, but it's going to be a long run home.

At 10:32 the BH-125 executive jet, with a crew of two and one guard sitting hunched over a steel case containing £13 million worth of uncut diamonds, took off from Heathrow.

By that time Pierre Tallon was assembling the Blowpipe—shipped from Harwich to Antwerp with a load of British Leyland accessories—in an apartment a quarter of a mile from the site where he had killed a man. He also had with him the Colt CMG-2 light machine gun and the .44 Magnum.

Ten minutes later he turned the keys in the double locks and drove a new Renault hired car to Deurne Airport.

At 10:45 Moses Ferguson left his small hotel near the nightclubs of Leidseplein, in Amsterdam, in an old Mercedes 250S saloon, picked up Rhodes at the Hilton, and headed for Schiphol Airport.

At about the same time an aircraft took off from an airfield in the forest near Munster—once used by the Luftwaffe and now owned by a flying club—with the German pilot Hans Muller at the controls. It headed south.

The executive jet from Heathrow made good time with a following wind, and began its final approach to Deurne just over an hour after takeoff.

The green security van passed Tallon, waiting in the Renault, and made for air-traffic control. Tallon drove away at a comfortable speed to the apartment.

Ferguson was at the wheel of the Mercedes. The leg he had injured falling in Fort Pierce hurt when he pressed the accelerator and brake. The pain was getting worse, but he didn't let Rhodes know.

Rhodes cradled a stopwatch in one hand. "You've got to remember that conditions will be different in December," he said.

Ferguson grunted.

"It could even be snowing." The thought of snow was comforting on this sweltering day, with heat lying in mirage pools on the road.

Ferguson said, "The trouble with our end of the rehearsal is we can't rehearse."

"We can do this part," Rhodes said.

"But not the part that matters."

"We can work out the timing, that matters."

In the apartment at Deurne, Pierre Tallon took up his position with the Blowpipe, standing with his left foot on a stool, the weapon resting on his right shoulder. He had studied the handbook—it was claimed that any soldier could operate the Blowpipe after a couple of lessons—and had fired one of the shark-nosed missiles on Dartmoor. This time there was no missile in the container: Tallon thought the temptation of sighting and tracking the security van might have been too much for him.

When the van came into sight, Tallon picked it up immediately and followed it, teeth bared. Again he heard the explosion, saw the flames. He licked his lips. Next time, he thought.

He locked up the Blowpipe and his guns, returned to the Renault, and drove away down the escape route at thirty miles an hour. The next time it would be eighty miles an hour.

Hans Muller checked his controls and sighed. The flight was little more than a hop: twenty-one minutes, allowing for takeoff and landing. To his right lay the sea, molten steel in the hot light; to the left Europe.

Regretfully, he banked and headed back to Munster. It was low adventure compared with the Congo, Biafra, and Vietnam. But the reward was the highest he had ever flown for.

Outside Schiphol Airport, Ferguson stopped the Mercedes. "We can't hang around," he said. "No point in getting busted for illegal parking."

Rhodes consulted his stopwatch. "It's the timing that counts," he said.

"So you keep saying." Ferguson pointed toward the entrance for authorized vehicles only. "They say they've got tanks hidden around here these days."

"They needn't bother us," Rhodes said. "We're not hijackers."

"I guess not," Ferguson said doubtfully.

"By the way," Rhodes said, as they drove back into Amsterdam, "when are you going to let me have that pink diamond back?"

Ferguson didn't reply for a moment. Then he said, "It was a sort of bond, right?"

"I guess so."

"Then I'll let you have it back when we've pulled off the job," Ferguson said.

Chapter 17

The batch of diamonds that had left London for Antwerp on August 15 was the seventh that year. There were three to go, which meant four months of tension for six people, particularly three men who didn't know when the heist would be made. The three were Nigel Lawson, Frederick Masters, and Benjamin Volkov, who had sent the anonymous tip to the diamond security bureau in London. But they had ignored it; they received so many, he supposed. What more could he do without involving himself?

Ever since Rhodes had called on him, Volkov had suspected he was planning a robbery. It could only be the big one in Antwerp that he had always feared would be pulled one day. His suspicions had been confirmed first by the killing of the small-time thief near the airport, then by the discovery of the pink diamond, which Volkov knew Rhodes had stolen in Brussels.

Volkov sweated before the arrival of each cargo from London. Rhodes had promised he had nothing to worry about. But what if Rhodes was caught? What secrets involving Benjamin Volkov would emerge from his past? I might even be accused of complicity, Volkov thought; at the very least, I would be tried by my colleagues, and my name would appear on a green slip of paper in the Bourse.

Pain stabbed Volkov's ruined testicles; he felt the flames in his fingers, as nails parted from flesh. He saw the diamond he was cleaving—together with the security he had subsequently built up—splinter into fragments.

Seven times this year Volkov peered into hell as the leisurely ritual of the sights, or sales, and the dispatch of the rough diamonds was conducted in London. During each ritual some 220 customers came to collect rough diamonds, which in one particular year had been worth more than £300 million—although since 1969, the figure had been kept secret.

At these sights each buyer is given a parcel of stones by the Diamond Trading Company that are believed to suit his requirements; he can't argue about what he's been given and can only query their valuation. The buyers are mostly rough diamond dealers or cutters.

Before the sights, the diamonds are sorted—first into general sizes and then the larger stones into eleven groups. Then they are sorted into crystal forms —stones, shapes, cleavages, macles, and flats. Next, the diamonds are sorted according to qualities—of which there are ten—the first five being gem stones. They are then sorted as to color—the browns having been removed already—of which there are ten categories (excluding fancies), from the rarest of rare blue-whites to pale yellows. With all these permutations, the Diamond Trading Company has, on occasions, sorted crystals into 2,500 grades.

After the two main sorting processes at the mines and in London, the crystals are weighed to one-tenth of a carat. After polishing, they are weighed to one-hundredth of a carat—a carat being one-fifth of a metric gram.

On the average, a customer leaves London carrying a parcel of rough gem stones worth £100,000. All the Antwerp customers' diamonds are transported together in the executive jet, which is why Benjamin Volkov had sweated seven times this year and didn't know if he'd be able to last until the end of 1974.

By the beginning of September, with the prospect of three more shipments before December 31, Volkov decided to fly to London to see Nigel Lawson, who was also sweating.

September was also a bad month for Moses Ferguson. Whenever there was a mugging, the police turned over the blacks, and there was no one blacker in Amsterdam than the Black Messiah. If they pulled him in and identified him as Henry Ballantine from Detroit, the game would be up. Why hadn't he reported the loss of the pink diamond—a diamond they would know by now had been stolen in Brussels?

So Ferguson moved from small hotel to smaller hotel and operated within the red-light area, where police and criminals had an arrangement so that peace and porn prevailed.

Half way through September, after the eighth cargo of diamonds had been delivered, de Gooyer tried to blackmail him. If Rhodes and Ferguson were prepared to pay him ten thousand pounds, de Gooyer reasoned, then the stakes must be much higher than that.

Ferguson listened to his threats and contemplated knocking the shit out of him and dumping him in a canal. But that wasn't the style of a gentleman cracksman, and in any case, the possibility of a minor accomplice getting smart—always the threat to an ambitious heist—had already been taken into consideration. Even Rhodes accepted that a little rough stuff was necessary at times.

Ferguson called Rhodes in London, and Rhodes told Daniel Tallon. Four hours later a black Citroen GS-1220 took off from Marseilles carrying three men in dark suits. They drove up the A6 to Paris and were in Amsterdam nineteen hours after leaving the Mediterranean coast.

They went straight to the club where de Gooyer's girl worked. Two of them walked down the red-carpeted corridor to reception, where a squat, blue-chinned man smiled a welcome at them. He stopped smiling when one of the men stuck a Beretta M90 in his chest. He raised his hands and pressed a button with his foot. From a doorway down the corridor behind the three men, a large, crew-cut man, about six foot four and just going to fat, emerged holding a pistol. The third man from Marseilles came up behind him and whacked him on the back of the neck with the blade of his hand. He fell on the deep carpet.

The receptionist said, "What the hell do you want?"

The man with the Beretta said, *"Ferme ta gueule."* He stayed with the receptionist while the other two pushed their way into the club.

Inside they were running a lesbian movie, and the

bar girls were moving in on a group of British publicans who had come to Amsterdam to visit its breweries. The two men walked swiftly across the dance floor; knocked de Gooyer off his chair as he went for his gun; picked him up; and carried him out of the club, legs trailing like a marionette's.

The Citroen accelerated down the cobbled street beside the canal and headed for the seamen's bars around the Zeedijk. They carried de Gooyer through a bar, where two men were fighting over a girl, and took him to an upstairs room. Two of them held him while the third cut him with a cut-throat razor, making sure they didn't disable him.

Two days later de Gooyer stared with hatred at Ferguson through a mask of sticking plaster.

Ferguson said, "Never try to blackmail a black." They were in the bar where they had first met.

"They didn't have to be so rough," de Gooyer said. "I'm not an informer."

"Next time," Ferguson said mildly, "they'll cut your head off."

Two weeks later Ferguson had his ambulance—or what looked like an ambulance: a Peugeot van painted white with red crosses. It was housed in a garage on the docks. Ferguson also had an assault rifle with a shortened barrel, weighing only eight pounds, complete with a grenade launcher and six gas grenades. The gun and grenades were locked in a tin chest designed to hold splints.

One other thing bothered Ferguson—his leg. It hurt like hell. A surgeon in London had told him he needed a cartilage operation, but you couldn't pull a heist with your leg in a cast. So Ferguson continued to conceal his limp from Rhodes and went regularly to church to pray that his leg would hold out.

Pierre Tallon had problems, too: his contact lenses. The left one covering the eye he used for lining up a target still didn't fit, and the eyeball was sore and inflamed.

On October 7 he flew back from Antwerp to London to get the lens fixed. But even without the lens, his eyeball remained inflamed; and he didn't think he cut much of a figure when he drove to Heathrow to pick up the Israeli girl, Raquel, who was acting as a courier for the Embassy in London.

Driving back to London, Tallon told her, "I'm going to buy you a diamond ring."

She kissed his cheek, expressed her gratitude, and said, "By the way, how's your son?"

"He's fine," Tallon said. "But he's a little tied up right now." Opposition from my own son is what I don't want, Tallon thought.

"What does he do?" she asked as they approached the Chiswick overpass.

"He's a gangster," Tallon said.

Raquel laughed.

He drove to a jeweler in the East End, which he had noticed on a previous visit. He said, "I'll buy the ring here." adding hastily, "But not with any strings attached."

"None?" She looked at him quizzically.

"Maybe one or two," Tallon said.

He paused outside the window. "Now, what we're looking for in the stone are four Cs: clarity, color, cut, and carat weight. The best color is blue-white, but beware when you see them advertised. There's only one blue-white, and they come from the Jagersfontein mine. Any other blue-white is a fraud."

"You know your diamonds," Raquel said. "You should come and live in Israel."

"Maybe I will," Tallon told her. But his mind was back in Denia in the soft evenings, as the shops opened after siesta and the fishing boats came chugging into the harbor; and he was wondering why the hell he had come out of retirement—a thirty-eight-

189

year-old deadbeat with a sore eye. "Now lesson number one," Tallon said, pointing at the window. "The lighting."

"It makes them sparkle?"

Tallon nodded. "And this jeweler is no fool. He's using white tungsten lights; and he's done nothing to stop vibration from the traffic, because that makes them sparkle better."

"Were *you* a gangster?" she asked.

Tallon laughed. "So we'll be looking for color and then clarity, which means we'll keep our eyes open for carbon spots and other flaws. Then we'll be looking at the cut. There are many cuts and shapes, but the main ones are baguette, pendeloque, emerald, marquise, and brilliant. We'll be looking at brilliants, which have fifty-eight facets. And they've been cut to get the best life and fire, the light that's reflected back *and* the light that's split into the colors of the rainbow—red, orange, yellow, green, blue, indigo, violet."

"Did you ever love a woman?" Raquel asked.

Tallon faltered. "That's a hell of a question."

"I've never heard you talk about anything the way you talk about diamonds. I think you prefer diamonds to women."

"You really think a Frenchman prefers compressed carbon to women?"

"When you talk about diamonds, you remind me of an Israeli talking about Israel."

"You mean they're more interested in their country than women? They're not good lovers?"

"They're superb," Raquel told him.

To his surprise Tallon found this annoyed him; in fact, the girl perturbed him. Such candor, such lack of posturing. If he'd told any other girl he was going to buy her a diamond, she would have murmured, "Pierre, you mustn't," meaning the opposite. Not this one, standing beside him in the October sunlight, slim and tawny in a heather-colored autumn outfit. She wanted a diamond ring. Why should she pretend she didn't?

"By the way," Tallon told her, "always be careful if you're looking at a diamond in anything that contains ultraviolet rays. They cancel out colors and you think you've got a blue-white. That's why experts examine stones at windows facing north, away from the rays of the sun. Also, watch out for a diamond set in blue sapphires; they improve the color, too."

"Shall we go in?" she said.

But Tallon hadn't quite finished showing off. "I'll be looking closely at the stone," he said, "to see if it's been cut to gain weight or make it look bigger than it is and to see if it's out of shape."

"It's the number of carats I'm bothered about," she said, pushing the door.

"*Carat* is from the Greek name for the carob, or locust tree—'keration.' " Tallon said. "They used to weigh diamonds with its seeds."

He followed her into the shop, and a smart young man in a trendy suit, with hair framing his face to disguise its sharp features, came to meet them, smiling and assessing.

Tallon said, "I want to buy a diamond ring."

"Certainly, sir." The young man began to feel his way. "Any sort of price in mind, sir?"

It was difficult to act the innocent when you had a face like Al Capone but Tallon tried, hoping that greed would override judgment; it often did.

He shrugged. "A good one. You know, no rubbish. I know a thing or two about diamonds," Tallon said, hoping to give the impression he knew nothing.

"Of course, sir. For the lady?"

Tallon nodded.

"Then it will have to be one of our most beautiful rings."

The young man brought out a tray of rings from

191

beneath the glass counter. They were set in white gold, one or two encircled with blue sapphires.

"I thought. . . ." Raquel began.

Tallon kicked her gently.

He picked up one ring and examined it through his bloodshot eye. The light was all wrong—it is said that in London you can only examine a diamond properly between 10:00 A.M. and 2 P.M.—and in any case, you can't value a diamond properly in a setting.

Allowing his French accent to thicken—because con men always presume a foreigner to be an easy touch —Tallon said, "It doesn't look too bad. How many carats?"

"About 1.75, sir."

"About?"

"Sorry, sir, exactly." The young man turned to Raquel. "He certainly knows his diamonds, madam."

"Miss," Raquel said.

"I beg your pardon?"

"Miss, not madam."

"Of course, how silly of me. Is this . . . an engagement ring?"

"None of your business," Tallon said. He picked up another ring. "How much?"

"For you, sir, one thousand two hundred pounds."

"Which means you'll let it go for a thousand?"

"I'd have to consult the owner first, sir."

"Then consult him."

The young man gazed doubtfully at Tallon's face. Such naïve stupidity, and yet that face. . . . Greed won the day. "Just a minute, sir." He disappeared behind the shop.

Tallon grinned at Raquel. "He's just gone to consult himself and pressed a button that locks the door at the same time."

"But why. . . ?"

Tallon put his finger to his lips. "Shush."

The young man returned shaking his head. "The

least we can let it go for is one thousand one hundred."

"Okay," Tallon said, "I'll take it."

The young man swallowed. "I wish I could always do business with someone as decisive as you, sir."

He slotted the ring into a cheap box lined with mauve velvet. Before handing it over he asked, "Will it be cash, sir?"

"Of course," Tallon smiled conspiratorially. "We don't want any complications with checks, do we?"

The young man smiled weakly as Tallon counted out the money in ten-pound notes. With the money tightly clenched in one hand, he bowed theatrically. "It's been a pleasure, sir."

Outside, Raquel said, "That wasn't much of a performance."

Tallon led her down the street to a café. "Wait here for five minutes," he said.

He went back to the shop and opened the door. The young man reappeared, looking puzzled.

Tallon said, "At least you didn't try and palm me off with paste."

"I beg your pardon?"

"At least you tried strontium titanate."

"I don't know what the hell you're talking about."

Tallon was patient. "The trouble with strontium titanate—also known as Fabulite and Starilian—is that it's too beautiful. This, as you know"—Tallon grinned at the young man—"is because its dispersion is .200 instead of diamond's .044. And, of course, it doesn't have any florescence under ultraviolet light. But that, of course, will be a matter for the police."

The young man sat down on a stool behind the counter. "Who are you?" he asked.

"It doesn't matter. But I think you'll get about five years."

The young man began to tremble, combing at his

hair and destroying its contours. "I only work here. . . ."

"*Merde*," Tallon said. "Give me back my money."

"And you won't tell the police?"

"Give me the money."

The young man reached into his inside pocket and handed over the £1,100.

Tallon said, "I think there's been some mistake."

"Mistake?"

"I paid fifteen hundred pounds."

The young man swore, hesitated, then went to the till and handed over another four hundred pounds in fivers and tenners. "Now get out," he said, his voice hissing.

Tallon tossed the cheap box on to the counter. "*Mazal u-brocha*," he said, using the Hebrew phrase that clinches a diamond deal. He went out into the sunshine.

In the café he told Raquel the diamond had been an imitation. "This afternoon," he said, "I'll buy you a diamond as big as the Ritz."

She sipped her coffee, grimacing at the taste. "That will be nice," she said.

"Aren't you surprised it wasn't a diamond?"

"No," she said, "I knew. My father's in the diamond business in Tel Aviv."

They made love in the service apartment Tallon was renting at Marble Arch, and afterward, she touched the bullet scars on his body and said, "You *were* a gangster, weren't you?"

Tallon propped himself on one elbow and looked down at her naked body with affection; the sex had been so different from the textbook couplings with his other girls, so complete.

"Let's say I've never been on the side of the law."

"I don't care what you were," she said.

"Not even if I'd killed someone?"

She didn't reply, and when he prompted her, she said, "I wouldn't want to know. It's what you are now."

He kissed her breasts, not wanting her to see the dishonesty on his face. This would be the last job, the big one. Then he would quit for good and return to Israel; and then, maybe, she would come to Denia to share those soft, mauve evenings.

But did she know anything? Had there been some sort of leak in the closely knit society of diamond people? He forced his thoughts in another direction, scared of what he would have to do if she did know anything.

Next day he returned to Antwerp.

They were tense months, too, for Johnny Rhodes, but the familiar excitement as time ran out was spoiled by the absence of Marie. He wrote to her from London but she didn't reply; in mid-November he flew to New York. He called her parents' home in Louisbourg Street, Montreal, and spoke to her, but they were like strangers discussing a business deal.

"Shall I fly up there?" he asked.

"There's nothing to stop you." A pause. "What are you doing in New York?"

"A business trip."

"The same business?"

"Yeah. Antiques."

"The same business you were doing when I left London?"

Anger sharpened his voice. "I'm an antique dealer, right?"

"If it's the same business, there's no point in your coming up here." A longer pause. "Still keeping fit, Johnny?"

"You could get your hands around my waist."

"But you're not going to change your immediate plans?"

"Nothing changes. I'm still aiming to write a book."
He hesitated and then said, "I miss you," just as she
put the receiver down. Rhodes went to Charley O's
and got drunk.

Chapter 18

The next morning Rhodes set about arranging one of
the most important details of any robbery—an outlet.
He knew it was going to be difficult. He had been
away eight years, and that's a long time in the underworld; men get shot, busted, retire, or, like old soldiers, just fade away.

He took a cab to Greenwich Village. It was the first
day of October, a Tuesday, and the leaves were turning in Central Park. He felt a sudden urge to visit
the country, to smell the mists of autumn, to kick
leaves underfoot. After he had fixed the outlet, he
decided, he would hire a car and drive up to Bear
Mountain, where, as a boy, he had once stalked
imaginery bears and Indians.

The cab stopped outside the address in the Village.
In eight years, Rhodes realized, a lot had changed.
The chic, two-story house—where Toni Ludi, the
leading New York diamond fence, had once lived—
had gone into a state of decline. Its faded yellow
shutters were hanging loose; the paintwork was blis-
tered; and on the wall, someone had volunteered
their opinion of the fuzz in red aerosol spray.

Rhodes knocked on the door. It was opened by a
fat blonde woman with bright blue eyes; she was
dressed in a white blouse, damp at the armpits, and

blue serge trousers. She had a cigarette in her mouth; she didn't remove it to speak. "Yeah?"

Rhodes gave her one of his winning smiles, but it was a wasted effort. "I was wondering if you could help me," he said.

"Just keep wondering," she said. "You the fuzz?"

"Do I look like a cop?"

"You can't tell these days, mister. When the bulls are out looking for drugs, you can't tell a cop from a pusher. Anyway, what do you want?"

"Eight years ago a guy called Ludi used to live here."

"Yeah, I heard tell a wop used to have this place."

"How long have you lived here?"

She shrugged. "Two years, maybe three. What's it to you?"

"I want to trace this Ludi."

"Can't help you. Sorry, mister." The door began to close.

Rhodes blocked it with his foot and slid a ten-dollar bill from his wallet. "Perhaps it just slipped your memory."

The woman took the bill. "Why, what's he supposed to have done? You know, I figure a guy's entitled to get lost without being chased by every sonofabitch from his past."

"You've had other callers?"

"Maybe, maybe not."

A boy of about seventeen with a parchment-colored face and inflamed eyes pushed past them. From down the corridor Rhodes smelled the unmistakeable odor of marijuana. Toni Ludi, the neat little Italian with the manicured hands and monkey face, would have turned in his grave—if that's where he was.

Rhodes handed the woman another ten-dollar bill.

"You must want to find the wop pretty bad," the woman said.

"I owe him money," Rhodes said.

"And *you're* looking for *him?* You sure you ain't from the mob, mister?"

Rhodes shook his head. "He did me a favor once."

"What's a favor?" the woman asked.

"When did he leave here?"

"About five years ago, I guess. He sold out to a Polack who rents the place to me."

"And you sublet?"

The woman stared at him suspiciously. "Yeah. Anything wrong with that?"

"Not that I know of," Rhodes said. "Any ideas where Ludi went?"

"I heard he went to California."

"Who'd you hear that from?"

"The Polack," the woman said. "And that's all I know, so you go asking your questions some place else."

"The address of the Polack?"

The bright eyes bored holes in Rhodes' wallet. He began to slide out another bill. "Well?"

She gave him an address on the Lower East Side off Houston Street. He gave her a one-dollar bill, and her abuse followed him down the path.

"Say," said the cab driver, "someone loves you."

Rhodes gave him the address.

"Jesus," said the cab driver, "the scenic route."

They headed east, pulling up outside a brownstone tenement with tattered lace curtains behind grubby windows and green paint blistering on the door. A girl with a jam-smeared face was playing on the steps.

Rhodes knocked and, after a long wait, it was opened by a thin man with a paunch wearing a dirty white vest. He was in his fifties, with a monk's fringe of grey hair and smooth cheeks that looked as if they had never needed a razor.

Rhodes said, "Are you the guy who owns a house

in the Village that used to belong to a man called Ludi?"

The Pole said, "What's it to you?"

"Look," Rhodes said, "it's nothing to me." There was a limit to the amount of plodding distrust you could take. "I just want to know where Toni Ludi is now, and you could help me, so why make a big deal of it? Why not just tell me where Toni Ludi went after he sold the house to you?"

"You'd better come in," the Pole said.

The passage was painted in flaking cream-and-brown. There were three numbered doors and a flight of stairs flanked by broken bannisters.

"A rooming house?" Rhodes asked.

"I guess that's what you'd call it."

"Why the hell do you live in a rooming house when you own a place in the Village?"

The Pole shrugged. "I liked to invest. You mind?"

They went into a room furnished with a bed, a table, two chairs, an old black-and-white television, a sink and a couple of cupboards.

The Pole said, "I got other property, too. Some in the Bronx, some in Queens."

Rhodes believed him. He was in the presence of a genuine miser. "Did Ludi ask a reasonable price?"

The Pole licked his lips. "He was a little greedy, you know. But I got a good deal because he was a little short."

This surprised Rhodes. Toni Ludi had been at the top of his profession, buying diamonds from the best thieves in the world. He had bought in quantity and gave a fair price—not a good price but a fair one by the going prices then. Rhodes could understand Ludi getting busted or even killed, but not short.

"What happened?" he asked the Pole. "He was always loaded when I knew him."

"Are you the fuzz?"

Rhodes sighed. Maybe you began to smell like the law after going straight for eight years. "No," he said, "I'm not the fuzz." He handed the Pole ten dollars.

The Pole stuffed the money into his trouser pocket. "You'd like a shot, maybe?" He picked up a half-empty bottle of cheap California white wine.

"No thanks. Just tell me where I can find Toni Ludi."

The Pole sat down in a rocking chair. "I heard tell that after he did a little time he headed for California and then upstate New York. Something to do with trading in hot diamonds, or maybe you know about that?" The Pole looked slyly at Rhodes.

"What did he get?"

"I heard five."

"Then he'd be out by now."

"I guess so." The Pole sipped his glass of wine; that way the bottle might last a week.

"Any idea where he'd be?"

"He had some family upstate somewhere."

"Like where?"

"What's it worth?"

Rhodes sat down opposite the Pole. The room smelled of dirty clothes, and the sunshine filtering through the grimy window had left behind its crisp October touch. He said, "I'll tell you what it's worth. It's worth me not going to the precinct and laying information that a property you bought from Toni Ludi, a convicted criminal, is being used for trafficking in junk with your consent. And it's also worth me not telling the cops that you've got places in the Bronx and Queens being used for the same purpose. I may even forget to tell the cops about the money you've got stashed away in this apartment to avoid paying taxes."

The Pole's mouth had opened, revealing broken

stumps of teeth. "I'm not responsible for what goes on in that dump in the Village."

"The lady says you are. And within a couple of minutes of me laying information at the precinct, the cops can be at the addresses in the Bronx and Queens before you've got to the end of the street." Rhodes followed the direction of the Pole's rheumy eyes: a miser with a hoard of money would have a gun somewhere. Rhodes said, "Do you have a license?"

"A license for what?"

"The piece you're thinking about pulling on me."

"Jesus," the Pole said, "are you psychic or something?"

"Because if you haven't got a license that's something else they could throw at you."

"Okay," the Pole said, "so you want an address. Okay, so I give you an address and then you beat it?"

Rhodes nodded, and the Pole gave him an address in Albany. "All I know is he had a sister there, so don't come back here threatening me if he ain't there."

Rhodes walked out into the sunlight illuminating the hopeless street.

"Where now?" the cab driver asked. "The morgue?"

Rhodes told him to stop at the first phone booth. He called the police and told them that the address in Greenwich Village was being used for drug trafficking.

The voice on the other end of the phone was polite but not impressed. "Thanks buddy, we'll look into it. You want to give us your name and address?"

Rhodes hung up and returned to the cab. "The Algonquin," he said to the driver.

"You got to be kidding," the driver said.

One hour later Rhodes rented a grey Mustang, drove across the George Washington Bridge, and headed north toward Bear Mountain, conscious that he was heading in the general direction of Montreal.

He parked the Mustang, booked into the hotel on the mountain, and went for a walk to get rid of the staleness clinging to him from the morning's inquiries. A stem of smoke arose from the red-and-gold trees on the opposite bank of the Hudson, and on the river, a tug towing a string of barges pushed aside shoals of sunlight.

The sleaziness lifted. Rhodes breathed deeply and walked energetically. There was only one thing lacking—a girl to share it with, and she was away to the north across the Canadian border.

He returned to the hotel, drank a couple of martinis, ate a steak, and went to bed. At 2:00 A.M. he awoke with his resistance low and almost decided to drive through the rest of the night to Montreal.

He paced the bedroom and gazed out of the window. The sky was bright with stars, and in their midst hung a solitaire moon. His strength—or was it his weakness?—flowed back. There were nearly three months of the year left, and by the end of December, the job would be finished and he could fly to Canada.

The next morning he drove to Albany.

The address proved to be a small, white frame house set among acres of fading flowers, mostly chrysanthemums.

The door was answered by a woman of about thirty, dark and pretty and beginning to get plump. Yes, she said, Toni Ludi, her brother, was at home. Who wanted him?

She went inside the house, and Rhodes heard a yelp of surprise. Toni Ludi came to the door; hair now greying, monkey face wizened, but the brown eyes still quick and humorous.

"Johnny." He shot out a hand. "What brings you here? Where you been?"

Rhodes gripped his hand and said, "Do you have a few minutes, Toni?"

"Of course, Johnny. A few minutes, a few hours. . . ." But his voice lacked enthusiasm, and there was a new wariness about him. To his sister he said, "Maybe you should go downtown and buy some wine, huh? Johnny is my great old buddy and we got to celebrate."

When she had gone and they were sitting in the neat living room filled with chrysanthemums and adorned with photographs of the Ludi clan, Toni said, "Well, Johnny, what can I do for you? You know I quit?"

"I heard," Rhodes said. "I also heard you had a vacation."

"That's right. But I had a good run, huh?"

"What happened, Toni?"

"I got busted."

"I always thought you were too cute."

"A bit too cute, Johnny."

"Tell me about it," Rhodes said.

Toni Ludi started his career as an apprentice diamond cutter on West Forty-sixth Street. But as he worked away, learning to saw an octahedral crystal in a cube plane or to polish a stone in a mechanical dop, he caught glimpses of men who made fortunes from diamonds far beyond the money a craftsman could ever hope to earn.

By this time Toni was smitten with diamond fever, and he knew that somehow he had to spend the rest of his life in the business; somehow he had to adapt to make the money that compressed carbon, properly handled, can accumulate.

But how? He hadn't the adventurous spirit to go prospecting. What chance would a little guy, who looked as if he should be playing an organ grinder or selling ice cream, have competing against the tough, brawling men who still scoured river beds for alluvial stones, the deserts for blue ground? In the underworld the aristocrats of crime were diamond thieves; but here again, Toni Ludi lacked the nerve. With knife in hand he could fight like a tiger when cornered, but his courage wasn't positive. Without capital, the chances of making a fortune honestly were remote—not that Toni ever seriously contemplated honest methods. After all, his parents, who had owned a delicatessen, had been honest all their lives, and now they were dying, and their wreaths would be fashioned from unpaid bills.

The answer came one day when a small-time operator named Rossi, who had been used by the mob in a minor capacity during a diamond heist, pocketed one of the smaller stones and accosted Toni Ludi on his way home from work.

"We've always been buddies, Toni, ain't we?"

"We haven't been enemies," Toni Ludi said. "What you want?"

"Maybe we could do a deal," said Rossi, who was just twenty.

"You working with the mob?"

"Sure. . . ."

"No deal," Toni said.

Rossi opened the palm of his hand, and the stone beckoned to Toni in the sunlight.

Toni said, "Like I said, no deal, but I'll buy you a beer."

They went into a bar off Broadway where the walls were adorned with pictures of old fighters, ordered two beers, and retired to a corner.

"Okay," Toni said, "let me see it."

He wished he had a loupe with him. But there were flaws visible to the naked eye: a little cloud, a small indentation of the girdle.

"Not bad," Toni said. "Not bad, not good. It's pretty small, huh?"

"It's the best quality," Rossi said, wiping froth from his downy moustache. "So don't give me any shit."

"No shit," Toni told him. "I don't give you any shit where diamonds are concerned," he said, realizing for the first time that this was true. "You know, maybe I pull a few strokes like any guy who wants to make it, but I don't tell no lies about the goods. You see," he explained, "they're maybe the purest goddamned things you can find. . . . Aw, shit, forget it."

"And this ain't pure?"

"That's a second piqué. Maybe first, giving you the benefit of the doubt."

"Don't give me this piqué crap," Rossi said. "What's it worth?"

Toni ordered two more beers. He was excited. His future was assembling in the corner of this bar filled with men with scarred faces and broken hands. He began to talk intuitively, although to Rossi it seemed as if he had been trained as a fence.

"Look," Toni said, "so I take the ice, okay? I take a big risk but I take the stone."

"How much?"

'Now look," Toni said carefully, "that stone's worth maybe a hundred bucks retail. You know, it's pretty small and the quality's not so good. It's also hot. . . ."

"A little stone, lousy quality, and you say it's hot?"

"Sure it's hot. It's stolen, ain't it? Now I'm not saying it could be identified. A bigger stone, yeah, because diamonds are like fingerprints and can be identified. So they have to be recut and polished a little if they're hot, which is one of the reasons you don't get a good price." Toni sipped his beer and stared speculatively at Rossi. "But you know, maybe you and me is going to do business in the future, and maybe that's why you got to accept the price I give you. I got the contacts, and I have to work on them."

Rossi said impatiently, "So what you offering?"

"The stone's worth a hundred bucks and I get maybe fifty for it, so I give you thirty," Toni said, wondering where he was going to raise thirty dollars.

"You mean sonofabitch," Rossi said.

Toni shrugged. "I give you a fair price, take it or leave it." They were phrases he was going to use a lot in the future.

The next day Toni borrowed thirty honestly earned dollars from his father and bought the diamond. He checked the list of his employer's customers, and found the name and address of one whom he had previously observed and instinctively assessed as crooked. This instinct was going to be Toni's strength, an instinct that was the natural partner of his dishonest nature. Sometimes he wondered how he had inherited this kink in his personality. It was, he supposed, born of the doomed honesty of his parents; he was like a convent girl who rebelliously takes to the streets.

He visited the jeweler, who had a shop near Chinatown, and got forty dollars for the stone. He paid back his parents the thirty and gave them five dollars interest. Toni Ludi had made five dollars from his first crooked deal. Toni Ludi was in business.

Six days later Rossi was driven to an address in the Bronx and methodically beaten up for stealing the stone from the thieves. Then, because he was only twenty, he was driven to a hospital and dumped there. He was detained for ten days. Not only was Toni Ludi in business, he had learned his first lesson: never cross the syndicate. Better still don't do any business with them—if that was possible, being an Italian with ambitions to be the biggest diamond fence in New York.

Within five years he had his own premises on Forty-seventh Street. He touched nothing on which there was a profit margin of less than five thousand dollars, and he managed not to aggravate the big-time mobsters, who, happily for Toni Ludi, were more interested in drugs, prostitution, and protection.

He first met Johnny Rhodes when they were both about quarter way up the ladder. Rhodes brought him a diamond he thought was a white river stone and asked a price. In his new office, not yet decorated, Toni picked up the delicate stone, holding it between manicured thumb and forefinger, and examined it through his loupe. Then he put it down on the new leather-topped desk and appraised the young man with the tough, attractive features to see if he was carrying a gun. He decided he wasn't.

"Where you get this?" he asked.

"They lent it to me at Tiffany's," Rhodes said.

"More like the Coke factory," Toni said. "The dump where they throw their broken bottles."

Then he explained to a rattled Johnny Rhodes that it was a bad yellow stone that had been burned to make it look white. "An old trick they discovered in South Africa a hundred years ago. So, you tell me where you *acquired* this piece of junk."

Rhodes gave him an address on Linwood Avenue, Fort Lee, New Jersey.

"Yeah, but where did *that* guy steal it from?"

"How the hell should I know?"

"You know, it would be interesting to find out. If there's a dentist in the block, then you owe me fifty bucks."

When Rhodes asked what the hell he was talking about, Toni explained, "They used to say that only dentists know the secret of burning yellow diamonds to make them white. I don't know if they're kidding, but I'd like to know."

Nine months later Rhodes traced the stone to an address in London. There a dentist's surgery on the third floor. Rhodes returned to New York, paid Toni Ludi the fifty dollars, and did business with him for the rest of his professional career.

But when Rhodes quit, Toni stayed on. He was supporting a wife and three children, but that wasn't the reason he kept going. He could never really believe that he possessed a fortune, and he expected it one day to vaporize—like diamonds do between 700 and 900 degrees centigrade. That—and his passion for the goods—forced Toni Ludi to carry on until the day he was arrested.

It happened when the syndicate decided to pull a diamond heist on Fifth Avenue. It was the heist Toni had feared all his working life; and sure enough, they came to him with the goods. He stared at them nervously and shook his head. The robbery had received a lot of publicity; the stones were big and beautiful and would be identified immediately, even if they had some work done on them. They could be cut smaller, but that would be sacrilege; and in any case, their value would drop dramatically.

Anyway, that's what Toni told the two men, although it wasn't completely true. The stones would be difficult to shift, but nothing was impossible if you were the top fence in America, possibly in the world. He would have the same difficulties as a bent art dealer trying to move a stolen van Gogh; but it could be done when you were the ruler of an empire. Brazil, Hong Kong, Switzerland—there were always markets for the flawless, beautiful currencies of the world.

No, there were other influences guiding Toni Ludi. He was a king and he wouldn't be commanded. Scared though he was he would fight; the knife, although invisible, was in his hand.

He said to the two men with the dark, dead eyes, "I could maybe shift them in a couple of years when the heat's off."

"Shift them now," one of the men said.

"Impossible."

"The big man says now." One of the men began to file his nails.

"I tell you, no way."

"We'll be in touch," the man with the nail file said.

That afternoon Toni sought the advice of a police detective he had been paying over the years. Three days later he was arrested and charged with receiving stolen property from two robberies six and nine months earlier. The detective had also been on the mob's payroll.

"Just out of interest," Toni Ludi said, "what you got to offer?"

"Forty million," Rhodes told him casually.

"Forty million what?"

"Dollars," Rhodes said.

A pause. "You kidding?"

"I kid you not," Rhodes said.

"There's never been a diamond heist like that."

"That's why I came out of retirement."

"Rough stuff?"

"Rough, the very best rough, not traceable."

"You gonna tell me where?"

"It's best you don't know," Rhodes said. "I wouldn't want to get you into any more trouble."

There was a pause while they both thought about $40 million worth of good-quality rough diamonds, each accepting that there was no deal, because in their league, once a man had been inside he was disbarred.

"I'm sorry, Johnny," Toni said after awhile. "In any case I couldn't have shifted forty million bucks worth."

"I have other outlets," Rhodes told him.

"Tel Aviv?"

Rhodes nodded.

"How many guys?"

"One."

"He won't take twenty million."

"Then I'll have to look around," Rhodes said. "Anyway, Toni, what's with you these days?"

"I grow chrysanthemums," Toni said. "Big, fat, twenty-carat mums." He lit a cigarette, holding it delicately with two fingers still coarse from prison. "After the mob called on me, I drew most of my cash and gave it to my wife. After I'd done two years she took off. I hear she went to Mexico City with the kids."

"I'm sorry," Rhodes said.

"Don't be. I figure the sort of broad who takes off like that ain't worth having anyway. You know, I miss the kids, but what the hell. . . . Still, I kept a little back, and now I'm in the mum business with my sister, who's worried stupid about you turning up here." He stubbed out the cigarette.

Rhodes stood up. "Don't worry."

Toni waved him to sit down. "Before you go, I got a couple of ideas that might help you." He stood up and walked around the room, examining the aunts and uncles and black-haired brides with smiles glued on their faces. "There's a guy on Forty-seventh Street who might be able to help you. . . ."

Two hours and two bottles of Chianti later, Rhodes took his leave. "Good luck with the mums," he shouted as the Mustang took off.

"I'm naming one for you," Toni Ludi shouted back. "Solitaire. How's about that?"

Twenty-four hours later, Johnny Rhodes had his New York outlet: a blue-chinned, businesslike, thirty-year-old Vietnam veteran named Schwartz, who had served an apprenticeship in diamonds before being drafted. Rhodes thought he looked like a White House aide.

They met for lunch in the Four Seasons on East

Fifty-second, and during the steaks talked about the diamond industry in America.

"In a state of decline," Schwartz said. He ate with determination, muscles flexing in his jaw as he chewed. "You know, the legitimate diamond business."

Rhodes knew.

Schwartz went on. "There are fewer and fewer kids coming into the game. You can let them loose on the small stuff, but we don't take much small stuff from the Diamond Trade Center these days —nothing much less than six grainers, and who's going to trust a new kid on a diamond that size? The old pros are still around, but most of them have gone underground for tax reasons. Okay, they're training Indians down in Arizona, and perhaps they'll make it someday; but at the moment it's mostly Puerto Ricans, and they're only good with the small stuff."

Over the fruit salad Rhodes said, "Toni Ludi sent me."

"I know." Schwartz poured cream thickly on his salad. He offered it to Rhodes who refused, and Schwartz said, "You on a diet?"

Rhodes nodded. "Are you interested?"

"Of course," Schwartz said, "or else I wouldn't be here."

"How much can you take?"

"Half," Schwartz said. "When?"

"End of December, beginning of January. Price?"

"Thirty percent," Schwartz said.

"Fifty," Rhodes said.

They closed at forty.

Rhodes said, "I guess you'll want to check me out."

Schwartz poured cream into his coffee. "No need. A recommendation from Toni Ludi is good enough for me. But I guess you'll want to check me out."

"No need," Rhodes said. "Toni Ludi's word is good enough for me."

The next day Rhodes called on a private detective named O'Hara, who used to help him in the old days, and asked him to get some background information for him.

"Schwartz?" O'Hara asked.

"How the hell did you know that?"

"Because he asked me to check you out," O'Hara said.

On Tuesday, October 15, Rhodes took an El Al flight from New York to Tel Aviv to arrange the second outlet. Israel had always been good for moving stolen diamonds. If the stones were already cut, they had the craftsmen to disguise them. More important, the Israelis had assembled in their country from every corner of the world, and their contacts were international.

As the jet crossed the Atlantic in the high blue sky above pastures of clouds, Rhodes thought about Schwartz. According to O'Hara, he was good, almost as good as Toni Ludi, whom he had replaced. But you couldn't be too careful, especially when the world would have read about the biggest diamond robbery in the history of crime. So he would follow the same procedure he used to follow when dealing with a possible security risk and would arrange a meeting ostensibly to conclude the deal. Maybe the meeting would take place on the boat that circled Manhattan from Pier 83; maybe at Staten Island Zoo; maybe at Coney Island. Anyway, on this first meeting any police or hoods who might be in attendance would find him clean.

For the trip to Israel Rhodes was traveling on a forged passport supplied by an old acquaintance in the Bronx. It was, he thought, refreshing to find that some of the old masters were still operating undetected. He had flown to New York under his own name and clinched a deal with a company on Madison for the import from England of rocking chairs he had imported from Spain. But the likelihood of antique business in Israel, where they were more concerned about importing Phantom jets, was remote. He was also concerned about the persistent friendship of Willis, who was quite capable of checking a suspect's movements between Timbuctoo and Peking. Hence the phoney passport. The subterfuge meant that he would have to return from Tel Aviv to London via New York to use the return half of the ticket booked under his own name. This would be a laborious process, but it was the sort of precaution that had kept Rhodes a free man.

Rhodes arrived in the afternoon, booked into the Hilton overlooking the sea, and went for a swim in the pool. The weather was sunny, and from the tanning bodies, he could have been persuaded that he was in Miami rather than a beleaguered country. It was only when he ordered himself a carafe of white wine in a café on Dizengoff and got talking to some Israelis that he found the tension and the spirit of the people.

The next day he went to Ramat Gan to seek out a New York Jew named Grose, who left America in 1950 to become an Israeli. Grose had taken with him two trades—diamond polishing and receiving. Much of the money he made he poured back into Israeli funds. He still did a little polishing in a small workshop not far from the towering Diamond Bourse Building, but he was in a depressed state when Rhodes met him.

Grose was a plump man with a sunburned pate, fluttering hands, and a perpetual smile. Today the smile was still apparent, but it had a sad, Mona Lisa quality about it.

As they walked along the beach, dodging the teenagers playing ball, Grose explained that five years earlier, Israel had been rife with diamond thefts occurring in factories, shops, security cars, airports, and aircraft. And so it was the good life for a fence with contacts in the United States, Belgium, Holland, Germany, Switzerland, Hong Kong, and Japan—Israel's principal diamond-export markets.

"And so what happened?" Rhodes asked, watching a couple of rotund, middle-aged men jogging and gasping along the water's edge.

"The Diamond Institute decided to get tough, would you believe." Grose gave a martyred smile at the treachery of his own kind. "They got together with the government, and everywhere they tightened up security. Now"—Grose fluttered his hands—"business is not so good."

By the time they had reached an open-air café where brown-limbed tarts knitted socks in between business appointments, the smile on Grose's face had become grotesque: Rhodes had offered him half the haul and Grose had accepted.

Forty minutes later, after they had parted company, Rhodes met an old business acquaintance emerging from the Diamond Bourse. His name was Joseph Kaplan.

"*Shalom*," Rhodes said.

Kaplan looked startled. "Another of you!" he exclaimed.

"Another?"

Kaplan said, "Don't tell me you don't know Pierre Tallon was here five months ago."

Chapter 19

Hans Muller, one-time ace pilot in Hermann Goering's *Luftwaffe*, stared with philosophical detachment at the wall of trees ahead. He presumed he would miss them by twenty feet as he had on the four previous occasions he had taken the jet up from the airfield near Munster. If he didn't, it was the predestined end, and that was just the way he had felt thirty-four years ago as he wheeled away from the armadas of Dorniers and Heinkels attacking London to do battle with the avenging Spitfires and Hurricanes. Goering had lost the Battle of Britain and Hitler had lost the war. But Muller had gone on winning in his own stoic fashion, awaiting the final defeat and not caring too much when it came, knowing only that when he could no longer fly, the sooner the defeat came the better.

Theoretically, the strip was eight hundred yards too short, but, with no load and no crew, Muller could just make it over the trees. The airfield was a private one, hardly used, and the owner was sceptical about Muller's ability to get the jet up in time. But 100,000 Deutsche marks and the laconic assurance Muller displayed while clinching the deal over schnapps in a bar in Borken, forty kilometers from Munster, convinced him—or at least persuaded him—of the stupidity of openly questioning Muller's ability. Muller was carrying out secret trials with the permission of the German aviation authorities, and if he wanted to scatter the jet and himself over the countryside, so be it.

The two Rolls Royce Bristol Viper turbojets screamed with power, and the aircraft cleared the trees as Muller had known it would. If it hadn't . . . Muller shrugged. He was fifty-four; and ever since he had learned to fly, at the age of seventeen, ever since he had shot down twelve British aircraft over the Channel and the green patchwork of southern England, he had shrugged when other men smiled or cried.

The only times he showed any emotion was when he was beating up a woman. Then his face contorted a little, and a dribble of saliva appeared at the corner of his mouth; in a way it made him appear softer, vulnerable to human weakness disguised as strength. But the emotion left his face as he tossed the money on the table and left the woman moaning on the bed.

The jet climbed steeply and banked, wisps of clouds scudding past like dandelion floss on a summer breeze. Hans Muller was at home. If he had any regrets, it was that he hadn't been born at the end of the last century. This would have enabled him to operate in the great days of pioneer aviation, flying with von Ritchoften in a biplane, shooting it out with the British over the muddy cemetery of the Somme. To have flown in the days before aircraft looked like underground trains with wings slotted into them. . . .

Muller reached his ceiling, headed southwest, turned, and began his descent. Four times he had completed this brief maneuver and he was bored with it. After the war he had done some commercial flying, but that had been tame—compared with the old days of, say, Imperial Airways—flying at one hundred miles an hour and taking a week to reach Nairobi, with the passengers sipping cocktails in their airborne pavilion. After that Muller had sought out trouble: Korea, Algeria, the Congo, where so many free-lance pilots gathered; Biafra and Vietnam, where he flew missions for the CIA in which it was necessary that no American be involved.

Then a man called Rhodes had come to him. It wasn't Muller's sort of assignment, but he respected Rhodes, trusted him as much as he trusted anyone, and the money was good. It was enough to keep him flying, enough to keep him well supplied with complaisant women until the end—which he now knew was not far away.

Muller descended to 2,070 feet above sea level. He

was five miles away from the airfield, lined up with the strip. At 4½ miles he was 1,410 feet up. Everything was going smoothly; Muller suppressed a yawn. Three-quarters of a mile away, he was down to 285 feet above sea level, 272 feet above the runway threshold. He touched down with the slightest of bumps. Five minutes later the latest monotonous rehearsal was over.

Muller walked to his improvised office at the end of the only hangar on the airfield, poured himself a shot of Bols gin from a stone bottle, and gazed through the window at the strip sprouting with grass. That was another hazard: would the strip continue to hold? And, of course, what would the weather be like on the day? Not that this would affect his course of action: Hans Muller would take off in an electric storm or an arctic blizzard.

Thoughtfully, Muller zipped up his ancient flying jacket—stained with sweat, oil, and blood—and went out to his old Mercedez-Benz open tourer. This car was his ally on the ground; with the winding driving at him as he topped one hundred miles an hour on the autobahn, it provided the nearest sensation to sitting in an open cockpit between wings emblazoned with black crosses.

As the car sped past a belt of pine trees, flickering like a silent movie, Muller glanced at himself in the driving mirror and stared deep into the faded eyes looking back at him. Their setting looked old and tough: skin that had been exposed to too much sun tight across the cheekbones; furrows deep from nose to mouth; cropped hair indecisive between blonde and grey. His was a hard face that would today look incongruous when Muller had to plead. If he had to abandon the pleas and threaten, then it would come into his own.

He parked the Mercedes-Benz between two beetle Volkswagens—thinking that they now looked like his fighter escort—and walked into the small bar in Munster, where Johnny Rhodes was waiting for him with half a liter of frothing lager beer in front of him.

Rhodes sliced into his venison and asked, "Are there any snags?"

"A few."

"Like what?"

"The strip's not long enough." Muller took a long swallow of beer and wiped the moustache of froth from his lips.

"Now he tells me." Rhodes felt as if he were listening to one of his pilots making his report on a Normandy airfield after a sortie across the Channel. Everything Muller said in his clipped English was precise, unemotional, disciplined.

Muller said, "There is a belt of trees at the end, but I can clear them."

Rhodes knew he was listening to a man past his prime trying to prove himself. "Is anyone getting suspicious?"

Muller shook his head. "As you know, the airfield's practically unused. It's in the middle of an estate, and the owner's only too pleased to take the money with no questions asked. The strip wasn't built for jets, but. . . ." He indicated that it presented few problems to a pilot of Hans Muller's prowess.

"What about the aviation authorities?"

Muller said, "No problems. Air traffic at Munster knows about the trials. I merely radio them a flight plan, if that's what you can call it."

A waitress in peasant costume served them coffee and brandy, bending low over the table so that they could almost see the nipples of her plump white breasts. On a small platform a pianist and violinist played anemic Vienna waltzes.

"There is just one thing more," Muller said, tipping the cognac into his coffee.

"You want the money now?"

Still Muller's features displayed no emotion. "How did you know?"

"This isn't my first operation. Someone always wants cash in advance."

"And do you pay it?"

Rhodes tossed back his brandy, followed it with coffee, stared into Muller's pale eyes, and said, "Tell me about the girl in the hospital in Hamburg first."

In between trials Muller had driven the Mercedes-Benz along the autobahn skirting Osnabruck and Bremen to Hamburg, a city that catered to most sexual appetites.

He drank a few schnapps with beer chasers and headed for the Reeperbahn, where the British Navy, on a good-will visit, was out in force. Before the night was out, Muller thought, there would be plenty of brawls; that was the way with good-will visits.

He went first to a club where brawny girls wrestled in mud. But Muller didn't want brawny girls, he wanted girls with sensual faces that looked as if they enjoyed pain even if they didn't, girls with voluptuous figures and tender flesh.

He moved on to a club with a dance floor made of mirror and hostesses with no pants beneath their skirts. He ordered a beer, picked up the cream telephone on the table, and dialed 9, the number of a table at which a well-built brunette sat, legs crossed, skirt up to her thighs. Muller was an honest man and he told her what he wanted. She slammed down the phone.

Muller went to a bar near a club where an unknown group, subsequently known as the Beatles, had once played. It was a very ordinary bar, with taped music and lights changing colors on the walls.

Its business was girls, and they draped the bar in attitudes of boredom, hardly bothering to solicit customers. But after all, did cattle in a market ogle the customers?

Instinctively Muller approached a blonde girl with smudged mascara. She wasn't his ideal, but it was geting late and soon he would be too drunk.

He bought her a drink, and she told him she was orphaned during the allied bombing of Dresden. She had been smuggled across the border into West Germany by a boyfriend who had subsequently left her. Sensing a catalog of misfortunes, Muller told her what he wanted and how much he was willing to pay. It was a lot of money for a girl in a bar like this; she looked scared, but she picked up her handbag and went with him.

In the cab she began to shiver. "Don't worry," Muller told her. "I know what I'm doing. I won't hurt you badly."

But he did. Perhaps he had drunk too much schnapps; perhaps her bones were brittle. After five minutes of submitting to him in her one-room apartment two miles from the Reeperbahn, she collapsed unconscious on the bed, face ashen, breathing stertorous, a trickle of blood oozing from her mouth. He tried to revive her but stopped, knowing that he might cause more damage. He swore and dressed, gazing speculatively at her naked body.

He didn't panic, he never had. First, he considered fleeing. But it was senseless to risk arrest for murder by leaving the girl to die through lack of attention. So Muller fetched his car, parked half a mile away, and took the girl to a doctor used by Hamburg criminals.

The doctor examined the girl in his office while Muller smoked a cigarette.

The examination didn't take long. The doctor, a

balding man wearing rimless glasses, straightened up and told him, "This girl is dangerously injured."

"But you can cure her?"

"She will have to go to a clinic where they have the necessary equipment."

Muller shrugged. "Then take her there."

"It will cost money."

"I paid you before," Muller reminded him, referring to an occasion when the doctor had treated him for a back injury after he had crashed in an old Dakota.

"It will cost a lot of money." The doctor bent down and lifted the girl's eyelid. "And we have to move quickly if the girl is to live. She will have to be operated on as soon as she gets to the clinic," he added.

"How much money?" Muller asked.

The doctor straightened up. "Fifty thousand marks."

"You're crazy."

"If you think so, get her out of here. But I warn you, you'll have a corpse on your hands. And"—the doctor moved nearer a drawer where he kept a Walther automatic—"as soon as you've left the office I shall call the police."

"And involve yourself?"

"Naturally I will call anonymously."

"I can't raise fifty thousand," Muller said.

"That's the price." The doctor watched Muller warily. "I have to use a good surgeon, I have to keep people quiet, and I'm taking a big risk."

The girl wrapped in blankets on the examination couch moaned softly.

The doctor said, "Come on, *Herr* Muller, make up your mind. There isn't much time."

"Thirty thousand?"

"Fifty," the doctor said, blinking behind his rimless glasses.

"I can't pay you right away."

"How much can you raise by tonight?"

"I could find ten thousand."

The doctor nodded. "Very well, get it."

The doctor made a telephone call, and when they arrived in Muller's car at the clinic on the banks of the Elbe, a surgeon and a nurse were scrubbed down waiting to operate. The doctor told Muller he would trust him to fetch the money after the operation. Muller drove back to Munster and was back at the office by noon the next day with the money.

"How is she?" he asked.

The doctor was sitting at his desk drinking coffee. "You know the phrase—as well as can be expected."

"Will she live?"

"She may with the proper treatment."

"And you'll see that she gets it?"

"That depends on you, *Herr* Muller," the doctor said, taking off his glasses and wiping them. "There is still the matter of forty thousand marks."

"You'll have to wait," Muller told him.

"I'm afraid the girl won't wait."

"Give me time."

"Three days," the doctor said, pressing a button on his desk.

His receptionist peered around the door. "Next patient. Please show *Herr* Muller out."

"So," Muller said, "you had me followed."

"In an operation like this," Rhodes told him, "I have to take every possible precaution. There are still imponderables, but I have to keep them to an absolute minimum."

In the corner the pianist and the fiddler tackled the "Blue Danube." Muller beckoned the waitress, who again bowed low before them. He ordered another cognac; Rhodes asked for a glass of water.

"You didn't trust me?" Muller asked.

"I don't trust or distrust anyone. In fact"—Rhodes picked up his black briefcase from beside the table— "I have a complete file on you. You had me worried for awhile because I don't like violence on a job. But your violence seems to be confined to women. And, as far as I can see, you always carry out orders."

"It is true," Muller said, lighting a cigarette and inhaling deeply. "I have to admire your thoroughness. Now, what about the money?"

"Also," Rhodes said, "I always stick to a contract, and I expect the men working for me to stick to it."

"But the girl. . . ."

Rhodes unlocked the briefcase and placed a green folder marked Hans Muller on the table. He opened it and rifled through typewritten reports, photostats, and duplicates of forms on which Muller could see the carbon copy of his own signature.

Rhodes took out the photostat of a long letter bearing an illegible signature. He scanned it and said to Muller, "If I gave you all the money now, what guarantee would I have that you would complete the job?"

Muller tossed back his brandy and replied, "I suppose you'd have to trust me."

"I need more security than that." Rhodes paused. "On the other hand, I don't want that kid in the hospital to die, so this morning I arranged for forty thousand Deutsche marks to be paid into your doctor's account. All you have to do is call him."

Muller drummed his fingers on the table. "So there's nothing to keep me now. What security have you got now, *Herr* Rhodes? What is to stop me from taking the jet and flying to Brazil?"

Rhodes smiled. "Its range for one thing. One thousand nine hundred forty miles, isn't it?"

"You should have been a German," Muller said.

"Also the following two reasons," Rhode went on. "After the job, I'll pay you the balance of what

I owe you, with the medical fees for the girl deducted."

"Maybe I don't want anything more to do with this lousy job of yours. Maybe I don't like bastards like you prying into my private life."

Rhodes' voice hardened. "Listen, Muller, you said you always carry out orders. You'll finish this job for me and I'll tell you for why. Only one thing gives you any kicks—apart from beating up girls—and that's flying. Right?"

Muller nodded, smoke dribbling from his nostrils.

"Okay, then this is how it will be if you blow it. You'll never fly again." Rhodes held up his hand as Muller tried to interrupt. "And I'll tell you why, old buddy. I'll have your flying license revoked, and wherever you go in the world I'll have you grounded. With my contacts I can do it, and you goddamned well know it."

Muller stubbed out the cigarette. "And just how would you do that when you admit I'm the best pilot you could find?"

Rhodes turned the photostat letter around so that Muller could see it; it bore the name and address of a doctor in West Berlin. "This is how, Muller. Because I know that, at the most, you've got one year's flying left. Because I know you're going blind."

Chapter 20

The ninth consignment of diamonds was dispatched from London on Friday, November 29. The last consignment would be dispatched some time between then and December 31, probably before Christmas.

Rhodes guessed it would be between the tenth and the twentieth. To be safe he had to arrange an alibi by December 5 at the latest.

In the old days Rhodes hadn't bothered with alibis. He hadn't been under suspicion, and if he flew from New York to Madrid to lift diamonds destined for the vaults of one of the big banks near the Puerta del Sol, there had been no need to establish his presence elsewhere, the necessity just hadn't arisen.

But this time he did need an alibi. Chief Detective Inspector Willis was still in evidence—not persistently, as he had been during the inquiries and prosecutions following the robbery at Covent Garden (three men—aged between twenty-one and twenty-eight—had received eight, ten, and twelve years), but frequently enough to arouse all Rhodes' instincts for survival. Everything about their friendship was plausible: they had met because of a crime, and Willis had prolonged the relationship because of his interest in antiques. Rhodes would have liked to assume he wasn't under surveillance on the grounds that Willis, the middle-aged trendy, was too astute to prejudice an investigation by overexposure. But assumptions had led many a good man to jail, and Rhodes refused to assume anything. Perhaps Willis, at the end of his career, was going it alone, seeking a sensational finale.

Rhodes considered the problems of an alibi while doing push-ups and sit-ups in his lonely bedroom. The perfect alibi, of course, would be to actually be somewhere else at the time of the crime. Obviously, this can only be done if you're employing someone to rob your bank, murder your rival gang boss, or kidnap a hostage. Rhodes had to be where the action was taking place, so he had to devise a plausible alternative.

In Rhodes' experience, most concocted alibis were usually disasters. They involve the use of witnesses bribed to swear on their mothers' graves that at the time of the mayhem, the suspect was one hundred miles away in a log cabin playing poker and drinking bourbon. One of two things happen: the police manage to intimidate the witnesses before they give evidence, or the witnesses are so transparently dishonest under cross-examination that their perjury gets the accused an extra two years.

Occasionally, the perjury is a little more subtle. One ploy is to use girls if the accused is a happily married man with three wonderful children. The girls give evidence that at the time of the crime, the defendant was in a motel on the other side of town taking part in an all-night orgy after watching a blue movie on closed-circuit television. Would the man being tried risk the breakup of his marriage if he wasn't desperate to prove his innocence? The alibi is further strengthened when the ashen-faced wife (who rounded up the girls) tells the jury that despite everything, she'll stick by her husband.

There are other ploys, each with its own hazard. For instance there's the alibi that depends entirely on speed and timing. The suspect is sighted eighty miles away from the scene of a crime at an hour that, theoretically, gives him no time to get there using regular methods of transportation. But in fact, he has a helicopter or a racing car and can just make it. Given enough time, a clever detective will finally work this out; but the criminal's ally is police under-staffing, and the dectetive often doesn't get around to it.

Variations include tampering with clocks so that the suspect is sighted at 12:35 P.M., the moment of the crime, when the time is really 11:35 P.M., and leaving a tape recorder in a flimsy-walled apartment with your voice on it. But these ploys are all gim-micky, fallible, and, in Rhodes' opinion, strictly for the birds.

With a grunt he made his fiftieth push-up and collapsed face down on the carpet. In all probability the alibi wasn't necessary—how the hell could Willis have learned anything?—but nonetheless, it had to be as near foolproof as possible.

Rhodes started on his sit-ups, hands clasped behind his neck, feeling the pull on stomach and thigh muscles. So, if he couldn't be elsewhere at the time of the heist, someone very much like him had to be.

Thirty-eight . . . thirty-nine . . . forty. . . . The strain was telling in his belly on the line of the naval. So, unless he chanced upon his double, he would have to find an actor—preferably dishonest—to impersonate him.

After he had finished his exercises, Rhodes showered and changed, had a snack at a coffee bar—where they served open sandwiches and coffee the color of tea—and caught a cab to a casting agency off Charing Cross Road.

"Someone about your height and weight?" the man behind the desk asked. His name was Matthews, and he was in his fifties, fat and white and smoking a large cigar. He frequently answered the telephone, calling the people on the other end of the line "baby." He picked up a thick book full of photographs. "Shouldn't be too difficult. What sort of part does he have to play?"

"An American businessman," Rhodes said slowly. "You know, a guy who's made it the hard way."

"And you say you're making some kind of movie?" Matthews blew out a thick jet of smoke, holding the cigar like a dart.

"A private movie," Rhodes told him.

"Dirty?"

Rhodes shook his head. "For a business corporation."

"We'll have to consult the union," Matthews said. He smoothed his sleek hair. "Everyone has to consult the union before they can do any business these days, even the government."

"Is it necessary? I mean, does anyone have to know?"

"I know, the actor will know."

"Sure, but does anyone else have to know?"

Matthews, cigar in the center of his mouth, stared at Rhodes through a lacework of smoke. "All right, perhaps we don't have to broadcast it if. . . ."

"The fee will be well above union rates."

"Why don't you have a look through the book," Matthews said, handing Rhodes the glossy, well-thumbed volume.

While Matthews talked on the phone—"Don't call me, I'll call you, baby"—Rhodes looked at the pictures of the actors, some posing like the stars they would never be; others accepting they would only be employed when a casting director sought an Italian waiter, an Irish barman, a South American revolutionary. Some wore silk cravats and pencil moustaches, looking as though they were seeking parts in an early Noel Coward production. In the flesh they would look twenty years older.

He picked three men, one of them American.

Matthews glanced at the photographs. He told Rhodes that one of them was on location in a Michael Winner movie, starring Charles Bronson. That left the American and an Englishman who had played a few American roles in the sixties.

Rhodes found the Englishman in a studio apartment off Kings Road and immediately knew he was unsuitable. His face was too familiar from TV plays, and his American accent, which he now used all the time, was as bad as Dick Van Dyke's cockney accent in *Mary Poppins*. Also he was an ardent union man and thought it irregular for Rhodes to visit him in his apartment. But when Rhodes said, "Forget it," he looked disappointed. Rhodes left him standing at the door of his apartment against a backdrop of photographs of himself.

That left the American. Rhodes called him from a phone booth. The voice that answered the phone was vaguely Bostonian, a telephone voice used until the actor had got an idea what was expected of him. When he heard Rhodes' unmistakable New York accent, he began to sound more like a cab driver from the Bronx.

The actor, whose name was Benchley, asked why the agency wasn't calling him. When Rhodes said it was something special, he hesitated, then agreed to a meeting in a bar in Regent Street.

Over martinis they assessed each other. They were the same build, about the same age, similar coloring. Rhodes was encouraged. Benchley's hair was on the long side, and he had an actor's manners; but presumably he could adapt. So what was so special about this engagement? he asked. They regarded each other warily. Rhodes hazarded a guess that Benchley wouldn't object to earning a dishonest penny. He arranged to meet him again in a week's time and sought the assistance of a private detective agency in Aldgate called Meeker and Warburg.

Five days later, reading the report on the agency's note paper in his apartment, Rhodes discovered that Henry Rawlinson Benchley's real name was William Beckert, born in the Bronx in 1934. He was a naturalized British subject, parted from his wife and two children, and was having trouble keeping up the maintenance payments on his apartment. He had made one county court appearance for debt and had come under suspicion after a box-office theft at a Shaftesbury Avenue theater, where he was appearing. Six months ago he had completed a series for TV, a stereotyped thriller characterized by salable mid-Atlantic accents. Benchley had taken the part of a mobster's bodyguard; since then he had been out of work.

Rhodes thought about the report while he poached himself an egg and brewed black coffee. Benchley was eminently corruptible, but his horizons were limited. A petty crook and an amateur. Rhodes only liked to use professionals and first-class crooks. Benchley, Rhodes decided, constituted a risk; but there was no alternative. It was up to Rhodes to minimize that risk.

Two days later he met Benchley in a pub near Smithfield market. The pub was full of big, meaty men discussing the price of turkeys. Rhodes remembered that it had been almost a year since he had landed in Antwerp and sought out Benjamin Volkov.

He slipped Benchley an envelope containing two thousand pounds in used ten- and five-pound notes.

"This," Rhodes said, "is what you have to do."

At 10:30 A.M. on December 4, a man carrying a passport belonging to John Robert Rhodes arrived at Heathrow on a red airport bus from the West London Terminal to catch the TAP flight to Lisbon, with a connecting flight to Madrid and Valencia. The man was William Beckert, alias Henry Benchley, and he looked remarkably like the mug shot of Rhodes in the passport. His hair was shorter, and his manner, helped by the expensive camel-hair coat, had authority. Henry Benchley was a good actor and might have made it, if he hadn't degenerated into a chameleon willing to take any part for money. Even today he was an understudy.

He bought *Playboy* and the European *Herald Tribune* and lined up for emigration. The official sitting at the desk flipped through the passport, glanced at the photograph, and stared at Benchley. A younger man standing at the desk leaned over and looked at the photograph. Benchley waited for the summons to the interrogation room. Still, he had paid the two thousand pounds into his bank, which canceled his overdraft, leaving him with a credit balance of £1,582.

The man sitting at the desk handed the passport back to Benchley saying, "The photographs are getting better these days."

At Valencia Airport, bathed in sunshine, Benchley was frisked before passing through customs and immigration. He caught a cab to the old Hotel Ingles, in the Marques de dos Aguas, opposite the Museum of Ceramics. A receptionist in black jacket and striped trousers took the passport and examined it. Benchley noted with satisfaction the mauve *entrada* stamp establishing the arrival of John Robert Rhodes in Spain on December 4.

Later he walked through the main square—with its fountain, flower market, and venerable buildings—to a small restaurant where crustacia lay in glistening beds of crushed ice in the window and lobsters flexed their claws in glass tanks of water. He ordered a plate of seafood and a bottle of white wine from Rioja, followed by coffee and two Ponche liqueurs. It was, he decided, the most rewarding role he had ever played.

Through the window he saw girls with long, slithery hair hurrying to their dates. Benchley sighed; one of the stipulations of the role was no women, no close contact with anyone who would be in a position to penetrate his disguise. He was here to negotiate the export of antique rocking chairs, and he was only to emphasize his presence in the city at times when there would be little opportunity for close scrutiny—by tipping lavishly, for instance, in dimly lit bars. Benchley had favored the wearing of sunglasses; in his last TV series, everyone traveling incognito had worn shades. Rhodes had taken them away from him saying, "We're not trying to establish the presence of the Mafia in Spain."

Vaguely, Benchley wondered about the object of the deception. Rhodes had hinted that some smart business deal was at stake. Benchley doubted this, but he didn't seriously question it. Not when a down payment of two thousand pounds with four thousand more to come and unlimited expenses was involved. It occurred to him there might be ways of extorting more money, but he didn't contemplate pursuing them. Benchley was a bit player, not a star. He ordered another Ponche and a Havana cigar, and when he departed, left a one hundred-peseta tip.

The day before Benchley left for Valencia, Chief Detective Inspector Willis called at Rhodes' shop. Rhodes was glad; he had been wondering how to engineer a meeting. When Willis arrived at 11:15 A.M. on a bitter grey morning, Rhodes was locking up shop.

"Bit early to be packing it in, isn't it?" Willis asked. He wore an overcoat, which flapped open to reveal a Gatsby-style suit, and the breeze teased the greying hair over his ears.

"My assistant's sick and a business trip's come up," Rhodes told him.

"Really?" A small frown creased Willis' forehead as they walked down Bond Street toward Piccadilly. "I should have thought Christmas was the time to sell antiques."

"Wrong," Rhodes told him. "The time to sell antiques is when the Americans are here in the summer. Winter's the time to replenish stocks."

They walked in silence for awhile, navigating their way through the crowds window-shopping in one of the most expensive streets in the world, defying inflation and devaluation.

"Where to this time?" Willis asked without displaying any great interest.

Rhodes told him Valencia.

"Flying?"

"I haven't made up my mind." If Willis was checking him out, then Rhodes intended to make it as difficult as possible. He certainly didn't propose to make it so simple that all Willis had to do was check departures on direct flights to Valencia. "I may fly via Paris, where I've got some business. Or I may even go to Rome and backtrack to Valencia via Madrid." He smiled to himself. "Or I may even go by train. I've always had a thing about trains. You know, the Alaska Railroad, the Canadian Pacific, the Trans-Siberian. . . ."

"I know what you mean," Willis said impatiently as they emerged into Piccadilly.

"Coffee?"

Willis nodded. They went into the Fountain Room at Fortnum and Masons and sat among elegant women who had started Christmas shopping in October.

Willis had coffee with cream and a chocolate cake; Rhodes ordered black coffee.

"Anyway," Rhodes said, dropping a Saccharine into his coffee, "what did you want to see me about?"

"I've bought some offices in Torquay in Union Street. Now I've got to stock up with antiques, and I thought you might have some tips for me."

It was all so plausible. Here I am, Rhodes thought, the policeman's friend, the hero who saved a cop's life—and an antique dealer into the bargain. What was more natural than Willis' anxiety to stay friendly?

"It's getting tougher every day," Rhodes said. "The stockpiles are running low, and the phonies are having a ball. It's not just two barrels of buckshot fired into an old chest these days; they're getting cute. Only the other day I nearly bought a Scottish snaphaunce pistol allegedly made for Charles I."

"But you didn't?"

"It was the best fake I ever saw. But they made one little mistake: the way the mainspring pressed on the toe of the cock. . . ."

"That was very careless of them," said Willis, who had no idea what Rhodes was talking about.

"So you got to know your stuff, old buddy."

"That's why I'm buying the coffee," Willis said, ducking as a woman tried to decapitate him with a bundle of parcels wrapped in fancy paper. He lit a cigarette and asked, "So when are you leaving?"

"Huh?"

"When do you go to Valencia?"

"Sometime within the next three days," Rhodes said. "Want to come with me?" Sometimes, he thought, I push my luck.

"Too much to do," Willis said. "You know, the winding-up process. When will you be back?"

"Nothing definite," Rhodes said, sliding the bill across the table to Willis. "But I guess I'll be back for your retirement party."

"Where's Marie these days?"

"Visiting her folks in Montreal," Rhodes said. He stood up. "Thanks for the coffee." He left Willis thoughtfully drumming his fingers on the table surrounded by predatory women.

Three days later Willis called a contact in Madrid with an apartment overlooking the Parque de Retiro. He was a retired plainclothes policeman who had helped Willis back in 1965, when a London bank robber had gone to earth in the Spanish capital. Willis asked him if he could check the immigration forms at Valencia Airport to see if a man named John Rhodes had passed through; and if he had, could he find out what hotel he was staying at.

It took the contact two hours to find out and call Willis back. John Robert Rhodes hadn't been through immigration at Valencia; he had checked in at Madrid. But he was staying in Valencia at the Hotel Ingles. "A three-star hotel," the contact said. "Very old, very pleasant."

"Did you get a description?"

"*Sí*. It is exactly as you described this Rhodes. American, tough looking but well mannered, blue eyes, pleasant manner—even the camel-hair coat is as you described it."

"And his passport was in order?"

"As far as I know."

"How long's he there for?"

"He's booked into the hotel on a weekly basis. But, of course, he can stay in Spain for up to three months without any trouble."

"Okay," Willis said. "*Muchas gracias*."

"*De nada*," said the contact.

Willis then put a direct call through to the hotel. While he waited for it, he paced his sparsely furnished office. Perhaps if he had been more of a stereotyped cop, he would have been retiring on a superintendent's pension. But it was too late for self-recrimination—too late by about twenty years. But at least he had the opportunity for a final coup.

The phone rang and he picked it up, knowing he would have to explain the call to accounts. He spoke to the hotel receptionist and checked out every detail about Rhodes he could remember. Everything seemed to fit except perhaps. . . .

"Whom shall I say called?"

"It doesn't matter," Willis said, replacing the receiver.

There didn't seem to be too much doubt that the man staying at the Hotel Ingles was Johnny Rhodes. Only one detail remained to be double-checked, and he couldn't to that until he was face to face with Rhodes.

Willis swore softly to himself, picked up the phone, and asked for Nigel Lawson's number.

The Britannia Airways Boeing 737 G-Avril was heading south crossing the high frequency beacon (VOR) at Midhurst on the first leg of its flight to Majorca on the Balearic Islands in the Mediterranean. It would cross the English coast near Brighton, the French coast near Le Havre along Upper Amber 34 airway to Limoges, and then along Upper Blue 31 to Palma.

The passengers on board were on a winter-sunshine package deal, their whole holiday costing much less than the return fare by a scheduled airline. They had just unbuckled their safety belts and were giving their drink orders to the stewardesses and discussing what to buy duty-free from the trolley. Ahead lay the sun, cheap booze, handsome men and golden girls, and the blue Mediterranean; behind lay strikes, bombs, rising prices, and winter. The atmosphere on the aircraft was heady with relief and abandonment.

The two middle-aged women with freshly curled hair from Muswell Hill in North London took their miniature bottles of whisky from the stewardess and poured the liquor into plastic glasses. The man with the Canadian passport sitting next to them emptied a little bottle of vodka into his glass.

As radio contact was handed over to French control, which would regulate the flight as far as the Spanish border, one of the women nudged the man and said, "How long you going for, mate?"

Two weeks, he told them.

"You a Yank?"

"No," he said, "Canadian."

"Fancy that," she said, "I used to go with a

Canadian during the war, before I met my Jack."

The man smiled politely.

"What you doing then going to Majorca from London? You know, I mean why didn't you fly from Canada?"

The man explained that he was a resident in London. He had been ill in the hospital, and the cheapest convalescence possible was a package-deal holiday.

The woman nudged him again. "We'll look after you, won't we, Florrie?"

The second woman said, "Watch it, mate. If she gets her hands on you, you'll find yourself back in the hospital again suffering from exhaustion."

The two women laughed uproariously.

The cart arrived, and the women each bought a bottle of Haig, a carton of Dunhills, and a cigarette lighter. The man bought a bottle of Smirnoff.

Conversation continued intermittently until the aircraft passed over the Pyrenees and the navigation receiver homed on the Barcelona VOR. With Majorca 110 miles away, the two women dozed as the crew carried out their flight-deck checks.

As the aircraft circled the nondirectional beacon over Palma, the women came to life again. What hotel was he staying at? the first woman asked. And when it was discovered that they were all under the same roof, she said, "But I suppose you'll be after the young stuff."

The other woman said, "The best tunes are played on an old fiddle, mate."

The crew selected the instrument-landing system on the navigation receivers and began the landing routine. As the aircraft passed over the middle marker and homed down on runway 24, the two women shut their eyes and gripped the arms of the seats.

The man took out his passport and flipped through it. Richard Walter Ogden. Birthdate, October 10, 1932. Issued at London on September 21, 1972. Passport expires September 21, 1977. Birthplace, Toronto. Hair brown. Eyes blue. And beneath the statistics was a photograph bearing the signature Richard W. Ogden.

Johnny Rhodes thought the likeness on the forged passport was pretty good.

The jet touched down. A brief reverse thrust of the engines and they were turning off runway 24 to the main parking area.

Half an hour later they were on the coach heading for their hotel. There was a lot of laughter, mostly relief at having actually arrived; and in the back of the coach, a young man wearing jeans, vest, and beads began to strum a guitar.

Rhodes glanced at his watch. Within five hours he had to be back at the airport. He had chosen the package-deal method of leaving England because it was safest: perfunctory passport and customs checks; identity submerged in boozy communal fun; and as yet, it didn't seem to have occurred to the police that the cheap charter was an ideal escape route for a fugitive.

At the hotel he consulted the courier. The courier was quite willing to accept the return half of his ticket. Rhodes knew that later he would resell it at half price to some stranded soldier of fortune unable to scrape together the full fare back to London.

Within six hours Rhodes was airborne again on a KLM jet bound for Amsterdam. As the jet took him back into winter, Rhodes pondered on the risks that had accumulated: the unknown quantity of the fence in New York; the elegant ferret Willis; a chrysanthemum to be named Solitaire—that was surely a coincidence; the second-rate character of his understudy in Valencia; the discovery that Pierre Tallon had made a trip to Tel Aviv without telling him—Tallon's prerogative, he supposed, but odd just the same. Tallon had explained that he was having an affair with an Israeli girl; with Tallon, that figured.

Once upon a time none of these risks would have occurred; but, coming out of retirement, he was out of touch. . . . *Touch the lion's paw, and good fortune will come your way.* Where the hell had he heard that? Then he remembered. According to legend it was said to bring you good luck if you touched the paws of the lion statues outside the headquarters of the Hong Kong Bank Group in Queen's Road Central, Hong Kong. Rhodes had once touched them as he entered the bank to draw funds to finance a successful robbery in Singapore. It was a good omen. Rhodes relaxed and slept until the jet touched down at Schiphol Airport.

Chapter 21

Nigel Lawson also guessed that the last consignment would be dispatched between December 10 and 20. With nine cargoes dispatched and one to go—his one chance to make a fortune—his nerve was giving out, and it required more and more scotch to revive it and calm the tic that had developed in one eye.

Over the past few months he had demanded five hundred pounds from Carmichael on the grounds that he was "onto something really big." Scared that he would be blamed if he didn't subsidize Lawson and something really big did happen, Carmichael paid up. But five hundred pounds was the limit, and now he wanted what he had paid for.

Lawson lost his last fifty pounds on the November Handicap and cadged twenty pounds from Willis. Willis, too, was becoming restless. "In just over one month," he told Lawson, "I shall be out to grass. Before I go I want that big break I've been paying you for."

Lawson's dilemma was further complicated by Benjamin Volkov, who had visited him in London. If Volkov panicked and told anyone about his suspicions, the last consignment would be held back or rerouted and there would be no reward. But why had Volkov held back his suspicions for so long? Lawson's instincts, delicately attuned to dishonest motives, told him Volkov was scared of something; he had a skeleton in the safe.

When they met in Trafalgar Square, Lawson hinted that he knew something of Volkov's past; he was rewarded by a flicker of fear in Volkov's eyes. "I should keep quiet about your suspicions, old man," Lawson told him. "These things are best left to us. We think it's going to be the last cargo this year, but don't tell a soul." Lawson put a brown-stained forefinger to his lips.

Volkov said, in his high-pitched voice, "Do you know anyone involved in it?" Pigeons and tourists swarmed around them.

Lawson said, "No, do you?"

Volkov hesitated. "No," he said, "just a feeling. I was worried about that killing at Deurne and that fancy diamond stolen in Brussels turning up in Amsterdam."

"What's the diamond got to do with anything?" Lawson asked.

"Well, it must have been stolen by a professional, and as it hasn't been recut, it must have still been in his possession. So it looks as if the thief was staying in Amsterdam, which is only 120 kilometers from Antwerp. Perhaps they're planning an escape route via Amsterdam."

Lawson laughed and said, "You have a criminal mind, Mr. Volkov. But don't worry, just leave it to us." He was glad Volkov had come to him instead of Carmichael; two of a kind, he supposed.

When he got home that night Lawson counted his money. He had £8 35p. He decided to go dog racing at the White City to make enough to tide him over until the day the tip came from Masters—the day he was back in the big stakes.

He won with forecast bets on the first three races, and with five large whiskies and three pints of bitter below his belt, he felt confidence flow through his veins. At times like this, he felt tempted to confront Rhodes and demand a corner of the takings; but when it came to it, when the counterfeit effects of the alcohol had worn off, his nerve failed.

He lost on the fourth race and decided to keep his capital for the last race. He drank a couple more whiskies, leaning on the bar with a faint smile on his face, calculating how much money he would get if he forestalled a robbery involving, say, £14 million.

On the last race he lost all his money except for sixty pence. He went home on the Central Line underground from White City to Chancery Lane. At Chancery Lane he lingered on the platform, as many desperate men before him had lingered, wondering if there was any light in the darkness that lay ahead if he stepped under a train.

Two trains came and went. Nigel Lawson went up the escalator into a cold night with mist blurring the lights. A cruel night, a Jack the Ripper night.

He walked slowly down Gray's Inn Road, hardly feeling the cold slip inside his open British Warm. He slept fitfully. Just before dawn he awoke and thought he saw rats scurrying around the room, but as he stared, they dissolved.

At 10:00 A.M. he walked to the office by way of the back streets, pausing to gaze into the window of a small jeweler's. It was then that the idea came to him.

The idea stayed with him all the way to the office. He knew his nerve had finally failed him; he knew he had to share his knowledge—and his idea. He spent two hours with Carmichael; then he phoned Willis.

The next day the executive jet took off from Heathrow bound for Antwerp. The date was Friday the thirteenth.

Part 3
PREMIERE AND FINALE

Chapter 22

Snow was beginning to fall as the BH-125—the color of a Silver Cape diamond with blue flashes on its wings—touched down at Antwerp's Deurne Airport at 11:33 A.M. on December 13.

Nonchalantly, Pierre Tallon strolled to the Renault S12 as the security van took off for the end of the runway. He parked the car three hundred yards from the apartment building and walked down the street, coat collar turned up, hat brim pulled down over his forehead.

The snow faltered in the air before touching the ground and melting. High above, gulls wheeled in the bruised sky. The lowlands were settling in for winter.

Tallon approached the building from the rear. He ran up the stairs, gave the code signal on the bell—two Victory Vs—and went into the apartment.

The gas grenades he promised Rhodes he would use were stacked beside two assault rifles equipped with launchers. The two men in the room—two of the three who had visited de Gooyer in Amsterdam—returned to their places at the window, one holding the Colt CMG-2, the other cradling the .44 Magnum.

One wore a dark blue Belgian police uniform, the other an asbestos suit and transparent helmet. Tallon stripped off his clothes, packed them into a white plastic suitcase, and put on a police uniform and black gloves. He opened the window, picked up the Blowpipe, rested it on his shoulder, and took up his position.

The man in uniform with razor-cut hair and expressionless eyes said, "Are you sure that's not too heavy for you?"

"Are you sure you haven't wet your pants?" Tallon said.

The man in uniform said, "I hope I live to be as old as you." It was his twenty-fourth birthday.

"Here she comes," Tallon said.

Down the wide street lined with small, square buildings Tallon saw the security van approaching. There was little traffic about and only a few pedestrians. Snow was beginning to fall more steadily, in cracks and hollows.

Tallon picked out the van through the sight. He was breathing slowly and steadily, mouth slightly open. He tracked the van as it approached, finger touching the trigger that closed the electric circuit and activated the batteries.

The contact lenses didn't hurt any more, but he was conscious of them. Snow blew in through the open window and settled on the canister of the Blowpipe.

He was alone now, the two younger men having gone down to the passage leading into the road.

The big one. The last one. He would marry Raquel and plant orange trees that grew. Then the old lust for destruction was upon him.

He squeezed the trigger. The missile sprang from

246

the launcher, tail fins opening on exit. Squinting through the monocular sight, Tallon guided the missile all the way to the security van—a matter of a split second, but it still gave him time to enjoy the delicate deliberation of the act.

The missile hit the van, exploding on impact, slamming it off the road onto the pavement, where it stood burning in the falling snow. It was right on target, just behind the driving cabin but in front of the hold, where the diamonds were lodged in case the intense heat damaged them.

Tallon grinned fiercely, picked up the Python and ran down into the road. Pedestrians were standing transfixed, a few cars were slowing down. Now it was only speed that mattered.

As the man in the asbestos suit climbed through the gaping hole, a Fiat 124 Sport skidded to a halt beside the van. The man with the Colt CMG-2 covered the two vehicles.

Tallon glanced at the driver and mate of the van. They were both slumped forward, and blood was oozing from the driver's face.

The Fiat edged up beside the hole. Tallon took the steel case from the man in the asbestos suit and dumped it in the trunk.

The man in the asbestos suit jumped, As he landed, his foot slipped on the snow; he fell against Tallon, knocking him to the ground. Tallon swore and jumped to his feet. But there was something wrong. The road, the burning van, the gaping pedestrians looked fuzzy. He closed one eye and the scene came into focus. *"Nom d'bleu,* my lens!" Tallon shouted.

He scrabbled around the curb looking for the missing contact lens. In the distance he heard sirens. The driver of the Fiat, the man who had carried the Beretta in the Amsterdam nightclub, shouted to him to get in.

Tallon made a last sweep of the curb, taking off

his glove to help him find the tiny lens. Nothing. He hurled himself into the back of the Fiat as it took off, tires skidding before they gripped. "God save us from old-age pensioners," the driver said.

The Fiat rounded two blocks, lurching wildly around the corners, and stopped beside the blue Volkswagen painted and equipped in a garage in Ghent to look like a police car and brought to Antwerp during the night in the back of a truck.

The man who had climbed into the security van was now free of his asbestos suit. The four of them, all in police uniforms, climbed into the fake police car, taking the steel case with them.

Tallon said, "Right, now we join the chase."

They edged out into the main street and turned right, aiming for the E3, which they planned to cross into the maze of streets in the Borgerhout area of Antwerp.

The driver swore. *"Merde."* There were police cars everywhere.

Tallon said, "They can't have got here that quickly."

"They didn't," the driver said. "It must be a trap."

The whole of the Deurne area was ringed with police cars following the information phoned the previous night by Detective Chief Inspector John Willis from Scotland Yard and confirmed by diamond security headquarters in Hatton Garden. The general alert reached the cars by radio telephone fifty-two seconds after the hit, and they began to close in from their positions in Merksem and the access roads on the E3, which separates the eastern districts from the main hub of Antwerp. Road blocks were thrown across the entries to the highway, and two helicopters rose from Deurne airfield, circling like two great dragonflies, incongruous in the falling snow.

"What the hell do we do?" the man with the machine gun asked, fear rasping his voice.

"Let me think," Tallon snapped.

The plan had been simple. By the time it was dawning on police that the Fiat had been switched for a fake police car, they would be on the far side of the Borgerhout area. There the driver, who had learned his stuff as a stock-car racer, would smash the car into a truck driven across the road by an accomplice. Tallon and the other three would leap out and disperse to three addresses arranged by Daniel Tallon, change their clothes, and emerge with forged papers as tourists.

But now Deurne was cut off like an island.

The driver said, "Here come two of the bastards." He pointed at two white traffic control Volkswagens approaching them.

"We've still got a chance," Tallon said. "They're not looking for a police car." He snapped his fingers. "Salute them as they go past."

The police drivers saluted back, pointing frantically in front of them, indicating that they were going in the wrong direction.

"We can't keep this up for long," the driver said.

"Maybe, maybe not," Tallon said. "They're not going to start chasing a police car when they've been told to pick up a blue 124 Sport."

The man who had worn the asbestos suit held the big .44 Magnum in two hands as if he were going to shoot. "They were waiting for us in the back of the security van," he said. "If we hadn't hit it with a missile and wounded them, they'd have got us."

The man with the Colt said, "Who the hell double-crossed us?"

The driver shrugged. "One of the three old men, maybe." He made a racing turn around a corner, tires sliding on the snow. He drove into the skid, righted it, and said, "Whoever it was, Daniel will take care of him."

The snow was falling heavily now, an ally. Another police car passed in the opposite direction, the occupants staring at them in astonishment. The helicopter lowered itself over them, almost touching the rooftops.

"That bastard knows," the man with the Magnum said, pointing upward.

"It doesn't follow," Tallon said. "He just wonders what the hell we're doing going the wrong way and why we haven't got the message right on the radio."

The man with the Colt said, "I didn't think it would be like this." He turned on Tallon. "You did this to us. . . ." The fear was turning to panic.

Tallon hit him across the face with the back of his hand. "*Ta gueule!* Get ready to use that thing," he said, slapping the barrel of the Colt.

Tallon took off his other black glove and clawed at the remaining lens. As he did so the car swerved; the lens came out grazing his eyelid and blood began to seep across his eyeball.

The man with the Magnum said, "There's a police car behind us now. They must have found the Fiat."

"We can still do it," Tallon said. He put on both his gloves, pawing at the blood.

The driver said, "There's the main road ahead. They've got a block up."

"Get your siren going," Tallon said.

Ahead, they could see police frantically signaling at them. There were two steel barriers across the road, which cut straight across the highway, and beyond the barriers a police car.

The police tried to move the barriers as the fake police car came at them, siren wailing.

"Get down," shouted the driver. "Here we go."

One barrier was out of the way. They hit the

second, knocking it off the road, and struck the hood of the stationary police car, spinning it around like a top.

Then they were over the highway heading for Bogerhout. Tallon looked behind him; through the veil of snow he could see the police at the roadblock with pistols drawn, but there were no shots. Above them they could hear the clatter of the helicopter's blades.

They crossed the railway at eighty miles an hour; the pursuing car was the same distance behind them. From side streets two other blue, general-control police Volkswagens took up the chase.

They were half way down Turnhoutse Baan when the driver saw the truck swing across the road and stop. He braked desperately and they hit it at thirty miles an hour.

They were running as the first of the pursuing cars skidded to a halt, the police shooting as they leaped out. The man with the Colt turned, the Colt gave a throaty roar, and two policemen dropped.

Tallon ran through the falling snow, Python in hand. He wished he had the big Magnum. He was blinded in one eye by blood, but the old exhilaration was on him.

A bullet sang past his head smashing the barred window of a jeweler's shop. More police had piled out of the other cars and were running toward him. Tallon turned snarling. He didn't have to close one eye to aim, the blood was doing it for him. They were shouting at him to give himself up. He fired twice and dropped one policeman. But without the lenses, everything was fuzzy, and the snowflakes were moths trying to blind his good eye.

He fired once more, the bullet smashing the wind screen of the first police car. Then he turned and ran on. The bullet caught him in the back of the neck. He remembered the girl Raquel, he remembered the oranges, and he died clutching the bars of the jeweler's shop separating him from trays of glittering diamonds.

Half an hour later the steel case that Tallon and his accomplices had left in the back of the fake police car lay on the long table of the Diamond Office in Pelikaanstraat.

Willis, who had flown in three hours earlier, was there, and Benjamin Volkov with several other diamond VIP's. There was a conference of diamond manufacturers taking place in Antwerp, and several of its luminaries from the diamond capitals of the world had been summoned from a reception at the town háll to witness the opening of the container snatched from the security van. But they had been summoned by officials who knew nothing about the messages from London the previous night.

There was an air of pleasant anticipation about the group gathered around the table. Once again the system had prevailed: the diamond industry was impregnable, and anyone trying to pillage its vaults, buttressed by honesty and integrity, deserved to die as Pierre Tallon had done.

Only Volkov was apprehensive. A robbery had been attempted, and if Rhodes was apprehended, it was still possible that he could become involved.

"Well," said a dealer from New York, "open up. Let's see the goods." He spotted Volkov. "Hey, Benny, don't look so scared. It's all over. Someone give Benny the keys."

The keys were handed to Volkov. Pale-faced, he stepped forward and inserted the key in the lock. But it didn't fit.

"Come on," said the American. "You're all fingers and thumbs. Give me the keys." He tried the key, but it wouldn't slide into the lock.

A few Antwerp dealers looked uneasy.

Willis stepped forward. "Let's have a look," he said. He compared the key with the lock. "It's the wrong key," he announced.

A Belgian security officer said, "It can't be, it's the only one."

"In view of what we know from London. . . ." Willis began.

"That's got nothing to do with the keys," the security man snapped.

It took them twenty minutes to get a locksmith; and it took the locksmith five minutes to open the container.

Volkov spoke first. "I don't have to tell you, gentlemen, that what you're looking at is quartz, common rock crystal worth next to nothing."

Shortly before the discovery of the quartz in the steel case, the executive jet with the blue flashes on the wings, which had landed with Hans Muller at the controls, took off again from Deurne Airport and headed back to Munster.

Chapter 23

Ten minutes after takeoff from London's Heathrow Airport that morning, the captain of the BH-125, which regularly flew the diamonds to Antwerp, had received a company message over the radio that mildly surprised him. Apart from routine instructions in the event of an emergency, such as a crash or bad weather, the pilot only reacted to a company message accompanied by the code number of the day.

The message was relayed to the captain by an air-traffic controller who had received five thousand pounds for radioing the message. The code word had been telephoned to him by Frederick Masters.

Captain Michael Rutherford, aged forty-nine, ex-RAF and civil-airline pilot, who had logged 21,000 flying hours, asked for a repetition of the message and the code number, VVS2 (taken from the Scandinavian system of diamond grading). Both were repeated: they were being diverted to Amsterdam.

Rutherford, a burly man with ginger sideburns, turned to his copilot, a sleek young man named Hawkins, and said, "I wonder what the hell's happened at Antwerp?"

Hawkins shrugged. "It isn't the first time we've been switched to Amsterdam."

"It's a bloody nuisance," Rutherford said. "Let's hope the snow holds off."

"Let's hope the whole place ices up after we've landed," Hawkins said. "I fancy a night out in Amsterdam."

Grafton, the third man on the aircraft, who was in charge of the steel case that was flown across the North Sea ten times a year, came into the cockpit.

"Everything all right?" he asked.

Over his shoulder, Rutherford said, "We've been diverted to Amsterdam."

Grafton, a balding, stocky man in the sort of nondescript suit favored by diamond people, said, "They must have got the wind-up at Antwerp."

Rutherford swung around. "Wind-up? Why the hell should they?"

"There was a report that there might be a holdup in Antwerp."

"No one told us," Rutherford said angrily.

"There wasn't any need to. The security van had armed guards inside it."

"I suppose they thought we'd refuse to land if we knew about it." Rutherford's voice was bitter.

"I don't know what they thought."

Hawkins said, "Who cares? We're well out of it, and with luck, we might be able to spend some time at the Blue Note Club."

They radioed ahead a revised flight plan as they passed over the VOR beacon at Clacton and headed across the North Sea, grey snow clouds beneath them. They were cleared to Spijkerboor, the Amsterdam beacon. They began to make their descent. From Amsterdam came the message: Clear to make approach to runway 19 right.

Snow was falling lightly, but heavy falls were forecast. "Look out, girls, here we come," Hawkins said.

The fake Peugeot ambulance proceeded at a steady pace through the center of Amsterdam. The festival of St. Nicholas was over, and with the falling snow, Christmas was beginning to touch the city. Rhodes imagined he could hear its chime on the cold air: peace, goodwill—and loneliness.

Moses Ferguson pointed to a bespectacled woman in uniform and bonnet walking along a side street with a couple of other uniformed women. *"De Majoor,"* he said. "A character in this town. Every year she runs up a bill in the neighborhood of ten thousand dollars for the old people, the homeless, the junkies. . . ."

"This year," Rhodes said, "she'll have twenty thousand."

"Thirty," Ferguson said.

Rhodes thought about Marie, and the loneliness entered the cab of the Peugeot, a replica of the make of the airport ambulance.

"What are you going to do with the rest of your cash?" he asked Ferguson.

"Count it," Ferguson said.

"And then?"

"You know, man, spread the good word. Catch a few fish. Buy another house. Look after a few people in Florida who need the dough." He paused. "We didn't really need the money, did we?"

"We needed to know we were still smart enough to get it."

"I guess so." Ferguson's leg ached, but he didn't massage it because he didn't want Rhodes to know how bad it was. "What will you do with your corner?"

"Much the same as you, I guess. Charity begins at home. Then I'll help out a few people. You know, a few kids maybe who haven't had it so good."

The ambulance left the city and joined the E10 highway to Schiphol Airport. Ferguson, who was at the wheel, and Rhodes both wore white uniforms.

Rhodes glanced at his stopwatch; it was 11:35 A.M. "The action should just be starting at Antwerp," he said. "If everything works out, that'll give us an hour." All the times had been worked out when they made the dummy runs in the Mercedes limousine.

Rhodes knew that as soon as the jet touched down at Deurne, word was relayed to Antwerp and London. When the heist was reported, alarm bells would ring in Hatton Garden as well as Pelikaanstraat. He smiled faintly as he visualized the panic that would be breaking out right now. But as soon as Tallon's car hit the lorry and the steel case was found on the back seat, they would relax. Boy how they would relax. The sweat would cool on their brows and the scotch would flow as the steel case was taken in triumph back to the Diamond Office. There would be no alarm about any diamonds snatched at Amsterdam. As far as diamond security was concerned, the consignment was safe in that steel box—the one Hans Muller had delivered in the jet from Munster, the one they had filled with quartz. By the time they had got a locksmith to the substituted box, he and Ferguson would be forty miles away from Amsterdam, with anything from £13 to £15 million of uncut diamonds taken from the diverted aircraft. The goods. The greatest heist in criminal history.

"Speed it up a little," Rhodes told Ferguson. "Did you ever see a meat wagon going slowly?"

Ferguson pushed his foot down on the accelerator and winced.

"Hey," Rhodes said, "what's the matter?"

"Nothing," Ferguson said, overtaking a Volkswagen beetle.

"Is that the leg you hurt playing Tarzan?"

"Yeah. But it's okay. Just a little twinge now and again."

Rhodes gazed at him suspiciously. "We don't want any little twinges when we make the hit."

"No sweat," Ferguson said.

In front of them a DC-10 floated down from the pewter sky—a predatory heavyweight, yet as vulnerable as a crippled eagle in those last few seconds before touchdown. Then it vanished behind the airport building, depositing three hundred or so people on the good, safe earth.

They were close to the entry for authorized vehicles only. Rhodes glanced at his watch again. "Any minute now," he said. Sweat trickled down his chest inside his uniform; his hands felt swollen inside his gloves. "How are you feeling?" he asked.

"Lousy. But then I always did just before I made the hit. Then, man, as cold and hard as the Cullinan."

Rhodes pointed through the snow, falling more thickly now. "Here comes our baby," he said.

In addition to the death of Pierre Tallon, there had been one other incident that no one had anticipated. Marie Tellier had returned to the apartment on Park Lane.

Rhodes' call from New York had destroyed her campaign to persuade herself that she could get along without him. The men she had been out with suddenly seemed like puppets.

She did some modeling in the big stores on St. Catherine Street, and went home at night to Lousibourg Street to watch television and talk with her parents.

After awhile she began to wonder if she had been wrong about Rhodes—knowing all the time that she hadn't. But just supposing? And even if she was right, perhaps there was one last chance that she could persuade Rhodes to change his mind.

She looked out the window one day in early December. The big cars were churning up the new, wet snow, and the children were throwing snowballs, a game that soon loses its novelty in Montreal.

Soon it would be Christmas. Marie remembered the ultimatum she had given Rhodes. She had said, "Marry me by the end of December or we're through." The ultimatum hadn't run out yet.

On December 12 Marie caught an Air Canada flight to London. She let herself into the apartment on Park Lane just as Daniel Tallon was taking a phone call from Frederick Masters in Hatton Garden.

She paused in the doorway and said, "Who are you?"

A man pulled her into the apartment and slammed the door. Tallon put down the receiver and said, "Who the hell are you?"

The man who had slammed the door jammed the barrel of a pistol in her back. Marie began to turn, but Tallon said, "I should keep quite still if I were you." He picked up a photograph on the writing desk. "So you're Marie?"

Marie said, "Get out of my apartment and take this thug with you."

"This is Johnny Rhodes' apartment if I'm not mistaken." Tallon put the photograph down. "We understood you were in Montreal. Rhodes miscalculated." He drummed his fingers on the desk. "Mr. Rhodes is getting old."

Marie said, "And you're still wet behind the ears. I'm leaving now, and I'm going to call the police."

Tallon took off his glasses and polished them, looking younger than before. He said, "Please don't move. If you do, you will be shot." He replaced his glasses. "Now, we have a lot to do, so please cooperate." He nodded to the man with the gun. "Tie her up."

The young man behind Marie stuck the pistol in his shoulder holster and pinioned Marie's arms. She struggled briefly and started to scream, but he clamped his hand over her mouth. She was dragged into the kitchen, where the man tied a dishcloth around her mouth. Then he bound her wrists and ankles with a nylon clothesline.

He dumped her in the bedroom just as Daniel Tallon got through to Amsterdam.

Captain Michael Rutherford cut the engines and stretched. They were on the runway about five hundred yards from the main building at Schiphol Airport. The steps were in position outside the exit; all they had to do was wait for the security van, which always had special clearance.

Hawkins opened the door and said, "There's an ambulance heading our way."

Rutherford yawned. "Can't be for us," he said. "Unless they're using it to take the diamonds."

"Traveling at a hell of a clip," Hawkins observed. "And the snow's coming down thick and fast. Don't fancy a takeoff in this, do you skipper?" He grinned at Rutherford.

The ambulance stopped near the steps, and the two men in front, one black, pulled white surgical masks over the lower parts of their faces. They climbed out of the ambulance, and the white man shouted, "Fumigation. Just stay where you are a moment, please."

Rutherford came to the exit. "What the hell are you talking about?" he shouted. "Fumigation? In Amsterdam? In this?" He pointed at the falling snow.

The two men were coming up the steps; the black man, who was limping, was holding a white case.

Grafton looked apprehensively at his own steel case. "Has this ever happened before?" he asked.

Hawkins said, "In some countries, yes. But we're not in the bloody Congo now." He shook his head. "Perhaps they think we've got foot-and-mouth disease."

The two men from the ambulance pushed their way into the cabin. "Go up to the cockpit, please," the white man said. He had an American accent.

Rutherford said, "I'm going up there anyway to find out what the hell's going on."

Hawkins asked, "Why surgical masks, for God's sake?" He thought about it. "And shouldn't we be wearing them if you're going to fumigate the bloody airplane?"

"I told you to get up to the cockpit," the white man said.

Grafton said, "There's something wrong. . . ."

The black man had unfastened the white case. Instead of a spray gun, he took out a rifle with a grenade-launcher attachment and fired a gas grenade. As the grenade exploded, he and the white man put on gas masks.

Grafton and Hawkins fell to the floor choking, but Rutherford had almost made it to the cockpit. He snatched a handkerchief from his pocket and stumbled forward toward the instrument panel. He was reaching for the pistol beside the pilot's seat when the black man hit him on the back of the neck with the side of his hand.

The white man pulled the heavy door shut while the gas finished its work.

Thirty seconds later Rhodes opened the door. They took off their masks, ran down the steps, and fetched three stretchers from the ambulance. Back in the airplane they replaced the masks and strapped the three unconscious men on the stretchers.

They got Grafton and Hawkins into the back of the ambulance easily; but Rutherford was a heavy man. On the last step, Ferguson's leg gave way. He stumbled and almost fell.

Rhodes shouted, "For Christ's sake, try and make it to the ambulance."

Ferguson shook his head. "It's no good."

Rhodes said, "Put your end down." Snow began to cover Rutherford's body. Rhodes thanked God for it; from any distance, he and Ferguson would be vague phantom figures.

Rhodes pulled the stretcher to the ambulance. Ferguson followed, dragging his leg. Rhodes climbed into the ambulance. "Pick up one end and try and lift it to me," he said. He was breathing heavily, and there was a small pain in his chest. So much for middle-aged men trying to keep fit. Finally they heaved the stretcher into the ambulance.

Ferguson climbed into the passenger seat and waited while Rhodes stuck a notice in red letters on the side of the jet. It said, in Dutch: Danger—Keep away—Smallpox. Then he fetched the steel case from the airplane and dumped it on the back of the ambulance, grunting with the exertion.

The ambulance took off across the runway. Rhodes

switched on the siren and saluted the puzzled guards at the exit.

Then they were on the highway heading south. The whole operation had taken four minutes twenty seconds, one minute twenty seconds longer than they had planned.

"I'm sorry, Johnny," Ferguson said.

"So am I," Rhodes said.

"But we made it, eh?"

"Maybe."

A white Porsche police car came up beside them.

"Shit," said Ferguson.

The police driver wound down his window and shouted in Dutch.

"What's he saying?" Ferguson asked.

"You tell me."

Rhodes smiled at the police driver, shook his head, and made a negative gesture with his hand.

The driver nodded and the Porsche dropped away.

"How did you know what the man wanted?" Ferguson asked.

"I guessed he was asking if we wanted help."

Ferguson pointed toward the back of the ambulance. "There's maybe $40 million worth of diamonds there. Maybe he was asking if he could go Dutch."

Near Leiden, forty kilometers from Schiphol, they left the E10. Five kilometers later they took a side road. The rented Fiat 850 was standing where they had left it, mantled with snow. Rhodes stopped the ambulance and cut the engine. They climbed into the back, stripped off their uniforms, and put on jackets, slacks, and overcoats. The three unconscious men slept peacefully.

"What about him?" Rhodes pointed at Rutherford. "I hope to Christ you didn't hit him too hard. That's what fouled up the train robbery."

Ferguson shook his head. "He's okay. We men of

God know how to slam a guy without hurting him too much."

They put the steel case in the trunk of the Fiat and headed for the one place no one would suspect the diamond thieves to head for: Antwerp.

And it was in the sitting room of a small house in the Berchem area of Antwerp that they finally opened the steel case and gazed at its contents: three trays of unremarkable crystals that, when cut and polished and pampered, would glitter with the icy fires of the Arctic. They would beckon millionaires, dazzle beautiful women, and seduce the cleverest criminals from the routine of conventional crime. And none of the thieves would ever guess that they were, in fact, dealing in stolen property, the proceeds of the biggest diamond heist the world has ever known—a fact that would soon have to be acknowledged by the *Guinness Book of World Records*.

Chapter 24

It was the last day of 1974 and Johnny Rhodes and Moses Ferguson, who was on crutches, were walking in Central Park. It was a bleak day, the grass drained of color, the sky pregnant with snow, and even the squirrels looked cold.

Rhodes said, "There's only one thing worrying me."

"What's that? How to spend the bread?"

Rhodes shook his head. "I've already got that figured out. A charity here, a charity there. No, what's bothering me is, what the hell happened to Lawson and Willis? Lawson's got a good criminal brain, Willis was hot on my heels, and yet they blew it."

"I guess we were just too smart for them," Ferguson said, staring at three youth in sneakers, jeans, and combat shirts and eyeing them speculatively. "That's all we need as a climax," he said. "To get mugged on New Year's Eve."

The three youths assessed the size of Rhodes and Ferguson and drifted away. Ferguson was crippled, but even on crutches, he looked lethal. Rhodes swung his arms around his chest to get warm.

"Rhodes pointed to Ferguson's bad leg. "Are you going to get that fixed?"

"Sure, when I get back to Florida. We've got witch doctors down there."

Rhodes still looked pensive. He said, "You see, what bothers me is that Lawson had it all figured out at Deurne. He guessed when and where the hit was going to be made, just as though he were pulling the job himself, and he advised the cops to cordon off the whole area. But you'd have thought he would have realized there was more to it than that. He knew he was dealing with the best operators in the world, and for Christ's sake, he should have known how we think because that's the way he used to think."

"Except he's a lush," Ferguson reminded Rhodes. "And he didn't reckon the guided missile, either."

"Who would?"

They turned and headed toward Fifth Avenue, drawn from the winter-dead park by a magnet.

"That Tallon," Ferguson remarked. "That bastard."

"He had to die that way," Rhodes said. "From the moment he was born, he had to die that way."

They left the park and joined the throngs of people on Fifth Avenue, everyone cold and grim as if anticipating tomorrow's hangovers.

Rhodes said, "I called Antwerp this morning."

264

"And?"

"No one's going to die. Tallon was the only fatality."

"Thank God," Ferguson said.

"So you should," Rhodes said.

"What now?"

"A new start, I guess. A new identity. Canada, maybe. I have a thing about Montreal. . . . And you?"

"Mr. Ballantine of Detroit leaves the stage," Ferguson said. "The Black Messiah returns to his flock with enough bread to bring Cuba into the diocese. As a matter of fact, I'm booked on a flight to Palm Beach tonight," he added.

Rhodes took his arm. "Just before you go," he said, "what about that pink diamond?"

Mumbling a little, Ferguson told him about it.

"You're getting old," Rhodes told him.

"And rich," Ferguson said. "It's downright disgusting."

They stopped outside the magnet: the window of Tiffany and Company at 727. The window was full of sprays of diamonds glittering as coldly as the day.

Ferguson peered in, shook his head, and said, "Doesn't look like quartz to me."

They shook hands. Then Johnny Rhodes went one way, the Black Messiah the other.

From the Algonquin Hotel Rhodes called Marie. When he had returned briefly to the Park Lane apartment on the morning of December 14—making sure that neither Willis nor any of his kind were in evidence—he had found her still tied to the bed. He had flown to New York, she to Montreal.

While he dialed the Montreal number, Rhodes still wondered about Lawson and Willis. Why hadn't Willis made any move in the last days before his retirement? When Marie answered the phone, he asked her to fly to New York.

"Why?" she asked.

"You know why." He paused, acknowledging defeat. Or was it victory? "Your ultimatum expires tonight, right?"

"But your promise. . . ."

Rhodes said, "Will you marry me?"

There was a pause in which he thought he heard her crying. Then she said, "On one condition."

"And that is?"

"No more jogging," she said.

"Jogging," Rhodes said, "is strictly for the nuts."

She seemed to be laughing and crying at the same time, and because he thought he might do the same, Johnny Rhodes hung up the receiver.

Ten minutes after speaking to Marie on the phone, Rhodes received two visitors in his hotel room—Nigel Lawson and ex-Detective Chief Inspector Willis.

"How the hell. . . . ?" Rhodes began.

"It was always your favorite hotel," Lawson said. "You're slipping, Johnny, becoming a creature of habit."

"What do you want?"

"A beer to start with," Willis said. "At least ask us in; we've come a long way to see you."

"On a charter," Lawson said. "Couldn't afford a scheduled flight."

"You'd better come in," Rhodes said. He ordered three beers from room service. "Now, to what do I owe the honor?"

Willis and Lawson sat down, Willis elegant in a velvet-collared overcoat that didn't seem to be quite right for retirement. "First of all," Willis said, "we want to congratulate you."

"For what?"

"For pulling off the heist of the century."

"It was very well done," Lawson said. He hadn't shaved, and he was wearing his usual shabby overcoat. "I couldn't have done better myself."

"Very droll," Rhodes said. "I'll play along with you. What heist?"

A waiter brought the beers, and they waited until he had gone. Willis took a couple of swallows of beer and said, "Let's not play games, Johnny. We're talking about the Amsterdam heist. You know, we know, so let's get sensible. We weren't quite as slow to catch on as you seemed to think."

"I don't know what the hell you're talking about," Rhodes said. He sat down opposite the two of them. "What Amsterdam heist? I'm a bit out of touch."

"On the contrary," Willis told him, "you're very much on the ball. By the way, did you have a successful trip to Valencia?"

"It was quite productive," Rhodes said. "Rocking chairs are swinging these days."

"According to the receptionist at the Hotel Ingles, you spoke fluent Spanish. I didn't know that was one of your accomplishments, Johnny."

"Then you haven't done your homework."

"Come off it," Willis said pleasantly. "Say something in Spanish, Johnny. Say, 'I'm innocent on all charges, officer' in Spanish."

"I don't have to say anything in any goddamed language."

"Just to put my mind at rest."

"*Olé*," Rhodes said.

"Is that it?"

"That's it as far as you're concerned, old buddy."

Lawson wiped some froth from his lips. "You see, it wasn't quite the perfect crime, Johnny—not the way it used to be. The pinky, for instance, led us straight to you. A trip to Spain meant Tallon; a trip to Florida meant Ferguson. You'll have to be more careful with your travel arrangements next time."

"Next time?"

Willis grinned. "That's what we came to see you about," he said, finishing his beer. "A business proposition. You know, I'm not really the retiring type. The point is that diamond merchants will be making new arrangements now to ship the diamonds to Antwerp, and Lawson here will know every move they make. We believe we can pull off a heist every bit as big as yours, but we need a partner. You—and maybe Ferguson as well."

"You know what I think?" Rhodes asked, sipping his beer, hardly tasting it. "I think retirement's gone to your head. You know, some guys go crazy as soon as their life's vocation is over, and that's what's happened to you—you're nuts."

Lawson gazed thirstily at his empty glass. "I knew you'd wait for the last shipment, Johnny. And I knew just where you'd hit in Antwerp. What bothered me was all the activity in Amsterdam. But I thought it was probably just an outlet, the most convenient city to work out of. Not that it really mattered."

Rhodes ordered more beer. When it arrived, he poured himself another glass and said to Willis, "How would you like to be paid off?"

"No chance," Willis said. "It's the thought of retirement that scares me. It's like this," he went on, an apologetic note to his voice, "I've got enough on you to put you inside for as long as the train robbers if you don't cooperate with us."

"I see." Rhodes thought that if Marie arrived tomorrow, they could be married by special license within a couple of days. He was rich beyond the dreams of ordinary theives; the future was theirs. "I'll think about it," he said. "I presume you want a cut now?"

"Just enough to get along," Willis said.

Lawson swallowed. "Just a few grand, Johnny."

"And by the way," Willis said, "we recruited—for want of a better word—a good man in Antwerp. A fellow called Benjamin Volkov."

Rhodes glanced at his watch. It was just past midnight. In London the first early morning joggers would be stirring. Rhodes shivered. He decided he preferred Brazil, where all the best villains retired incognito, where a fortune could still be made prospecting for diamonds.

"So you're in?" Lawson asked, brushing dandruff from the collar of his coat.

"I don't have much of an option, do I?"

"Not much," Willis said.

EPILOGUE:

In September 1975, ex-Detective Chief Inspector Willis and Nigel Lawson, described as a security officer, appeared at Bow Street Magistrates Court, London, charged with conspiring with persons unknown to steal £14 million worth of rough diamonds destined for Antwerp. They were tried at the Old Bailey. In their court statements, both the accused implicated an antique dealer named Rhodes, who vanished from London in December 1974. At the request of Scotland Yard, it was said, the FBI had checked various New York hotels, including the Algonquin, but the only man answering Rhodes' description was a Canadian named Richard Walter Ogden, who had left the city several weeks earlier leaving no forwarding address. The Bow Street Magistrate was also told that the information that had uncovered the alleged conspiracy had emanated from an Antwerp diamond merchant named Benjamin Volkov. (Although it wasn't stated in court, the Magistrate was told privately that the

Dutch and British police had agreed that Volkov would not be prosecuted for his part in the conspiracy—or for any other indiscretions of which he might have been guilty in the past.)

In the garden of his palatial home on the outskirts of Rio de Janeiro, the new adviser to the city's largest diamond dealers read a report of the committal proceedings in an old British newspaper and grinned. Then, with a smile still creasing his pleasant, slightly crumpled features, he went and told his wife. She laughed a lot, then returned to her book on diamonds. They had just returned from a trip into the interior of Brazil, where she thought she had spotted alluvial diamonds in a dried-up river bed. She had a bad attack of diamond fever, and her husband wondered how the hell he was going to cure her—although he didn't really. The disease was incurable; they would just have to share the symptoms.